THE WORLD OF JACK DENNISON-DETECTIVE
(THE FINAL CHAPTER)

by

ALBERT E. FARRAR JR.

PITTSBURGH, PENNSYLVANIA 15222

The contents of this work including, but not limited to, the accuracy of events, people, and places depicted; opinions expressed; permission to use previously published materials included; and any advice given or actions advocated are solely the responsibility of the author, who assumes all liability for said work and indemnifies the publisher against any claims stemming from publication of the work.

All Rights Reserved
Copyright © 2012 by Albert E. Farrar Jr.

No part of this book may be reproduced or transmitted, downloaded, distributed, reverse engineered, or stored in or introduced into any information storage and retrieval system, in any form or by any means, including photocopying and recording, whether electronic or mechanical, now known or hereinafter invented without permission in writing from the publisher.

RoseDog Books
701 Smithfield Street
Pittsburgh, PA 15222
Visit our website at *www.rosedogbookstore.com*

ISBN: 978-1-4349-8689-4
eISBN: 978-1-4349-7685-7

BOOK SYNOPSIS

A DETECTIVE ON THE LOOSE

JACK TAKES A MUCH NEEDED VACATION AND MEETS A LADY HE KNEW IN HIGH SCHOOL. HE SEES FRIENDS IN CLEVELAND, HELPS SOLVE A CASE AND THEN TRAVELS TO SWITZERLAND WITH MARIAN A LADY HE ALMOST MARRIED.

TRAVELING THE COUNTRY

JACK ENCOUNTERS A MARRIED LADY IN MUNICH WHO IS LOOKING TO CHANGE HER LFE STYLE. ACROSS THE U.S. HE STOPS TO SEE MO AND JANE IN KANSAS CITY. LATER HE MEETS A TEENAGER WHO WANTS TO GO WITH HIM AND ALSO ENCOUNTERS TWO LADIES AT THE GRAND CANYON.

THE RYMAN/ORVETT CASE

JACK RETURNS TO THE MURDER OF SEVERAL LADIES. A NEIGHBOR'S FRIEND TRIES TO DEVELOP A RELATIONSHIP. THE CHIEF SENDS HIM TO MIAMI TO SOLVE AN OLD CASE. AND WHEN HE RETURNS, HE LEARNS THAT MARIAN IS KILLED WHILE SKIING.

WHAT?

JACK LEARNS HE IS GOING TO BE A FATHER. A LADY FROM HIS PAST SUDDENLY APPEARS AND HE WINDS UP SAVING HER FROM JUMPING OFF A BRIDGE. HE RE-OPENS AN OLD CASE AND THE NEW MEXICO TEEN SHOWS UP. TWO LADIES PROPOSE MARRIAGE. JACK IS RECRUITED TO SAVE AN UNKNOWN MAN'S DAUGHTER AND HE IS LATER SHOT IN HIS FRONT YARD.

SADNESS AND HAPPINESS

JANE IN KANSAS CITY DIES. JACK GETS A BIG CHECK FROM THE MAGAZINE. A LADY IS KILLED LEAVING A BANK AND JACK LEARNS MORE ABOUT HIS DECEASED WIFE'S FAMILY. AN OLD COUPLE IS MURDERED IN THEIR HOME. JACK GOES TO GERMANY TO RETURN THE HERALD BOY. HE PROPOSES MARIAGE TO HIS HIGH SCHOOL FRIEND.

ACKNOWLEDGEMENTS

IT'S IMPORTANT TO ACKNOWLEDGE THOSE WHO HELPED ME PUT THIS BOOK TOGETHER. FIRST I NEED TO THANK MY WIFE ALICE FOR HER TIME IN READING MY STORY AND FINDING MY ERRORS IN SPELLING AND GRAMMER AND OTHER THINGS SHE THOUGHT I SHOULD CHANGE.

THANKS TO ALL THE PEOPLE IN MY WRITING CLASS. ALICE, BARBARA, KAREN, BEVERLY, LORETTA & MARGARET, WHO HAVE GIVEN ME ASSISTANCE ALONG THE WAY,

THEN I AGAIN NEED TO THANK MY DAUGHTER, FRANCINE AND MY SON KEVIN, FOR THEIR COMPUTER KNOWLEDGE.

I ALSO WANT TO THANK THE READERS WHO CHOOSE TO READ MY HUMBLE EFFORTS. I TRULY HOPE THEY HAVE ENJOYED THE THREE BOOKS OF THE JACK DENNISON SERIES AS MUCH AS I ENJOYED WRITING THEM.

THE JACK DENNISON SERIES
ALBERT E. FARRAR JR.
(2009-10)

JACK DENNISON – BOOK ONE

1. FOOTSTEPS ON THE GRAVEL PATH
2. THE CRYSTAL GOBLET
3. CABIN IN THE TREES
4. THE SENATOR'S DAUGHTER
5. A FATHERS MISSION

(2010-11)
JACK DENNISON – BOOK TWO

1. THE KIDNAPPING AND THE WIDOW
2. DRAMA AT GOLDEN GATE
3. A COMPLICATED LIFE
4. A CHANGING LIFE STYLE
5. DESTINED TO BE ALONE

(2010-11)
JACK DENNISON – BOOK THREE

1. A DETECTIVE ON THE LOOSE
2. TRAVELING THE COUNTRY
3. THE RYMAN/ORVETT CAS
4. WHAT?
5. SADNESS AND HAPPINESS

OTHER STORIES BY THE AUTHOR

1. THE END OF AN ERA
2. A NIGHTMARE ADVENTURE
3. THE ANGEL OF CRYSTAL FALLS
4. THE SECRET LIFE OF SISTER PAUL
5. THE GREATEST GOLFER WE NEVER HEARD OF
6. A STRANGER FROM THE PAST
7. SEARCHING FOR SALLY
8. CHARLIE'S MOMENT

MINI STORIES BY THE AUTHOR

1. A BROKEN CLOCK
2. THE MYSTERY ROOM
3. THE DARK STAIRS
4. A WISH UNFULFILLED
5. CHURCH IN THE WOODS
6. THE BIG YELLOW HOUSE
7. NEVER ENDING LOVE
8. THE LADY & THE DOG
9. I HATED HIM
10. THE PEARLY GATES
11. MAX & MYRTLE (PUBLISHED)
12. A REAL COOL GUY
13. TWO OLD CARS (PUBLISHED)
14. THE STORY OF CHEAP
15. THE OLD MAN & THE LITTLE GIRL (PUBLISHED)
16. FLIGHT TO?
17. THE MINNESOTA SNOW
18. AM I RICH OR POOR
19. THE NEIGHBOR I NEVER KNEW
20. THE LAUNDRY

A DETECTIVE ON THE LOOSE

CHAPTER ONE
TIME TO GET AWAY

Jack and Don watched as Marian headed down the road to return her airport rental car and then fly home to Virginia. She didn't leave until Jack promised to fly with her to visit her parents in Switzerland. She knew he liked them and hoped that perhaps the two of them being together again, would re-kindle a relationship that almost resulted in something permanent between them, such a short time ago. Marian knew it was too soon after the passing of his wife for him to consider anything between them just yet. But there almost was at one time, and she hoped there could be again.

She loved him from the first time they met. She was certain of her feeling for him and that hadn't changed. At least as far as she was concerned and now she needed to try and make him see her as the one person he wanted to be with. She needed to be there for him. She had to be available and to make sure she was still the person he almost; the person he almost chose to marry.

In a few weeks after he'd taken what he felt was the necessary journey to "clear his head", he would arrive at her home in Virginia and they would fly to Switzerland to visit her parents. A couple of weeks together and he'd return to San Francisco and his work.

Maybe she could go there for awhile. Maybe if he found her available, he would gradually decide he liked the arrangement.

She drove on toward the airport her mind filled with these plans and these thoughts.

After watching her drive away, Don turned to his friend and said.
"She's stubborn Jack. She wasn't going to leave until you promised to go with her to visit her parents."
"Yes, I guess so," Jack replied with a laugh. "Well they are special people."

Don caught Jack turning his head again to look down the road where Marian's car disappeared.

"She wants to make sure she sees you again and she felt getting you to see her parents, was one way to do that."

"Well, I do like them," he replied. "I guess I can take some time from my vacation to visit them."

"So, have you decided just where you are going?" Don asked changing the subject.

"Not for sure. I'm going to head in the general direction of Wyoming and Yellowstone Park. I've never been there. Then I think I'll drive to Cleveland to see some friends."

"We were in Yellowstone many years ago and it's really something to see," Don said and then changing the subject he asked. "You are coming to my wedding aren't you?"

"Of course, but you'd better make it on my days off." Jack said. "After all this vacation time off, I might be hard pressed to get away."

It wasn't long before they said goodbye and Jack was on his way. Marian would be almost to the San Francisco airport by now he thought as he reached the main highway taking him east toward Reno, highway 80 and on to Salt Lake. Since he'd agreed to visit Marian's parents, he wondered if he should have done that now and then taken the rest of his vacation later.

It was the middle of the afternoon before reaching highway 80 east. Traffic was miserable.

However it was partly clear and sunny with cumulous clouds floating overhead, and that made driving a little more tolerable.

I guess I'd better find someplace near Reno tonight he thought to himself. Getting a late start like I did, that's probably as far as I'll get. I know with travel season here, I had better not wait too late in the day to find someplace. In and around Reno motel's can fill up pretty fast and since I don't have a reservation I don't want to be sleeping in my car. I'm getting too old for that.

The miles went by fast and before long the buildings of Reno loomed in front of him. As he looked at the fast approaching skyline he commented, "Boy, it sure looks like it's grown since I was here last. What's it been? Seven, maybe eight years?" His mind dug back into its memory attempting to pin down the correct time frame. No. I guess it's been longer than that. It must be twelve or thirteen years since I've been here.

Yes, that's right. I remember now, he said under his breath. I'd just turned twenty four and I came here with two friends. It wasn't long after I joined the police force. And look at the freeway going right through town now. You don't even have to drive down the main street anymore.

He wondered if he should stop and look it over, but he didn't and drove on looking at everything as he headed east. It wasn't long before the city faded behind him and the growing outskirts of homes and businesses seemed to line the highway for some distance.

"Guess you'd better find a place to stay old boy. It's after 5p.m," he said out loud.

Looking to one side and another Jack decided on a two level private motel that was not one of the big chain establishments. It was on his side of the highway and he noticed a restaurant next door and a lit vacancy sign. Jack pulled off the highway and down the slight slope into the driveway and past the sign that said. "HOIT'S MOTEL." He pulled up in front of the office door.

Prying himself from the front seat with a bit of effort, and feeling a bit stiff from the long drive, he walked to the office door and pushed it open.

"You must be getting old Jack old boy," he said in a voice loud enough that anyone who might have been close by could hear. "These long drives never used to bother you."

As he walked through the door he noticed a fairly trim attractive lady he guessed to be about his age. She was seated in a room behind the counter. At hearing the door open she looked up, rose from her chair and walked toward him.

"May I help you?" she asked.

"I see your vacancy sign is still lit. Hope that means you have a room available."

"Yes. We still have a few. A single?" she asked.

"Yes," he replied.

"One night?" she asked.

"Yes," he answered again.

"Just fill this out card," she directed as she pushed a small card across the counter.

Jack picked up the pen she'd provided and filled out the card, giving his name, home address and license number. Returning the card along with his credit card, he smiled. A few moments later she handed the credit card back to him along with a key to room 210. Without looking at the credit or registration card, she said.

"I hope the second floor is okay."

"Oh yes. That's just fine. Is that restaurant good?" he asked, and nodded in the direction of the nearby eating establishment.

"Yes," she replied and handed him a small card with the motel name emblazoned on it. "If you eat there, give them this card and they'll take two dollars off your bill."

"Thanks," he replied and turned to leave.

"Jack Dennison!" he heard her say in a surprised voice.

He turned, looking back in her direction and noticed her looking at the registration card.

"You aren't by any chance, the Jack Dennison who attended Jefferson High School in the bay area in 1954 are you?"

"Yes," he answered a bit surprised by the question.

"You probably don't remember me," she said. "Betty Brady? Everyone called me Bunny."

"Bunny Brady?" he questioned, a bit surprised.

"Yes," she replied.

"Sure I remember you."

"Really?" she answered.

"Oh sure. You sat two seats in front of me and in the row next to the windows in the Biology class."

"How do you remember that?" she asked.

"Because you were always talking to Delores... what was her name?"

"Delores Thomas," Bunny replied.

"Yes, Delores Thomas. I remember the teacher correcting the two of you many times."

Bunny laughed. "You remember that too?"

"Sure," he replied laughing with her. "And the teacher finally separated the two of you. She put Delores on the other side of the room."

"Yes she did. I'm surprised you'd remember that."

"I also remember you were always looking back in my direction when you weren't talking to her."

Bunny looked down as if embarrassed and then asked.

"Where do you live Jack?"

"Oh, I'm still living in Frisco."

"What do you do for a living?" she asked.

"I'm with the Police Department."

"Really? Do you like it?"

"Yes. It's very interesting and very challenging."

"Dangerous?"

"At times," he replied and then changing the subject asked her.

"How did you get here Bunny?"

"My husband Don was from here. He was a truck driver and when we got married, well I just came with him."

"And now you're working in a motel."

"Actually the motel is mine. Well, mine and the banks," she said laughing.

"Your husband still driving trucks?" Jack asked.

"Don was killed last year in a truck accident," she answered.

"I'm sorry Bunny."

"There was a big dust storm in the Imperial valley. I understand from what I was told, it came up very sudden. There were quite a few cars and trucks involved. Maybe you heard about it."

"Yes. I think I do remember hearing something about that," he replied and then repeated. "I'm very sorry Bunny."

"Thank you," she answered. Anyway I've been too busy here to think too much about it. Besides I have two boys to look after."

"Really? How old are they?"

"Jeffery is ten and Michael is eight." Then hesitating a moment she said.

"I'll be done here in a few minutes Jack. Someone is coming to relieve me. I live right next door and I have to fix dinner for myself and the boys. I'd like it very much if you'd join us. It's not often I get to see someone from my high school years and I'd love the opportunity to visit and just talk. Will you have dinner with us? You can meet the boys and I know they'd like that."

He didn't hesitate more than a moment. He knew it would be nicer than sitting in a motel room.

"Sure," he replied. "Why not? "I'd enjoy that too."

He showed up at her door forty five minutes later and a young boy about ten answered.

"You must be Mr. Dennison," the young lad said.

"Yes I am," Jack replied.

"My mother said you'd be having dinner with us. She told me to let you in and she'd be out as soon as she finished her shower."

"Thank you," Jack replied. "You must be Jeffery."

"Yes," he replied. "My mother said to help yourself to a drink if you like. It's over there." He pointed toward a cabinet in the corner of the room.

"Thank you," Jack responded. "Where's your brother?"

"He's in his room. He's shy around strangers."

Jeffery sat on the couch, turning his attention toward the TV. Jack walked to the corner cabinet, and reached for a bottle of bourbon. As he did so, he heard a familiar voice from the hall.

"I'll have whatever you're having."

He looked up and there she stood in a full length flowered dress that looked like spring had arrived. It was cut in half by a two inch red belt hooked together with a brass buckle.

I hope I gave you enough time before I showed up."

"My replacement arrived ten minutes early, so I left," she replied. It shouldn't take too long for dinner. The boys don't like to wait too long to eat, so I usually get it ready earlier in the day."

He handed her the glass of bourbon. Taking it, she clicked it against his and said. "Here's to old friends."

"To friends," he replied. "But not too old," and they both laughed slightly. She took a sip as did he and then she walked into the kitchen. A few moments later he heard her call out.

"Jeffery will you help me set the table?"

"I can help," Jack called as he stepped into the kitchen just ahead of Jeffery.

"Thanks Jack, but Jeffery is used to helping and besides he knows where everything is."

Jeffery eased himself past Jack and walked to the cabinet in the corner of the kitchen. He removed dishes and silverware and brought them to the table.

"You said you're with the Police Department. Just exactly what do you do there?"

"I'm a Lieutenant in the homicide division," he answered.

She looked up from where she stood in front of the stove.

"Really? Do you like that?"

"I've been doing it for a dozen years, so I guess I must enjoy the challenge."

She looked up and laughed. "I guess you must. Isn't it kind of dangerous?"

"It can be at times," he said, not telling her about having been shot at several times recently.

"I didn't ask if you were married. I guess since you arrived alone, I just assumed…"

He didn't answer immediately, but took a few steps closer to the stove where she was standing.

Bunny looked up waiting for his answer.

"I was," he replied. "Until a few weeks ago. We were married only a bit over a year. She was diagnosed with what is called Creutzfeldt-Jakob disease. It is incurable. Hers was the first in this country detected in anyone at such an early age. They don't know how she contracted it. She was adopted at an early age and there is no known history about her family."

"Oh Jack," she said putting down the cooking spoon and taking the few steps and wrapping him in a big hug.

"I'm so sorry. That's terrible… I'm so sorry."

"I'm taking some time to get away from work and everything else for awhile."

She moved back to the stove and continued stirring.

"Would you like another drink?" he asked. "I wouldn't mind one if you don't mind."

"No of course not," she replied handing him her glass still half full.

A few minutes later he was back, drinks in hand. Handing hers back to her, she took it, clinked it against his, took a sip and said. "That's good. I think dinner is ready. Why don't you sit down Jack?" Then turning to her older son Jeffery, she said. "Get your brother honey."

The conversation at dinner centered with talk about the boys, her life until recently, how she liked running the motel and what she did since high school. Once they finished eating, Bunny told Jack she'd join him in the living room in a few minutes.

"Can I help you clean up?" he asked.

"Thanks Jack, but no. Jeffery will help. Why don't you go into the other room and I'll be there shortly."

He took a seat on the couch facing the TV. It wasn't long before she appeared and sat down on the same couch facing him, while the boys disappeared into their rooms.

"Has it been difficult since you lost your husband?" he asked not sure if he should even have poised that question.

"I've hated being alone, but having to run the motel and take care of the boys, I didn't have much time to grieve. It kept me busy. Of course with him being a truck driver, he was gone much of the time. The boys keep me busy and while the insurance helped pay off the truck, the only bills I have are the payments to the bank for this business we bought. Fortunately business has been pretty good and I've managed to save a little so the boys will get a decent education."

"Perhaps you'll find someone else one day," he said.

"I haven't had time to think about that. The boys and this place take up all my time. Running a motel and keeping good help is a full time job."

"Yes. I suppose it is," he replied.

"So you're taking time off?" she asked changing the subject.

"Yes. I just felt I needed some time to get away. I visited my sister in Oregon and another friend of mine, and now I'm heading east. I got a late start today so I didn't get very far."

"That's a lucky break for me," she interjected and smiled at him.

She hesitated a moment before speaking and then noting his empty glass asked.

"Would you like another drink?"

"Oh sure. Why not? I won't be doing any driving tonight."

Bunny got up and fixed another drink for each of them and then returning to the couch she said.

"I have a confession to make."

"Really?" He asked. What's that?

Bunny hesitated a moment and looking up at him smiling, she said.

"I had the biggest crush on you in high school." She turned slightly pink as she said it.

"You did?" he replied.

"Yes. I did," she was laughing just a bit now.

"I never knew that. I guess I was too wrapped up in sports at the time to notice."

"I always wanted you to ask me out, but you never did," she said.

"Well back in those days I never had much money. Between sports and working and helping at home and trying to get my school work done, there was never any time for much of that. In fact I never dated much."

"I remember you took Mary Sullivan to the junior prom and I was devastated," she laughed again and so did he.

"You remembered that?"

"Yes."

"Now that I've seen you again, and what an attractive lady you are, I guess I missed out back then."

Bunny turned slightly pink once more at his compliment.

"So how long have you had the motel?" he asked changing the subject.

"My husband and I bought it five years ago. We thought it would supplement our income. Trucking is kind of,…kind of uncertain at times.

"Yes, I guess it can be," Jack replied.

"Anyway, I've been doing okay. I'm keeping the bills paid and putting a little away."

They paused for a moment, neither saying anything before Bunny broke the silence.

"Where did you go to college Jack?"

"Well, I did have two years at a junior college and I took law enforcement courses while there. When I learned the Police department was accepting applications, I applied."

"And they hired you," she said.

"Now right away. I wasn't quite twenty one and I needed to be that old. It was close to my birthday so I applied anyway. Turns out I was almost twenty two before I got hired."

"She took a drink from her glass and asked.

"Did you like it right away?"

"No. I really wasn't sure at first. In fact I almost quit once, but decided to stick it out awhile longer. Then as things turned out, I just kept hanging on and on and on," he laughed. "And I'm still there."

Bunny laughed along with him.

"How did you meet your husband Bunny?"

"Quite by accident. I was in a beauty shop getting my hair done and he came in to see a lady he was dating. She happened to be doing my hair as it turned out and he talked to her for a few minutes. I noticed he kept looking at me and after he finally left, Millie, the lady doing my hair, told me she didn't know whether or not she wanted to keep seeing him."

"Did she say why?"

"Yes. She said he wanted to get married and she didn't feel she was ready. He was six years older than her. She was only nineteen and she just wanted to do other thing before getting married. She said he was a really nice guy, and maybe she'd be sorry, but she just didn't want to get married yet."

"So how did you get to know him?"

Bunny laughed at the question.

"He met me outside the shop when I left," Bunny laughed again and Jack laughed with her.

"Anyway he asked me for coffee and that's how it started."

"Did you ever go back and get your hair done there again?"

"No," she said laughing once more. Bunny looked at him and he looked at her for a few moments, neither saying anything until he said.

"I think I'd better go, I could use some sleep. I'd like to get an early start tomorrow since I didn't get as far as I expected today."

"Don't go yet. Let me put the boys to bed. I want to show you something. It will take only a few minutes."

"All right? Jack answered.

He finished his drink and placed his glass on the coaster sitting on the table. It didn't take long before she returned. Bunny came carrying a large photo album and she sat down right next to him on the couch.

"I wanted to show you some photo's before you go," she said.

Bunny opened the book. The first few pages were of her and her family when she was quite young, but pretty soon there were pictures of her high school years. Jack spotted some of her in her school sweater.

"I remember those sweaters," he said.

"They could be pretty uncomfortable in warm weather, but they were okay during the cooler time of the school year," she replied. He saw photos of her and some of her friends.

Then she turned to the next page. There across the whole page was a large picture of Jack in his high school football uniform. On the opposite page was a picture of him in his suit standing next to an attractive brunette lady.

"What are you doing with a picture of me and Mary Sullivan?" he asked.

"Remember I said I had a big crush on you?"

"Yes. I remember you said that."

"But how come you've got a prom picture of me and Mary?"

"I ordered it thinking I'd paste a picture of my face over hers."

"Ha! Ha! That's funny. You really did?" he asked.

She was laughing and looking up at him. "I guess I was kind of silly."

Bunny was very close now and looking into his eyes as she spoke. He stared back at her and the Alcohol from earlier was beginning to take effect on both of them, she inched forward just a touch and as she did, he moved instinctively in her direction. A moment later the photo album fell to the floor.

Jack pulled back a few moments later.

"I'm sorry Bunny."

"I'm not," she replied. "I've waited a long time to kiss you. Every since high school."

"Still I shouldn't have done that."

"Why not?" I wanted you to kiss me and it wasn't like you forced yourself on me. I don't regret it and I'd do it again. So don't feel like you need to apologize."

"Still?" and he hesitated a moment more, but bunny was determined not to let it end with just one kiss. She'd waited too long and now he was here in her home and she wasn't going to be a bit shy. She leaned forward and touched her lips once again against his. He didn't resist.

"Don't get up Jack," she whispered. "I've got to get the boys off to school. I'll be right back."

He felt her get up as he rolled over still not quite awake, but enough to see the last fraction of her bare skin through his foggy eyes as she slipped into her robe.

She headed for the bedroom door, closing it behind her. It was getting light outside he noticed as he blinked the haze from his eyes. Light peeked through a crack in the curtain and reflected off the wall next to the door she'd disappeared though a few moments before.

"Oh! What happened?" he said aloud. "The last thing I remember was sitting on the couch looking at photos. We were sitting next to each other looking at her photo album and we laughed at her thought of putting a picture of her face over Mary's in the prom picture. Then she kissed me. I guess I shouldn't have had that last drink. I don't remember what happened next. And how did I get here? I don't remember that either. I think we both had too much to drink. I'd better get up. I didn't mean for this to happen."

He rose up on one elbow just as the door opened. She saw him and said.
"Don't get up. I'll be right back. The boys are having breakfast."
"Bunny," he said and she interrupted.
"Never mind and don't apologize. Just lay back down. I'm coming back in a few minutes."

He started to protest again, but she stopped him, pushing him back down and kissing him as she did.
"Stay there Jack. I'll be right back," she was up and out the bedroom door again.

He lay there on the bed as she disappeared through the door once more.

His eyes were closed. His mind was thinking he should get up because she would return just as soon as the boys were gone. Instead he lay there wondering how the two of them ended up here in the first place.

He knew when she returned from the sound of a squeak as the door opened and light from the hallway poked through the open space as she entered. He opened one eye to see her standing next to the bed and as he looked, he noticed her robe slipping onto the floor. He quickly closed his eyes once more and a moment later he felt her body pressing against him. It was easy to tell she wasn't wearing anything.

"The boys are off to school and I'm back." she whispered into his ear.
"Bunny," he started to say.
"No words," she said. "Unless you have something sweet and enduring you want to say." He could feel her arms around his warm body pressing herself against him. He turned to face her. She was hard to resist... He didn't.

Bunny fixed a very nice breakfast for the two of them. She was seated across the kitchen table from him still in her robe and not saying much but you could tell she was very pleased with the situation. Jack wasn't saying much either except to tell her how good the breakfast was, as his mind tried to formulate words to apologize for the night the two of them just finished. It had never been his intention to let this to happen. But it did. As he looked across the table he could tell from her demeanor that she was ever so pleased. In his mind lingered the idea that he must apologize. Still he knew she was happy it did.

Bunny had a crush on him in high school and when they graduated, she knew she'd never see him again. Then all of a sudden many years later, here he was and best of all they'd spent the night together. She was more than just pleased. She was ecstatic. They sat there quietly finishing their food. From time to time she would look up at him and he'd look back at her. Neither said a word except on Bunny's face was a happy smile.

Finally as he took the last piece of food from his plate and slipped it between his teeth, he sat back in his chair, and looking across at her he said.

"Thank you for the lovely breakfast Bunny. It was very good. I really enjoyed it."

She smiled and replied with a grin on her face.

"I thought you might need a hardy meal."

Her smile was even broader after she spoke, while she tried to control the sound of her giggle.

"Bunny," Jack started to say, "I."

That was as far as he got before she stopped him.

"Don't apologize Jack. You have nothing to apologize for. If you feel guilty about last night, then don't. You didn't take advantage of me. I can assure you of that. Remember I had a crush on you since high school and for me, well last night was like a dream come true."

"I know Bunny, but I do feel guilty."

"Well, don't," she replied.

He got up from the kitchen chair and she did as well.

"I should probably go. If I'd left as I planned, I'd be down the road quite a ways by now."

"I don't suppose you could stay? Even a little while? Perhaps another day?"

He looked at her a moment thinking it might not be so bad, but thinking better of it, said.

"I'd better go."

"Will I ever see you again?" A bit of disappointment in her voice.

He looked down at her thinking what a nice person she seemed to be but knowing that he couldn't promise to come back. Before he could answer, she spoke again.

"If I thought there was ever a chance for us, I'd" she hesitated before continuing. "I'd sell the motel and move."

Jack took her hold of her arms just above the wrists and slightly caressing the skin with his thumbs, replied.

"I'm flattered Bunny. I really am." Somehow just now she looked even more attractive than at any time before.

"Is it my boys?" she asked.

"Oh no Bunny," he exclaimed. That would never be a problem. It's just that right now; well I just don't know. After losing my wife I just need to be alone and get away. At least for awhile."

"It's okay Jack. I understand. Really I do." she said, but he could see the disappointment in her face. After last night she hoped there might be a chance for the two of them. She remembered the young man she'd had a crush on so long ago and now he was here. This handsome man who was single came into her life again and they'd spent the night together. It had fulfilled a dream she'd dreamed so long ago. It was as if the God's had destined it to be.

They stood there briefly. He was looking down at her and she was looking up at him but neither saying a word until finally Jack broke the silence.

"Bunny! I have to go."

As he started to pull away, she put her arms tightly around him hanging on desperately one last time. Slowly after a few moments, she released her grip and stepped back and reluctantly said.

"Good bye Jack. Best wishes."

"Good by Bunny," and he turned to walk away. Jack opened the car door and turned toward her one more time. She was still standing in the same spot looking across the open space between them.

As he started to step into his car, she called out.

"I love you Jack."

He did not respond, but waved from the car door. Then getting in, he started the engine, put the car in gear and backed out of his parking spot. As he drove away he could see her standing in the same place watching his car.

It would have been so easy to stay he thought. I never meant for last night to happen, but it did. It wasn't fair to her. Years ago she'd had a crush on me and now after all this time, apparently she still did. She'd lost her husband in a tragic accident and now with two young boys and needing someone, who should come along but me.

"Damn" he uttered aloud. "Damn, Damn, Damn. Of all the places to stay."

His car slowed and stopped just before entering the highway. He sat there a few moments his mind ablaze with thoughts about her and what happened racing back and forth in his brain.

Then after what seemed like a long time, he stepped on the gas pedal and picking up speed turned onto the freeway heading toward Salt Lake. He glanced down at the motel as he passed it one last time. She was still standing in the same spot looking up at the highway.

The thought of her standing in front of the motel looking up at the highway stuck in his mind for some miles down the road. It was like the plague and it wouldn't leave him. Temptation to turn around kept creeping into his mind. His eyes kept registering on the spots he passed where he might turn around and go back. But on he went and it wasn't until a passing car cut too close in front of him that his mind snapped back to reality. Forced to slow quickly to avoid a possible accident he was finally able to think more about driving and less about what happened last night.

CHAPTER TWO

YELLOWSTONE HERE I COME

The sun was out again and the same cumulous clouds dotted the sky. Traffic wasn't too bad and the miles piled up rapidly. A rest stop sign appeared and he pulled in for a few minutes to get out and stretch but he was soon on the road once more.

The miles went by faster than he realized and before he knew it, the sun was getting low in the western sky. It was late in the afternoon now and Jack thought he'd better stop for the night. It was the late start he got this morning after waiting for the breakfast she'd prepared. He wasn't quite going to make it to Salt Lake today, so he picked the first town across the Utah border. The sign said Wendover. Perfect he thought. The vacancy sign at the first motel was lit and he noticed a place to eat not far away so he pulled in and stopped.

After checking in, he turned on the TV and while it was coming on, Jack made his way into the bathroom. When he returned a few minutes later, the news was on. They were reporting an accident on the highway he was traveling just short of Salt Lake. As they finished that story, the announcer switched to a reported robbery of a motel on the highway just east of Reno.

Jack stopped in his tracks. He recognized the camera picture as Bunny's motel or at least he thought he did, and then as the camera scanned the area, he could see the sign advertising "HOIT'S MOTEL." A reporter was talking to an employee, who said that two men came in and robbed the motel. In the process the owner, a lady named Betty Hoit had been assaulted by the pair. She'd been taken to a Reno hospital and treated. No further information was available on her condition.

"Damn." Jack exclaimed as he stood momentarily in front of the TV. Then grabbing his travel case he headed back to his car.

It was a bit after midnight when he pulled into the Hoit motel parking lot. The office was still lit and the vacancy sign was still on. He couldn't tell who the person was in the office other than he was sure it was female.

Getting out, he walked to the door and pushed it open. The lady seated in the inside office heard the door open, got up and turned around to walk toward the counter.

It was Bunny.

"Jack," she exclaimed surprised at seeing him. "You came back," There was overwhelming joy in her voice at seeing him.

"Bunny," he said. "I heard about the robbery on TV. I was concerned. Are you all right?"

"Yes. I'll be fine," she replied as she made her way round the counter to give him a big hug, overjoyed at seeing him again.

"You came back," she exclaimed once more.

"Are you sure you're okay?" he asked once more.

"You came back," she repeated once more hugging him even tighter and then answered. "Yes. A few bruises but I'm going to be okay."

"I was worried," he said.

She squeezed him again, overjoyed at his being there and ecstatic at the thought that he'd come back.

"You were worried and you came back," she repeated once more.

"I'm glad you're okay."

She was smiling a broad smile as if this were the highlight of her life. She wouldn't let him go but finally she did release him, and he asked.

"Have you got a room? I'm pretty tired. It's been a long day."

"You bet," she replied. "I know of a place right next door."

Sensing what she meant, he responded.

"I'd better not Bunny. I'm really tired and I need some rest."

"I'm closing up now," she said and she reached behind the counter and turned off the vacancy sign and the office lights. "Yes. Just come with me. All the motel rooms are full Sir, so I'll have to find another spot for you."

"Not all the rooms are full," he said sternly.

"It's my motel and I say there're all full," she replied forcefully.

She led him outside, locked the office door and holding his hand tightly led him toward the house next door.

"This isn't a good idea Bunny," he said.

But she led him up the stairs to her house, still holding his hand tightly so she wouldn't lose him. "I'm really tired."

"It's the best idea I've ever had," she replied.

"You came back," she repeated once more dragging him behind her.

Once inside, Jack took her hands and turned her to face him.

"Bunny. I came back when I heard the news because I was concerned about you. Besides, I like you. Now don't take anything from that. I was just concerned, but I still have to go."

"I know. But you did come back. That means a lot to me." She paused a moment and then continued. "Jack even if we don't make love tonight, I'm going to sleep with you. And tomorrow when you leave I will have experienced another day with someone I've thought about many times over the years. And even if I never see you again, I will have memories that are a very important point in my life that I will never forget. Now my dear, you know where the bedroom is. Go and I'll be there in a few minutes."

CHAPTER THREE
HEADING EAST ONE MORE TIME

She fixed him a good breakfast again and it was earlier in the day this time when he started to leave. She walked him to the car and he turned to face her once more. Before he could say what he wanted to say, Bunny spoke.

"Have a good and safe trip Jack. And,... And thank you for caring enough to come back and check on me. That means a lot. It really does."

Jack squeezed her hands and smiled, then said.

"I've enjoyed seeing you again Bunny. I wish I'd taken the time to know you better in high school."

"I do too," she replied. "If you get this way again, I hope you'll stop by."

"You can count on it," he replied.

With that he gave her a big hug which she returned and as he pulled back slightly, he noticed her looking up and not letting go entirely, so he bent forward and kissed her one last time. Bunny returned his kiss with as much effort and desire as possible. Then suddenly she stepped back and said.

"You'd better go while you can."

He got into his car, started the engine and drove from the motel lot toward the highway. As he glanced down one more time, she was still looking up at his car watching it disappear from sight.

By mid afternoon he'd returned to the spot where he'd stopped the evening before, but since it was now earlier in the day, he kept on driving. Finally after passing through Salt Lake he turned north on Highway 84 and eventually onto Highway 15 that would take him through Pocatello and Idaho Falls and tomorrow into Yellowstone park. By now it was getting late again, so he selected a large motel chain in Idaho Falls and called it a night.

The next morning he stopped at West Yellowstone, a little town just outside the park and had breakfast. Then it was the grand tour stopping to view everything he could. Finally as the day started to wind down, Jack decided he'd better find some place to stay. Since it wasn't quite summer vacation for families, he found space at one of the buildings at Mammoth Hot Springs.

The next day he was off again heading east. It took him a whole week to reach Cleveland with stops en route to see as much as possible. Places like the Custer battle field, the Black Hills of the Dakota's and many other locations he found interesting along the way. When he finally reached Cleveland, he called Zeke and Gail, and their first question was:

"Where have you been? We thought you'd be here a few days ago."

Gail opened the front door when he reached their house and standing beside her was their first child hanging onto the bottom of her dress. Jack noticed right away she was expecting a second child.

"Come in Jack. Zeke is at the store. I sent him to get some things." She hugged him and said softly. "I'm so sorry." Meaning of course the loss of his wife Jacquee. She knew he was taking this journey to get away for awhile.

"Did you bring any luggage?" she asked as she noticed he was empty handed.

"It's still in the car," he replied.

"How long can you stay?" she asked.

"I'm not sure. I promised Marian I'd call when I arrived here."

Gail looked a bit surprised. She didn't know Jack had been in touch with her friend or that he'd promised to fly to Switzerland to visit her parents.

"Really? I didn't know you'd been in touch," she said.

Jack told her Marian had come out to California to see him. They had visited and he'd promised to go see her parents. Gail was very pleased because she'd always hoped the two of them might get together. About that time Zeke came through the back door, his arms full with three bags of groceries.

"Hi friend," he called out. He put the bags on the table, and walked over to give Jack a hug and to shake his hand.

"Guess what honey?" Gail asked and then without stopping went on. "Jack and Marian are flying to see her parents."

"Really?" Zeke replied.

Jack went on to explain the situation once more. They visited a bit and when Gail went to fix dinner, Jack asked. "How are things going at work?"

"They aren't bad except for one case that is really bugging me."

"What's that?" Jack asked.

"A couple of months ago, a young child of 2 years disappeared from the front yard of its home. The mother, a widow lady who'd lost her husband just six months previous in an industrial accident and still grieving over that, was sitting on the front porch watching her child when the phone rang. The phone was just inside on the living room table about a half dozen feet away, so the mother went inside to answer it, knowing she could still see her child from the living room window. She answered the phone and a moment later turned to look out the window and she couldn't see her child. She said she parted the curtain because at first she thought the curtain obscured her vision, but when she did, the child was nowhere to be seen.

She told us she dropped the phone and ran outside and still no child. She screamed the child's name and started running around the house thinking her child might have gone around the side. When she didn't find him, she came back to the front calling his name but he was nowhere to be found. Neighbors came when they heard the scream to see what the problem was but the child was nowhere in sight. Many of them started helping her look without any luck. That's when we were called. We don't have a clue. We've talked to all the neighbors, but we've learned nothing."

"That's not a very wide time frame you describe to not have the child in sight and then not be able to locate it," Jack said.

"No it isn't. That's what's so frustrating. We have talked to all the neighbors several times, examined the yard thoroughly, checked with friends and one relative, but we've learned nothing. It's driving me crazy."

"Why don't you let me look at the file tomorrow? A fresh pair of eyes might help."

"Sure Jack. Be glad to."

"How's the mother doing? Jack asked.

"Not good. She's just going through the motions of living now."

Gail called them for dinner and they enjoyed the rest of the evening visiting and talking about many things.

The next morning after breakfast, Zeke took Jack down to his office and introduced him to the other detectives. After meeting everyone and seeing where Zeke worked Jack asked.

"Okay. Where's that file?"

Zeke picked it up off his desk where he'd been looking at it every chance he got. I really appreciate your doing this."

At lunch time Zeke opened the door to the office where Jack was still busy pouring over the information in the child disappearance case.

"Want to get some lunch?" he asked.

"Do all the neighbors in the area still live there?" Jack asked.

"What do you mean?" Zeke questioned.

"Well, I was thinking. If any of the neighbors moved away shortly after, were they checked and asked why they moved?"

"Yes, there was one. The Ramos family. But we checked and he'd gotten a job across town. They wanted to be closer to his work."

"How many children do they have?"

"Two I believe. Why?"

"I don't know. I guess I have a suspicious mind. By the way, where did they live in relationship to where the widow lady lives?"

"They lived right next door. Why?"

"How long had they been thinking of moving? And how long has he worked for the company he's working for?"

"He's been working for the same business for about four years. They said they wanted to move every since he learned his job was permanent. What are you thinking Jack?"

"Well... Like I said. Maybe I just have a suspicious mind." He took one last look at the folder and finally putting it down said.

"Okay. Let's get some lunch."

While they were eating, Jack turned to Zeke and said.

"How about taking me over to where the disappearance took place. I'd like to see the area."

"Sure." Zeke answered. "Be happy too."

"Here we are," Zeke said as he pulled the car to the curb. "That house is where the missing child's mother lives," and he pointed to the tan colored house across the street. "The Ramos family lived just there on the other side," and he pointed to the run down two story house painted in a fading green color. It had two broken steps out front and dried up grass behind a wooden fence that needed a coat of paint in the worst way.

"The homes here are pretty close together," Jack said.

"Yes they are."

"I notice the ladies yard is not fenced in front."

"No," replied Zeke.

"Are there many kids in the neighborhood?" Jack asked.

"Why?"

"I don't know except your information indicated school was out and it happened to be a warm day."

"Yes, that's right. What are you getting at Jack?"

"If kids were home from school and it was a warm day, why were there not kids outside playing? Did anyone check on that?"

"We did talk to a few but none of them said anything important."

"Were their parents present when you spoke to them?"

"Yes. Why?"

"Let's talk to all the kids in the block without their parents present. We just might learn something. I've learned that sometimes kids are reluctant to say anything in front of parents."

"Okay. I'll have our people do it right away."

"Okay let's go," Jack said. "I just wanted to see the area."

As Zeke started to pull away, a rundown looking pickup truck stopped across the street. A man got out and walked around to the back of the truck and opened the rear tailgate. As Zeke's car started to turn the corner, Jack looked back to notice the man taking a mowing machine from the rear of his truck.

"Stop," Jack ordered.

Zeke did and asked. "See something?"

"Look. That man apparently is going to cut someone's grass. Did anyone talk to him?"

"I don't remember that we did. I didn't know he was even mentioned in our investigation."

"Let's go back and talk to him now. Today is Thursday and if I'm correct, the disappearance happened on a Thursday."

"Yes it did," Zeke replied.

He turned his car around and pulled in behind the man and his truck.

"Excuse me Sir," Jack said when they got out of the car. "You're cutting grass here?"

"Yes. Why?" he replied.

"I'm detective Dennison," Jack said. "This is my partner. We're looking into the disappearance of a young child here a couple of months ago."

"Oh yes. I heard about that. It's terrible," the man said.

"Do you cut lawns here all the time?" Jack asked.

"Yes. Every Thursday."

"How many lawns do you cut on this street?" Jack asked.

"Just this one. The William's are the only ones I guess who can afford to have someone do this for them."

"How long does it take you to do their lawn?"

"Oh, not more than thirty minutes. Why?"

"Are you here about this time every Thursday?" Jack asked.

"Usually," he replied.

"Were you here at the time the child's disappearance took place?"

"I was just finishing when the lady came out screaming. I didn't stay since I was in a hurry to get to my next job. I saw several neighbors checking on her so I didn't worry."

"What is your name sir?"

The man reached into his pocket and pulled out a card and handed it to Jack. On the card was the following information.

MARIO'S LAWN SERVICE
REASONABLE RATES

There was also a phone number on the card.

"You're Mario? Jack asked.

"Yes. Mario Penavar," he answered.

"I'll need your home address," Jack said. "Have you seen anyone that may have been a stranger to this neighborhood when you have been here?"

"I don't know all the people who live around here. I see people at times when I am working but I don't know where they live. I'm just busy trying to get done because I have two other yards yet to get done, just like today, so I don't pay much attention."

"Do you remember seeing anyone walking here on the day the child disappeared?"

"No. Not that I remember. I just keep busy and I don't always see what's going on."

"Okay," Jack said. "Thank you. I guess you can go on with your work."

Jack and Zeke walked back in the direction of their car.

"Check him out," Jack instructed Zeke.

"I will. I don't remember even seeing anything in the report about a lawn service."

"I don't remember anything either when I was looking at the information."

Back in the office Zeke went to check on the lawn service person while Jack returned to reviewing the file information once more. When the day was finished, Zeke drove them back to his and Gail's home. Dinner was almost ready when they arrived.

"Marian called," Gail announced when Jack walked in. "She wanted to know if you were here yet."

"I'd better call her after dinner," he replied.

The following day Jack and Zeke went to his office again. Jack once again read everything trying to see if doing so would enable him to catch something he'd missed the day before. Zeke had other business to attend to in the morning part of his shift, so when Jack finished reading the file, he went to get a refill of his coffee cup.

Standing there ahead of him was a lady detective. She looked up when she became aware of his presence.

"Hi. I'm detective Gloria Glassman. I don't remember seeing you before. Are you new here?"

"No," Jack smiled and answered. "I'm Lieutenant Jack Dennison from San Francisco. I'm just here visiting Zeke and his wife. I've just been looking at the file on the child disappearance case. Thought maybe a pair of fresh eyes might see something."

"Pleased to meet you Lieutenant. I've been gone for the last week, so I guess that's why I didn't see you before. Are you staying long?"

"No. I'll probably only be in town a few days."

"That's too bad," she said. "We could use a good looking Lieutenant here," and she laughed and then went on. "Don't tell Zeke I said that."

Jack laughed with her and replied. "I won't."

Just then Zeke walked in and noticed the two of them together.

"I see you've met Gloria," he said seeing them together.

"Yes," Jack replied. "We just met."

"I've got to go," she said. "Nice meeting you Lieutenant."

"Nice meeting you Gloria," he replied.

As she walked away, and Zeke and Jack turned toward his desk, Zeke said.

"Gloria's a pretty good detective. She lost her husband last year in a shoot out. He was a detective here also. They met on the job, got married and were together about three years before he was killed. She took time off after and came back to work right after last Christmas. She was gone last week to care for her mother. Gloria had to put her in a convalescent home."

"Gloria doesn't look too old," Jack said.

"I think she's thirty," Zeke answered. "Her mother is about sixty I think, but her mother's had some health problems. Gloria's the only child and she really hated having to put her mother someplace to be cared for.

"Gloria doesn't have any kids?" Jack asked.

"No. She and Glen were going to wait awhile. Then he got shot. Too bad."

"What do you say we go to lunch?" Zeke asked.

After lunch two detectives approached Zeke to report about talking to the children of the neighborhood and to fill him in on the background of the lawn service man. When they left, Zeke went to the office Jack was using.

"Here's what we learned," he said. "Several of the children remembered seeing the man cutting grass and seeing the child in the yard. No one saw anyone take the child. Mario's lawn service seems to be legit. He's been in business for about eleven years and we are now talking to some of his other customers. His wife and he have two children. He has a sister who just moved in with them and she has one child."

"I think you should talk to the missing child's mother again," Jack said. "Find out if she saw Mario's lawn service truck. She may not have noticed it with the William's house just on the other side of the Ramos' house. Anyway park a vehicle where we saw his today, and then from inside her living room window, see if it's visible. If Mario took the child, he might have been close enough and had sufficient time. It's worth a shot."

"You think this Mario may have taken the child? Zeke asked.

"I don't know, but now that we know he was in the neighborhood and the time frame fits, we need to see if there is a possibility."

Awhile later Zeke took a phone call and then turned to Jack and said.

"We did verify that Mario cut grass on the day in question at other locations."

"Was he at the other locations at the approximate same time he always is?"

"According to my detectives, yes he was. Why?"

"Well, if he took the child, it seems like it would have been necessary for him to take the child someplace. He wouldn't have kept the child with him all the rest of the day."

"That makes sense," Zeke replied.

"Anyway, talk to the mother again and see if she saw his truck. If she was looking for her child, she may not have seen the truck, but she may have. We need to know."

"Okay. What's next?" Zeke asked.

"We don't know of any stranger in the neighborhood at that time. Do we know the ages of Mario's children?"

"I think they are six and eight."

"And find out how old his sister's child is?"

"Okay," Zeke answered. "I'll have someone check on it.

Just then Zeke's phone rang. He answered it, then hung up and turned to Jack.

"I've got to go talk to someone. I won't be gone long. When I get back, let's take off the rest of the day."

"Okay," Jack replied.

When Zeke was gone, Jack looked around the office and his eyes fell on Gloria at her desk working. She looked up and saw him looking at her, so she smiled and said.

"Do you have any opening in your office Lieutenant?"

"There's always an opening for a good detective," he replied as he walked toward her desk.

"What are you working on?" he asked.

"Dull and boring stuff, but someone has to do it. Just a couple of robberies. I think I know who might be responsible, but I don't have any evidence. At least none that I can make stick. I'd really like to get my teeth into something interesting like a multiple murder of some wealthy industrialist of something like that. Do you have anything like that out where you are Lieutenant?"

"Once in awhile. Mostly it's just routine work like everyplace else."

"How long are you going to be here?" she asked.

"Probably only until the first of the week," he answered.

"Too bad. I noticed you're not wearing a wedding band. Am I being presumptuous in thinking you're not married?"

"My wife died a short time ago. I've been taking some time off."

Gloria's face changed and she stood up.

"I'm sorry. I didn't know."

"It's okay," Jack replied. I just decided to drive around the country and see some things that I've never taken the time to see before. Zeke and I met in F.B.I. school awhile back and that's how I know him. He and I met his wife Gail and another lady one evening and Zeke wound up marrying his wife Gail."

"And you married the other lady?"

"No. As it turned out I married someone else."

"Oh!" Gloria answered. "You didn't like the other lady?"

"Yes. I liked her a lot," he replied. "It was really difficult trying to decide which person I wanted to marry."

"Perhaps now that your wife has passed away, maybe you can find her again."

"I'm going to see her in a few days," Jack said.

"Oh!" Gloria said softly seeming a bit disappointed.

Just then Zeke came in.

"Are you harassing my detective Jack?" he asked in a laughing voice.

"I was just asking if he had any vacancies in California," Gloria said.

"You're too late Gloria." Zeke said. "I think he may have another lady in mind."

"Too bad," she answered smiling and turned back to her work.
As Jack and Zeke walked away, Jack said.
"Maybe I should transfer here,"
"Let's go home," Zeke said laughing just a bit.

After dinner Gail asked. "When you talked to Marian, Jack, what did you decide about going to meet her parents?"

"I told her I'd probably fly down on Monday to meet her and we could leave the next day. I told her I was helping Zeke here but if we aren't finished on his case by then, I'd leave anyway."

"Then we have the week-end," she replied. "We should plan something."

"Right," Zeke said. "Tomorrow is Friday so we have a day to plan. Do you know what you'd like to see in our part of the country Jack?"

"No. I haven't any idea what is here to see. You go ahead and plan and I'm sure it will be new and interesting to me whatever you decide."

Friday morning Zeke was greeted by two of his detectives who told him the missing child's mother doesn't know if there was a vehicle parked on the street or not. The lawn cutter's kids were verified to be six and eight years of age. Mario's sister's child is two.

"Is there anyone else in the neighborhood that has a two year old child?" Jack asked.

"I don't know but I'll find out," Zeke replied. "Do you think another family in the area might have taken the child?"

"Probably not, but it's something I want to find out."

"Okay. We'll check it."

"And you'd better have them check all the houses on streets close by."

"You think someone just happened to be walking by and picked up the child and walked off with it?" Remember the mother was out of sight of her child for only a minute or less."

"Have any other ideas?" Jack asked.

"Well no... Okay I'll have them check."

"There's been no ransom request so that means someone just wanted a child."

"That's what it sounds like. And one more thing," Jack said.

"Who is the child's doctor?"

"The child's Doctor?" Zeke asked puzzled by the question. "Why?"

"Because if someone living close by took the child and wanted to take it to a doctor, it's possible they might accidentally take it to the same doctor the mother took her child to. Especially if the doctor's office is nearby."

"That makes sense. I never thought of that. Okay, I'll find out."

It didn't take Zeke long to return with the information.

"The baby's Doctor is Preston Gomez. His office is only about a half mile away."

"Okay. Make sure he knows and have him watch for anyone new coming into his office. He might be able to help."

Just then Gloria Glassman walked in.

"Good morning Lieutenant," she said looking at Jack with a glistening smile and a sparkle in her eyes.

"Good morning Gloria. Solved any of those cases yet?" he asked.

"Not yet, she replied. "I could use some help. Are you available to lend your expertise to a poor lady detective?" her smile was almost a chuckle.

"I don't think you really need me," Jack replied. "Zeke tells me you're very capable," Jack was smiling back at her.

"You don't need Jack's help Gloria." Zeke said.

"You've got outside help. Why can't I have some?" Gloria asked, still with a smile as she looked at Jack.

"Maybe I should give her a hand," Jack said in jest.

"No! She doesn't need your help Jack," Zeke said and then went on. "I'm going to take you to see a couple of our other Police stations this morning.

"I can do that," Gloria chimed in still smiling and trying to worm her way into getting to know Jack better. "Besides, boss, you're too busy."

Zeke just looked at her, then turned toward Jack and said. "Let's go."

As they walked out and down the hallway, Zeke said.

"She can be impossible sometimes."

"I'll bet she's not," Jack replied smiling at his friend.

Zeke just looked at him and said in smiling. "Maybe not."

When the detectives Zeke sent to Doctor Gomez's office returned, he brought some unexpected news.

"Doctor Gomez is gone. He took three months off to work with a charity organization that is sponsored by his church. There is a Doctor Lawrence Ward taking his place. I spoke to Doctor Ward and he told me he wouldn't know the child. I talked to the nurse and she said there were two new patients the week after Doctor Gomez left. One came in for only one visit. She was supposed to return but so far has never come back. The nurse said she tried to call to see how the child was, but the phone number had been disconnected."

"Could the nurse describe her?" Jack asked.

"Yes. She was mid thirties, dark hair and eyes and appeared to be from one of the Hispanic countries."

"Did she have a name?"

"Yes. Anna Avila."

"Did the nurse see the child and did it have the approximate same skin color as the mother?"

"The nurse told me she wasn't sure about that. The child was bundled up in a hooded jacket and she wasn't with the doctor when he examined the child."

"Okay, see if we can find an Anna Avila," Jack ordered.

"And by the way," Zeke jumped in. "Did the nurse think the lady seemed nervous or edgy?"

"The nurse didn't say and I didn't think to ask. I'll check back, the detective replied.

"How did she pay for the visit?" Jack asked.

"Cash," the nurse told me. She thought that was a bit unusual."

"That is a bit unusual," Jack answered. "Okay, let's see if we can find her."

The detective left and Jack turned to Zeke and said. "Well that's something but it's not much. Let's get a notice out to all pediatricians to watch for a lady who might be a new patient and would pay cash and might be Hispanic."

"Okay. At least it's more than we had a week ago."

The day came to an end without any new information on the case so they returned to Zeke and Gail's home.

The week end went by fast. Jack got to visit all the interesting places his hosts thought he might enjoy seeing including several in other parts of Ohio.

It was Monday morning before they knew it. The sun was out early and already showing signs of being a hot day. Gail turned on the air condition early as she felt it was a bit stuffy in the house.

"Are you still planning to leave today?" Gail asked Jack while they were seated at the breakfast table.

"I probably should since I told Marian I would, but I'm interested in that missing child's case and I'd like to see if there is any news today."

"Just like a detective," Gail said laughing. "Get him interested in a case and he can't let it go until it's finished."

"I think I'll call her and postpone it one day. You don't mind if I stay another day do you?"

"No, of course not. We love having you."

Jack called Marian as soon as he finished eating, to tell her he was staying another day. She was disappointed as she was looking forward to his arrival, and she'd already made plane reservations and now would have to change them. He promised that he'd come the following day no matter what.

There wasn't any new information when Jack and Zeke arrived at his work location, so as Jack reviewed the known information one more time, Zeke went on to attend to other work related items. As he was seated at Zeke's desk, Gloria walked over.

"How about taking me to lunch Lieutenant? She asked.

Jack smiled a bit and then replied.

"I think Zeke has plans for us."

"Oh! Darn. I was hoping we could visit. Are you going to be here tomorrow?"

"I don't think so Gloria. I'm pretty sure I'm leaving tomorrow."

She was disappointed and replied. "Too bad for me I guess. Oh well. That's life." She turned and walked back to her desk. She sat there for a moment then called across the room.

"If you get an opening out at your work place, let me know."

At 10a.m., Zeke was scheduled to attend a meeting and invited Jack to come along. After meeting several other members of the Cleveland Police department and being quizzed about things on the west coast, it was lunch time.

"I want to take you to Gerry's place for lunch." Zeke said. "She's the wife of an old friend of mine from college. She's got a great little sandwich shop not far from here. I go there every once in awhile."

"Okay." Jack replied.

The drive took only about ten minutes and was located in a busy section in west Cleveland. It was away from the city center but in a location that still contained many active and busy businesses. It was tucked between a ladies apparel shop on one side and a travel agency on the other. Zeke managed to find on street parking around the corner and they walked back toward the sandwich shop. Once inside, Jack noticed it was already crowded, but there was a table for two in the corner, so they made their way there and sat down.

"Hi Zeke," the young lady said as she arrived to greet them. Looking down at Jack, she asked. "Who's your handsome friend?"

"This is my friend from San Francisco, Lieutenant Jack Dennison. He's with the Police department out there. He's visiting us for a few days." Then turning to Jack, he added. "This is Ginny, Gerry's sister. She helps out here sometimes."

"Pleased to meet you Lieutenant Dennison. Going to be in town long?"

"No. In fact I'm leaving tomorrow."

"Oh!" she replied acting a bit disappointed. "That's too bad. If you change your mind and would like to stay a bit longer, I'd be glad to show you our wonderful city."

"Sorry Ginny, but I've really got to leave."

She took their orders and after she left, Zeke said.

"Be careful Jack. She's looking for a husband," he said laughing as he said it.

"Thanks a lot," Jack replied.

Gerry Gertsen, the owner came by later to visit and her sister arrived moments after with their order.

"Lieutenant Dennison is leaving us tomorrow." Ginny told her sister in a voice that sounded like she was unhappy.

"Well, Lieutenant you must come and see us again," Gerry replied.

"If I can, I will," Jack replied.

"How are things in your world Zeke?" Gerry asked.

"Oh, I'm keeping busy and out of trouble," he replied.

"I supposed that's good," she answered. "You need to come in more often. Bring your wife. Take her out once in awhile."

"Yes. I'll do that," he replied.

Gerry walked away to attend to another customer she saw come in.

Ginny returned a few minutes later to fill their coffee cups and see if there was anything they needed.

"You don't get in here very often Zeke. At least I never see you. Busy at work?"

I don't always eat lunch out Ginny. Today is special with my guest in town."

She turned toward Jack and said.

"It's too bad you aren't going to be here longer. You might like to try some of the other items we have. We offer many good selections and some of the best ones aren't even on the menu."

She was smiling as she turned to walk away.

"That sounded like an invitation," Jack said.

Zeke laughed and replied. "Yes it did. Sure you don't want to stay another day?"

The both laughed.

Zeke knew she'd always been a flirt and since she and her husband were now divorced, she was free to use her flirtation to attract a handsome man. He'd felt that even when she was married, her teasing of some of the more attractive men might have been a contributing factor in her divorce. But then, he never knew what she saw in Bert, her ex anyway.

Bert was rather rough, loud and not very likeable. He'd heard rumors that she only married him because she was expecting and he was available. After she lost the baby, not much time went by before she divorced him.

When Zeke and Jack finished their lunch and were returning to their parked car, they passed several people, among them a lady pushing a stroller with a small child. Jack looked at her as he saw her approaching, and noticed she appeared to fit the description of the lady they knew was in Doctor Gomez's office. Then as he looked down at the child it too, seemed to meet the criteria they knew about the child. It seemed to be about the right age. But then, he thought, there must be many ladies and young children that fit the category of the missing child and the lady from the doctor's office. Besides he couldn't know if this was the person who took the child. There are many people who would fit the description given by the nurse.

Jack glanced at the lady once more, smiled and she smiled back. Then he noticed the ugly looking scar on her right fore arm.

"Did you see that scar?" he asked Zeke.

"Yes. It looks like it wasn't very old. I didn't get a good look, but enough to know it was ugly."

"It's terrible," Jack said. "I wonder how it happened."

"Not an angry husband, I hope." Zeke said.

When they returned to the office, one of the detectives stopped them.

"The nurse from Doctor Gomez's office called. She wanted to let us know that she just remembered something about the unknown lady with the young child that she was telling us about."

"What's that?" Zeke asked.

"She remembered that the lady had an ugly looking scar on her right arm. She said she forgot all about it when we were talking to her. She thought it might be important."

Jack and Zeke looked at each other.

"We may have just seen her," Zeke told the detective.

"Where?" the detective asked surprised by the answer.

"We were having lunch over on Euclid at the Tip Top café."

"I'd better take a few people and go check the area," the detective replied.

"She may be gone by now but if she is living around there, we can keep an eye on the area."

"I'll go look now anyway. She may still be shopping in the area."

The afternoon didn't result in any new information. The detectives returned a couple of hours later without finding the lady in question and when the day ended Zeke and Jack returned to another very good meal prepared by Zeke's wife. Gail had invited a few Friends over for the evening and it turned out to be a very enjoyable.

CHAPTER FOUR
SWITZERLAND

The next morning Jack bid Gail farewell and Zeke drove him to the airport.

"I'll be back in a week to get my car and hopefully you will have solved this case."

"Yes, I hope so. We may find the lady with the badly scarred arm and hopefully that will help us find the child. Not sure how that's connected if at all, but we can hope. Anyway thanks for the help and have a good trip. Tell Marian hello for us."

"I will, he replied.

Jack's flight to Virginia was uneventful and Marian was waiting in the baggage claim area to greet him.

"You're here at last," she said. "I was beginning to think you weren't coming. You detectives just can't leave a case alone even when it's not yours."

He laughed as he replied. "I guess not, but it's what friends are for, helping one another."

"Well, you're here," she exclaimed as she threw her arms around him. He gave her a gentle hug in return. "Our plane leaves tonight so we've got a few hours to kill. What would you like to do?" I thought we'd grab some lunch, take my car home and then take the shuttle back to the airport. How does that sound?"

"Whatever you think," he replied.

"We have to change planes in Paris. There is a short layover of two hours, but we will arrive at the Embassy tomorrow afternoon."

"I'll be glad to see your parents," Jack said.

"And what about their daughter?" she teased. "Are you glad to see her?"

Jack laughed as he looked down at her. "Yes of course. I'm glad to see their daughter too."

The embassy car was waiting when they arrived and it took them directly to the home of the Ambassador and Mrs. Johnson.

"It's good to see you Jack," the Ambassador said as he extended his hand. "I'm pleased you were able to make the trip."

"Yes Sir. I'm glad I was able to come. Marian was pretty persuasive."

"Hello Jack," Evelyn said.

"Hello Evelyn," he replied as he remembered her telling him more than a year ago to call her by her first name. I hope it's all right to still call you Evelyn even though you're the Ambassador's wife and not the Senator's wife.

She laughed. "Of course it is." Then she stopped him and looking up at him said. "Jack. The Ambassador and I just want you to know how sorry we are about the loss of your wife. It's a terrible thing. And after such a short time. We're so sorry."

"Thank you. It was terrible. So unexpected," he answered. "It's why I've taken time from my job. I just needed to get away for awhile."

She gave his hand a squeeze. "We understand Jack. Well come in," she continued. "I'm sure you must be tired after that long flight. After you've had a chance to freshen up, we will have dinner. I've had the staff prepare something really special for this occasion."

They mounted the stairs and walked into the huge lobby of the Ambassador's residence.

"Would you care for a drink Jack?" the Ambassador asked.

"Yes sir. That sounds good."

"Your usual?" he asked.

Jack nodded and as the Ambassador turned he noticed Marian was already preparing drinks for the four of them even as her father was asking. She knew that he as well as the rest of them might enjoy something to relax with after the flight.

After they were seated, the Ambassador turned to Jack and said.

"I have invited someone, an old friend of mine, to dinner tomorrow. I want you to meet him. I told him you were coming and he wants to meet you as well."

"Really?" Jack answered a bit surprised.

"Yes. His name is Henry Mullins. He's a writer of detective stories. I suspect he wants to talk to you about some of the cases you've been involved in. He may want to have you partner with him in writing about some of them."

Jack laughed a bit and then asked. "Is there really any money in that?"

"Well Henry says there is. In fact he's made a pretty good living at it for many years. Anyway when I told him you were coming, he adjusted his schedule to be here. I hope you don't mind."

"No. I don't mind at all. I just never thought about something like that."

Marian distributed drinks to the four of them and then sat next to Jack and said.

"Well, I finally got him to come here."

"And were glad you did daughter," the Ambassador said.

"How long can you stay Jack?" Evelyn asked.

"I don't know. Not very long. I have to go back to Cleveland and pick up my car and then drive back to San Francisco. Along the way I'd like to take in some of the southwest. I've never really done that. And time is running out on the time I have available. I guess only a few days."

"That's too bad. We were hoping you might be able to stay at least a week."

"Well, I'd really like too, but I'd better not. Perhaps another time if your still here and I'm invited."

"You'll always be welcome Jack," Evelyn said. She and her husband still had hopes that he and their only daughter might one day marry. They knew it almost happened once and now with the unfortunate death of his wife after such a short marriage, perhaps he would feel that Marian, their daughter, was the lady he'd like to marry.

"Dinner is ready," the announcement came from a member of the kitchen staff.

The next morning after a good night's sleep, Jack wandered down stairs and found Marian and her mother lingering over the remains of their breakfast.

"There you are," Marian said. "We decided to let you sleep. I thought you might need some extra rest."

"I guess I really did need it. I think I was so tired that if some attractive lady had wandered in, I never would have known it."

"Boy you must have been tired," Marian replied laughing.

"What's on the agenda today?" he asked.

"Well, after you've had something to eat, Marian is going to show you around town and tomorrow she plans on showing you some other parts of Switzerland," Evelyn said. "I don't need to tag along and the Ambassador is too busy, so Marian will do the honors. Besides you don't need us tagging along," she said a twinkle in her eyes and thoughts in her head that the two of them needed to be alone. "Anyway we've seen most of it during our time here."

"Well, that sounds great to me. I hate to put everyone to so much trouble."

"It's no trouble at all," Marian chimed in. "So what would you like for breakfast?"

The day went fast. She showed him all of Bern which is not the largest city in the country. They stopped for tea and talked to a few tourists. The met a couple of locals who Marian knew and before they knew it, the whole day suddenly came to an end.

"Bern is not the most interesting city or has the most interesting places to visit." Marian said.

"Tomorrow I'll drive us to Zurich. We'll go up Mt. Jungfraujoch. You'll be able to see much more there. Perhaps the next day we can go to Lucerne. There's also allot to see there. I just wish you had more time."

"Perhaps I will another time," he replied.

"Will there be another time?" she asked quickly seeming to pick up on his indication that he'd come again. Perhaps with her she was thinking.

"Yes. I think I'd like to spend more time here one day," he replied.

"I could show you a lot more someday," she answered hoping there might be some hint that he would think it was a good idea to have her as his guide.

He looked down at her beautiful face and could see in her eyes how happy she was.

"I'd like that," he said simply.

Those words sent a tingle of joy through her. It was the first real indication he might want to be with her for a longer period of time.

He turned to her as she stopped the car in the front of the embassy. Looking across the front seat into her eyes, he said.

"Marian. I know it was difficult for you when I decided to marry Jacquee. It wasn't that I didn't love you, it was… well…I don't know what it was. I just felt a stronger love for her at that time I guess. I just decided she was the one I wanted to be married too. It really wasn't that I didn't care about you, didn't love you, because I did. I did feel you and I could have been very happy together. I felt terrible about how you must have felt when I decided to marry her. I knew in my mind that you loved me and it did bother me for some time when I would think about it. From time to time I wondered how you were doing and when I heard you were engaged, I really prayed for you to be happy."

Jack paused for a moment, and then continued.

"After Jacquee's passing I wasn't really thinking about anything. When you showed up in California at Don's cabin, I was really surprised. But almost immediately, seeing you and being with you, I began to feel that same attraction that I felt before when I was with you. Maybe that sounds strange since it was such a short time after Jacquee's passing, but I couldn't help it."

The joy of hearing him say he was still attracted to her sent a tingle through her whole body. Her face was sober but she was smiling inside from head to toe. At that moment, listening to him, she could sense that she would once again have a chance to win him.

"Anyway," he continued. "I just need to let you know how I feel. I don't know what you think about it, but I do need some time before I can get on with my life."

"I've always loved you Jack," she said. "Even after you married Jacquee. I was saddened to hear of her illness and I really prayed for her recovery because I loved you and wanted you to be happy. When it didn't happen and she died I really felt bad. I knew you would grieve, but still loving you I needed to let you know I was still here. I needed to find out if you felt you cared enough that we might have a chance. I'm really sorry you lost her. I truly am." She paused a moment and then said. "Do we Jack? Do we have a chance?"

There was silence for a few moments in the car as she watched him. He was looking away thinking about what she said and the questions she'd asked him. Then, looking back at her, he answered.

"Yes. Yes I think so," he said. "But I need some time. I'm not ready. Not yet."

"I know," she replied soberly. Inside, joyfully she knew the man she loved just told her they had a future if she was just patient a bit longer while he dealt with the loss of his wife. It was more happiness than she'd known in a long time.

Finally after sitting there for a few minutes, he said.

"We'd better go in."

"How was your day?" Evelyn said when she saw them.

"It was really nice," he replied.

"It was wonderful," Marian replied not thinking about the day, but about what happened a few moments ago in the car.

"What are the two of you going to do tomorrow?"

"I'm going to take him to Zurich. There's a lot to see there. Maybe we'll even go up Mt. Jungfraujoch. He'll be able to see a great deal and perhaps the day after we'll go to Lucerne. We'll see."

"Well, dinner will be ready soon. Mr. Mullins is with your dad and he wants to meet Jack, so the two of you should get ready."

"Okay," Marian replied as she took his hand and led him up the stairs toward their respective rooms.

When they returned, the Ambassador and his wife were in the dining room along with their other guest.

"Jack," the ambassador said when he and Marian arrived. I want you to meet Henry Mullins, a friend of mine. He writes detective stories for a well known magazine. He asked to meet you when he learned you were a detective."

Greetings were exchanged and dinner was announced, so they all sat down to eat. Following the delicious meal, everyone retired across the hall to a large sitting room to enjoy a drink and some conversation.

"How long have you been a detective Jack?" Henry Mullins asked.

"About fifteen years."

"All in San Francisco?" he asked.

"Yes."

"You must have come across some very interesting cases."

"Well, I guess you could call them interesting. Challenging is more the word I would use."

They all chuckled slightly and then Henry went on.

"My friend, the Ambassador here thinks you might have some cases I would be interested in. I believe he told you I write stories for a magazine based on actual crimes across the nation. I recently have been working with detectives in New York, Philadelphia, Atlanta, L.A. and a couple of other places.

I'm looking for another big city that might have some interesting cases I could write about. Do you think there might be any like that out where you are?"

"Well, I don't know. I've certainly had some strange ones over the years."

"What I do Jack is take the information and write a mystery story. I use the basic information, changing the names and places and try to make the story as real as possible without actually using too many facts that would identify the actually place or people.

The public seems to like them and I, as well as my magazine have made quite a bit of money from these stories. Of course the detectives I work with make quite a bit of money as well. I get paid a percentage of sales and I share fifty/fifty with the person who provided the information for the story. If I write more than one story, you would get paid fifty percent from each."

"There must be pretty good profits from this I take it," Jack said.

"Oh yes. My magazine is eager for me to bring them stories each month. I just sent in one story from Dallas and now I need to come up with another for next month's issue."

"Once the monthly issue hits the market, isn't last month's issue dead and the profits end for it? In other words don't the sales stop on old issues of the magazine? I would think profits end with old copies." Jack asked.

"Not exactly Jack," Harry said. "You'd be surprised how many older issues sell many months after they first hit the market. In fact when copies hit the overseas market, it's like a brand new infusion of sales. These stories are really big in some countries. Even with old issues. Last quarter on my statement from the magazine, I made two thousand dollars from an issue that came out last year. That may not sound like much but, look here," he said as he reached into his pocket.

"Here is a copy of my last quarter's statement. It will show you how much I made from across this country as well as from other countries."

Jack took the paper Henry handed him and first looked at the total figure near the bottom.

It surprised him. His eyes glanced up the page at other figures on the sheet.

"And this is your share of profits for the last quarter?" Jack asked.

"Yes. Of course my partners; the detectives I work with, also get a statement just like that for the same amount. I've made enough money in the ten years I've been doing this that I could retire. But I see no reason to do that yet as long as the public seems to like them and I feel like writing them."

"Can I see that?" Marian asked.

"Sure," Henry said and Jack handed it to her.

"If I choose to help you," Jack asked. "And since I don't write, just what would I do?"

"You give me the case information, I write the story, we consult about the facts and I send the finished copy to the magazine and they take it from there."

"And that's all?"

"That's all Jack," Henry replied.

"This is pretty impressive," Marian said.

"Well, what do you think Jack? Is it something you might be interested in doing?" Henry asked. "I am looking for a new area to write about and it seems to me that San Francisco would be just the place."

"Let me think about it," Jack replied.

"Okay," Henry answered. "I need one now for next month's issue, but perhaps you and I could get together for a story for month after next. When are you going to be back in Frisco?"

"I think I'll have to leave here in a couple of days. I have a few weeks left on my time off, so I'll be back just after the first."

"Okay. I'm leaving tomorrow. How about if I call you then?" Henry asked.

"Okay," Jack replied.

"I think you should do it honey," Marian remarked talking to Jack.

Evelyn and the Ambassador both noticed her use of the word "honey." It was something she'd not done so far in conversations with Jack. They looked at each other approvingly and smiled slightly.

The next two days Marian and Jack traveled to Zurich and Lucerne. She showed him all the most interesting sights available in the limited amount of time available. When they returned to the embassy, she turned to him and suggested.

"I was thinking. I could fly back with you tomorrow and we could visit Zeke and Gail and then I'd drive back to the coast with you."

She already knew she didn't want them to be separated again ever.

Jack looked at her. He needed to tell her he didn't want her to come back with him. He knew she wanted to, but he needed to finish this journey alone. He needed that time. That's what he really intended to do, but somehow he ended up in Cleveland and now here. Still he needed some time to spend alone just to remember his dearly deceased wife. They had been together such a short time and he missed her so much. He never knew he could. At least as much as he now seemed too.

"Marian, my dear," he started.

She knew she wasn't going to like what he was about to say.

"I don't want you to come with me," he said. It sounded harsh and he didn't mean it too, because being with her from Virginia a few days ago until now, he knew he still really did love this lady. If that were possible he didn't know, but she'd asked him to come and in a moment of haste, he'd said yes. Well, he needed to keep his promise and he had gone to visit her parents, but now he must complete this journey alone.

Soon he'd be back at work and busy and that would help him. Being busy would keep his mind off his dearly beloved wife. It was difficult knowing both Jacquee and Marian at the same time and he was drawn strongly to each of them. He hated telling Marian he'd decided to marry Jacquee and not her. It was difficult. Very difficult. Now she was here again trying to convince him she still loved him, and he was sure she did and he was equally sure the two of them could be happy, but he just wasn't ready.

"I need to spend some time on my trip alone. I really do," he said. "My two months time alone has not turned out the way I intended. I did intend to see my sister and Don, but it wasn't in my original plans to go to Cleveland or come here."

"But I persuaded you didn't I?"

"Yes you did. I was surprised to find you at Don's cabin and when you asked me to come, I just couldn't refuse."

She was smiling at him as he said it.

"Anyway," he continued. "I don't want you to come with me. I need to finish this journey alone. I've spent almost half my time so far and I've not done all I intended."

"How about I come out when you get home?" She asked not putting up much resistance.

"I don't think you should do that either. When I get back, I'm going to be extra busy for awhile catching up on things. I'll be working long hours and I'll either be working or sleeping most of the time. I won't be much company. And since you don't know anyone there, you'd be alone and bored to death. If you want to come, then give me a chance to get caught up and settled into my routine."

"I love you Jack." she said breaking into his conversation. "I want to be with you. I know it's not been long since Jacquee's passing but I loved you too and I know that you loved me. I know you loved me once, I'm sure you did. Do you love me enough to want to be with me? I want to know if you think we have a chance. The two of us. Do we?"

He looked at her. He certainly didn't want to hurt her. He knew he loved her when Jacquee was alive and that's what made his decision at that time so difficult. But it was different now. Yes, when she showed up at Don's cabin, he was surprised, but happy and inside there was that feeling again. But now he just needed some time. Then perhaps they might pick up their relationship again. Having her around even for this short time was enjoyable and perhaps it is the way to go. Still, he wasn't ready and he still needed some time alone.

"Yes. Yes I do think there is a chance to pick up our relationship again," he said. "I must admit when I saw you at Don's, I did have those same strong feelings again. I guess that's why I agreed to come here."

"Okay," she responded. "I'll let you go and when you're ready, call me and I'll come. Just don't keep me waiting too long."

TRAVELING THE COUNTRY

CHAPTER ONE
ROCHELLE

The flight from Bern to Munich was short. Only about an hour. Once there, he had a three hour fifty minute wait before catching the long flight across the Atlantic to Toronto. Why Toronto he didn't know, but that's the way he was booked to go. He would arrive at two thirty five p.m. Toronto time according to the schedule. The flight was listed as eight hours and forty five minutes and he wasn't sure why, but anyway he'd be back across the Atlantic. There was another two hour wait until the plane departed to Cleveland and then it was only an hour's flight and finally he'd be there. It would be five thirty P. M. local Time in Cleveland. Back in Bern however, it would be two a.m. the next day. He knew he would be tired, but at least Zeke could pick him up at the airport and he'd be able to get a good night's sleep before heading once again back toward the west coast and his job.

Once in Munich, Jack headed for the first place he could find that offered him some breakfast. He hadn't eaten before he left Bern. It had been too early. The food at the airport restaurant here in Munich was pretty good for airport food. He remembered in his past experiences not all airport eating places were what he considered the best tasting or quality. Of course the prices were outrageous. Still he needed something. He was sure they would be feeding on the plane, but to be sure he picked up a few things at one of the airport stores he found on his way to the loading gate. Now he had only three hours and fifteen minutes until the next leg of his journey.

Picking up a newspaper, (the English version) he sat down to read and see what was new in the world. He wasn't really interested, but he had time to kill, so he decided he might as well be reading. Of course there were the screeching headlines of crimes, government problems in several countries and a myriad of other things, but he looked past those and tried to find something that might be more interesting to read. He'd almost finished the paper when he heard a voice ask.

"Are you an American?"

He looked up to see a middle aged lady, perhaps a bit older than he, but not by much, standing a few feet away.

"Yes," he answered.

"Do you mind if I sit here with you? I'd like to talk to someone without a German accent."

Jack chuckled a bit and said. "They almost all speak English here."

"Yes, but some of them, at least most of the ones I've spoken to, don't do it very well. "I'm Rochelle Alexander," she said as she extended her hand.

"Jack Dennison," he replied as he shook her hand gently. Her hand shake was weak to almost nonexistent.

"I'm sure going to be glad to get home. I didn't really want to come here, but my husband insisted."

"He did?" Jack asked surprised.

"Yes. He was born over here and he wanted me to see his relatives one more time. I own several stores that specialize in beauty aids for ladies. Perhaps you've heard of Rochelle's house of beauty."

"No I don't think so," Jack replied. I don't pay much attention to those things."

"Well, anyway he's from Germany and we've been married ten years. I've only been to see his parents and relatives once, and he insisted I come again. I tried to tell him I was much too busy, but he insisted."

He noticed she seemed to be studying his face. Then changing the subject she said.

"You have lovely looking skin. Do you do anything special to take care of it?"

"I shave and wash every day."

"And that's all?"

"Yes, that's all."

"Well, you're very fortunate," she replied.

"Where are you headed?" she asked.

"Well, I'm going to Cleveland first and then on to San Francisco."

"Oh!" she replied. I have two shops in the City by the Bay."

"Where are you headed," he asked.

"I'm waiting for a plane to Saint Louis to see my sister and then it's back to Frisco and work."

"Where is your husband now?"

"He's staying here for another month, but I have to get back. I've been too busy to be gone, but he insisted, so I made arrangements to come. Anyway I really have to get back. I'm stopping for two days to visit my sister only because I figure that after spending three weeks visiting his family, I can spend a couple of days seeing my only relative."

"Are you married, Jack?" she asked abruptly.

"No. My wife died a short time ago."

"I'm sorry to hear that," then pausing a moment, she asked. "What do you do for a living?"

"I'm with the San Francisco Police Department," he replied.

"Why are you going to Cleveland?" she asked.

"I left my car there with friends. I'd been on a road trip and I got talked into visiting people I know in Switzerland. I left it there while I flew across to Europe. I'm picking it up and driving home so I can go back to work."

"Oh, I'd love to do that some day. Drive across the country."

She was silent for a moment and then said.

"I don't suppose you'd be interested in picking me up in Saint Louis?"

Her face was serious and he looked back thinking she might be joking.

"I thought you were in a hurry."

She laughed a bit; then said. "Well actually I am, but it sounds really tempting. I would like to do that one day."

They sat there for about an hour, talking about nothing in particular, but mostly her work and finally she asked.

"I see the bar just opened. Can I buy you a drink?"

"It's a bit early in the day isn't it?" he asked.

"Well, yes it is, but sitting here this long waiting for a plane with nothing to do; well I'm just looking to do something besides sitting and I thought it might break the boredom. How about it Jack? Let me buy you a drink. I've enjoyed having someone to talk to that doesn't sound German."

"Okay," he laughed conceding to her request. "I'm tired of sitting here as well."

They walked over to the just opened bar she'd seen a short distance away and ordered their drinks. Rochelle pulled out one of the several credit cards he noticed in her purse and handed it to the bar man. They waited while the drinks were prepared and then took them and sat at a nearby table.

She took a long drink. "Umm. That tasted good. I don't usually drink in the morning, but somehow today I need it." They sat there for some time and she asked him about his life, which he didn't usually discuss to any great detail. She emptied her glass rather quickly and while his was still half full she proceeded to order another drink for the two of them. Then after taking a large swallow from her second, she looked across the table into his face, and asked. "If I change my flight and go to Cleveland with you, can I ride back to Frisco with you?"

Jack was startled by her surprising question.

"I thought you were going to see your sister in St. Louis?"

"I can see her another time. We're not very close anyway. Besides if I could drive back with you, it might be much more interesting."

He noticed the smile on her face as she looked at him. She apparently was being affected by this second drink, or so he thought. After all, they only met an hour ago, and she was a married woman. At least that's what she said. Now here she was making a play for him in the airport bar. He wondered what her reaction would be if he agreed to take her along. Would she jump at the chance, or would she make an excuse? There was always the chance she would go with him and, - - - well, he didn't want her along no matter what.

She reached across the table and took his hand. He did not pull away but looked down at her hand on his.

"What about it Jack?"

For a moment as he looked back at her, and then down at her hand on his, he wondered; would she really go with him if he agreed to take her?

She was quite attractive, he thought, but he wondered what was below the makeup on that face? After all she was in the beauty business. Maybe she wouldn't be as attractive as she now seemed to be once it was all removed.

"Rochelle," he said. "You're married. What are you doing?"

She let go his hand without saying anything, and then taking another long drink and signaling the bar tender for a refill, she said.

"I'm bored Jack. I find you very attractive, and I hate my husband. I only stay with him because he financed my business, but now that's its doing very well, I'm thinking of divorcing him. He's really not very interesting." Rochelle hesitate a moment, then continued once more.

"I need to bring a bit more excitement into my life. It's certainly not going to happen with Rolf. I just know it would happen with you. How about it Jack? Take me." she hesitated a moment. "Take me back with you."

He didn't answer her, but sipped a bit of the drink he didn't really need thinking he should just get up and leave.

The next order of drinks arrived rather quickly and after the bar tender took the empties; she took another long drink and continued.

"How about it?" she asked leaning across the table.

Jack took a second sip from his second glass not yet empty and staring back at her said.

"Rochelle. I just met you. I think you've had too much to drink. You don't know me and I don't know you and besides you're married. I'm not going to take you with me."

He stood up and said.

"Thanks for the drinks Rochelle Alexander," and he turned to walk back to his previous seating area.

She stood up as well seeing that he was leaving and not wanting him to. Stepping forward she stumbled over the table leg, causing her to fall toward him. He grabbed her to keep her from hitting the floor, and as he did, she wrapped her arms around him.

Then looking up at him, she said.

"Kiss me Jack."

Jack steadied her on her feet and separated himself from her. She looked into his face and began to cry as suddenly she seemed to realize she was making a fool of herself. Then grabbing her purse and removing a tissue she began to dab at her eyes. He stood there watching to make sure she was going to be all right. Finally after a few moments, she said.

"There goes my damn makeup. Now I've got to go redo my face."

With that, she turned and headed toward the ladies room without saying another word. He watched her walk away not knowing if it was all an act or was she all of a sudden too embarrassed. Was she really trying to start something with him or was she not much of a drinker and the three drinks made her say things she really didn't mean.

Jack took a walk around the area to kill some time hoping that maybe he'd not see her again. When he returned to the area where he was first seated, there she was sitting in the same place before they went for drinks. When she saw him, she motioned him to come over. He hesitated a moment, but went back and sat down next to her.

"I'm sorry," she said and after a moment's hesitation and went on. "I really was trying to get you to take me with you. I really wanted to go. My life is so boring sometimes and Rolf, my husband is such a drag. I saw you, a handsome man, and all of a sudden I had this desire to spice up my life by having an affair with you. Then after a couple of drinks I had the courage to try harder and all I did was embarrass myself. I'm sorry Jack. I've never done that before. I don't know what possessed me. Sudden desperation I guess. I'm sorry."

He said nothing, and after she fumbled a moment with the tissue still in her hands, she said. "I wish I had someone like you in my life." She looked at him, dabbed her eyes once more and then turned away.

"It's okay Rochelle," he said. "Really it is."

"I'd better go find someplace else to sit," and she started to stand up.

"Sit down Rochelle," he ordered. She did, not really wanting to leave. She knew nothing was going to happen between them but sitting there made her feel better.

"Tell me about yourself before Rolf," Jack said.

They talked for some time. She'd been married before Rolf, but that didn't work out. She'd met him at a party and he'd pursued her and convinced her to marry him. The marriage was okay for awhile, but he was gone a lot and when she opened her first business they gradually drifted apart. After a couple of years the business failed and a few months later she met Rolf. She moved in with him and they lived together for awhile. He agreed to finance her second effort in her field of beauty products. She opened a new business under its current name and it was doing wonderfully. They got married, perhaps because she was grateful, and Rochelle soon learned that Rolf was boring to be around. He was involved in his business ventures and she in hers, and perhaps that was part of the problem. When they were together, it wasn't very enjoyable. Still she stuck it out, grateful that he'd been willing to help her get started. Often she thought of leaving him. He'd taken her to meet his parents and other relatives and she knew she didn't like it there or them.

She wanted to know all about him but Jack insisted there wasn't much to tell. Rochelle said she was sorry about his losing his wife and admitted that in the short time they were talking, she found herself attracted to him. Before long the speaker announced her flight. She stood up, grabbed her purse and looking down at Jack, she said.

"Rochelle's house of Beauty Jack. I'd like it if you'd come by," she hesitated a moment. "I really would like to see you."

"You're married Rochelle. I won't do that," he replied as he stood up to send her off.

"Would you come to see me if I wasn't married?"

He hesitated a moment before answering. "I don't know."

She took a step closer and before he could react, she reached up and pressed her lips to his passionately. Then stepping back she said.

"There goes my damn lipstick again." She turned and walked toward the gate to catch her flight. Jack watched her go and after she handed her ticket to the airline agent, she turned one last time to look in his direction as if to get one more look at a man she felt she would never see again.

CHAPTER TWO
THE SOUTHWEST

His flight to Toronto was long and boring. He slept for part of it and was glad when they arrived. They did feed them on the flight across the ocean as he suspected.

Enough flying he thought as he waited for the flight to Cleveland.

Zeke met him at the baggage claim area when he arrived.

"Boy am I glad to be back," were Jack's first words. "I'm not going to be doing that too soon again," then without stopping Jack asked.

"Did you ever find the baby?"

"Yes," Zeke replied.

"Tell me what happened after I left."

"We found the lady with the scar on her arm. At first she denied everything. She said the child was hers, but we checked and found out it wasn't. Then later we learned that her boy friend wanted them to have another child. They had one older child, but she couldn't have any more. He had been after her for a long time and threatened to leave. She said she was desperate and when she was walking down the street thinking about it and what she was going to do, she saw the lady go inside and leave the child outside in the yard.

She told detectives that she didn't know what possessed her, but she just grabbed the child and ran between the houses and down the alley and home."

"What did her boy friend say when she showed up with another child?"

"She told me he was unhappy. He wanted her to have a baby but she told him she couldn't take it back. She said he finally agreed to let her keep it."

"So I imagine the mother was happy to get her baby back."

"Oh yes."

"What's going to happen to the lady and her boy friend?"

"Well, she's being charged with kidnapping and he as an accessory."

"Then the case is over," Jack said.
"Yes, except for the trial."

It was morning when Jack pulled away from Zeke and Gail's house after spending the evening and having a good breakfast, he headed west and south toward Kansas City. The sun was out and headed toward being another warm day. It became a bit boring driving down the main highway, but he stopped a couple of times to get out and stretch. He knew it would be tomorrow before he'd arrive in Kansas City for a short visit with his friend Mo Harrison, his staff and of course, Jane, the office lady he knew very well. He wanted to travel as many miles as possible each day as he felt his vacation time was running out. In his mind were thoughts that if he'd not taken the trip to Switzerland there would have been more time to visit some of the many interesting sights across the country, but all in all it had been an enjoyable journey so far.

He stopped in Terre Haute, Indiana, for the night at a motel along the main highway. After a meal nearby, Jack quickly climbed into bed hoping to be up early for the drive to Kansas City knowing that it would take most of the day.

He fell asleep quickly, but In the middle of the night he was awakened by the sound of someone twisting the door knob to his room. He'd been careful to place a rubber door stop on the floor close to the door that would keep the door from being opened easily if someone tried to break in. It was a habit he'd gotten into years ago after learning from a friend's family who told him they always did that when they traveled.

His room was totally dark except for the little green light in the ceiling smoke alarm. Jack reached for his revolver on the night stand and waited. He could hear someone still trying to open his door. Then all of a sudden there was a loud bang as the door was broken open. The chain hook on the wall connected onto the door broke. The door stopped quickly as the rubber door stop on the floor did its job. Then as he lay their quietly, there was another loud crashing sound as the door was apparently broken off its hinges and went banging against the wall opposite his bed. Suddenly the room light came on as one of the intruders hit the switch lighting up the room. Jack saw two men dressed in dark clothes with their faces partly hidden by make shift masks and slightly off balance from the break in.

"On the floor," Jack ordered pointing his service revolver in their direction.

They hesitated at seeing his gun. They were not expecting to find someone pointing a gun at them, but instead thinking they'd find a tourist they might rob.

"On the floor," he ordered once more. "Don't even think of doing anything else. I can kill you before you reach the door."

He eased himself from the bed and stood up as the two partially masked people positioned themselves on the floor face down.

They lay flat arms extended as jack dialed a number on his room phone. Within Minutes several police cars arrived.

"We've been looking for these two, Lieutenant," One of the officers said after learning Jack was a police lieutenant. "They've been robbing several motels around here for the last few months. I guess this time they picked the wrong motel room."

Jack got off to a late start the next morning after stopping to file a report. His drive to visit Mo would be a day late. Terra Haute to Kansas City could take him seven hours he thought and by the time he filed the report and eaten, it was too late to try and arrive in the same day.

When he walked into the F.B.I. office in Kansas City, there she was sitting at her desk as usual.

"Hello Jane," he said as he stepped through the door.

Immediately at seeing him she was up from her desk and moved quickly to embrace him.

"Jack," she said as she threw her arms around him. "It's so good to see you."

"It's good to see you too," he answered.

"How long can you stay?"

"Not long. Perhaps long enough for lunch," he answered.

"Not overnight?" she asked.

"No afraid not. I need to get back to work and I don't have as much time as I thought I might."

"You really need to visit us longer than that. We enjoy seeing you. Especially me!" She answered with a big smile on her face as she gave him another big squeeze.

Jack smiled down at her remembering their first meeting when he was assigned here awhile after his school in D.C. She hadn't liked him at first, but after a bit their relationship became closer than he ever anticipated. Jane was a few years older than him. Actually about twenty years older, but that didn't seem to detour her from wanting a much closer relationship.

"Is Mo in?" he asked.

She didn't answer at first wanting to just hang onto him. Finally, and reluctantly she said.

"Yes, he's in."

"Can I see him?" Jack asked as he tried to pry himself loose from the lady who seemed determined to not let go.

"I'm so glad to see you, I don't want to let go," she answered.

"I can see that," he answered.

Finally she took his hand and led him down the hall to Mo's office.

"Look who I found," she announced when they reached his door.

Mo got up from his desk and walked around to greet him "Good to see you Jack. I'm glad you could stop."

"Well, I could hardly pass by and not stop. Unfortunately I can't stay long. I'm behind schedule and need to get back to work."

"You've got time for lunch don't you?"

"Oh yes. I can do that. I need to stop for lunch somewhere, it might as well be here."

"Okay. Let's go. I know a good place nearby,"

"I'll get my coat," Jane answered.

Mo looked at her a moment, then said. "We need to keep the office open Jane. There's no one else here."

Not wanting to be left out, she responded. "I'm coming. It won't hurt for the office to be closed for a couple of hours. Besides when are we ever going to see Jack again? I'm coming along Mo, and that's it."

Mo looked at Jack and smiled saying. "I guess the office will be closed after all. Jane's decided that you're more important than our staying open."

Lunch was over all too soon and the three of them returned to the F.B.I. office. As Jack prepared to leave, Jane said.

"Will we ever see you again?"

"I don't know Jane. Right now I need to get back to work. Besides that, I have many other things I need to do."

She wasn't ready to have him walk out of her life because she knew she'd never see him again. She wanted him to stay. She also knew she's go with him if he wanted her to. Even though she was almost twenty years older than he was, Jane felt such a strong love for this man that she was willing to leave her job and home and following him to the coast or wherever he was going.

But it wasn't going to happen and deep inside she knew that. Still there was the hope that he'd look at her and say, "Come with me Jane."

"It's been good seeing you Mo," Jack said as he extended his hand.

"Good seeing you, Jack. If you ever decide to come back and work with us, I'd be glad to have you. Best of luck."

Jack turned to Jane and extended his hand, but she wasn't going to settle for a hand shake. She put her arms around him and hugged him in front of Mo and looking up she said.

"I love you Jack."

Not quite sure what to say, he looked down and answered. "I love you too, Jane, but I've got to go."

Jack separated her from himself and turned toward the door.

"I'll walk you to the car," she announced as he moved to the door with him.

Just then the phone rang.

"The phone's ringing, Jane," Mo announced as if she didn't hear it. But she was too busy and really didn't care.

"Then answer it, Mo," she ordered not caring at that moment that he was the boss and she was only the employee.

Jack waved one last time as he and Jane disappeared through the door that would take them to Jack's car.

She clung to him desperately not wanting to let go of the first person she loved since her husband died many years ago. She knew she would never see him again.

"I've got to go, Jane," Jack said after they reached his car.

"I don't want you to go," she answered and continued to cling to him as they stood on the walk.

Finally he was able to separate himself from her.

"Jane," he started to say.

"Can I have one final kiss?" she asked.

"Sure," he replied thinking it might be a way to bring this to a halt.

It was the most passionate of kisses and one of the longest lasting he'd ever experienced. She didn't want it to end and was doing her best to make sure he'd remember her.

One more time Jack pulled himself away. "I've got to go Jane."

"I know," she replied weakly. "Will I ever see you again?"

"I don't know Jane. I don't know."

He could see her on the walk watching as he drove away.

CHAPTER THREE
THE TEENAGER

He stopped in Liberal Kansas on the Oklahoma border that evening. It was late but he managed to find a place to stay. The sun had already disappeared into the west by the time he arrived. It was a nice sized city, but he didn't really get to see much. It had taken seven hours from Kansas City to drive the four hundred or so miles.

In the morning after a good night's sleep he was up and heading southwest across the upper corner of Texas toward Tucumcari, New Mexico. First it was breakfast, so down the road in a small Oklahoma town called Guymon, only about forty miles from Liberal, he stopped to eat. It was typical of many small towns. The area was flat and desert like with a scattering of trees and bushes that looked like they could use some water. It was dry and he was sure no rain had fallen here all summer. There wasn't any breeze and the heat was already starting to scorch the land once more. The main street had the usual businesses, not yet open, and except for the tiny eating establishment and a gas station across the street, it was quiet and deserted. A man was pumping gas into an old broken down looking truck that must have been thirty years old or perhaps even more Jack thought.

He was the only customer in the tiny eating place at the moment, and the lady who took his order didn't seem too interested in conversation. There was a man in the kitchen that he could see through an opening in the wall. He seemed to be doing what anyone who did the cooking might do, so Jack guessed he must be the cook.

The food came and it was nothing special, but it did fill him. Jack paid his bill and walked outside. The temperature was already in the seventies he noticed as he looked at the temperature gauge on the outside wall of the eating place. Getting back into his car he could tell the inside of his vehicle was already many degrees hotter than the outside temperature. He started the engine and as he did, two old cars drove by, each headed in a different direction and each stirring up a bit of dust. The old truck at the gas station across the street was just driving away after having spent more time than necessary to purchase a tank full of fuel. The attendant hobbled back inside out of the heat, aided by what appeared to be an old wooden cane. Jack suspected he would wait in a cooler environment until another customer might arrive and require his services.

As he started to leave the town of Guymon, it occurred to him that perhaps he should check his map once more time to examine his line of travel. Pulling over to a wide spot on the road near the end of town and unfolding his map, he looked first at where he was and then where he was heading. All of a sudden it occurred to him as he looked at his map; that he was going to miss seeing the Alamo in San Antonio if he continued in this direction. Certainly, being this close he didn't want to miss going there.

"I'd better make time to go there," he said out loud. "If I didn't stop and see that, I'd always regret it. Who knows when I might get back?"

Jack turned around and headed back to intercept highway eighty three toward Abilene. He'd stay there tonight and could make San Antonio the next day. The drive was uneventful as was the stay. He noticed the heat temperature outside registered 103 as he passed through a small town in north Texas.

The next day he left Abilene and headed south toward San Antonio and the Alamo. The distance was only about two hundred twenty five miles, so he knew he'd arrive early in the afternoon. Several places to stay were right in the middle of town and within walking distance of that famous place. Finding one with a vacancy was not a problem. After checking in, he took a stroll through the area and that brought him to the River Walk where he spent time exploring the river that ran through the middle of town. He discovered many eating places along the river banks and finally selected one that specialized in typical southwest food. It was here that he had his evening meal. Afterwards he walked past the Alamo to take a look at it from the outside.

The next day his visit to the historic Alamo proved interesting to him. Jack tried to put his mind back to what it must have been like in those days. It was difficult to imagine. It took him. Most of the day and then it was back to the River Walk once again to enjoy the unusual, but interesting surroundings. He selected another of the many fine eating establishments that lined the river to have his evening meal.

The next morning came too early. The hotel offered everyone a continental breakfast, so after a bite to eat, it was on the road again. He enjoyed his stay so much, that he wished he could linger here even longer. West on Highway ten he drove and then north toward New Mexico. He finally decided to stop at Pecos, a small town not far from the border. He'd gone about three hundred twenty five miles and was now less than one hundred from Carlsbad and the caverns of New Mexico. He could easily see them the next day and then be in Santa Fe the day after. It was a place he'd heard a lot about and thought he would have to see it for himself.

The motel in Pecos he selected was the typical southwest style of stucco construction with a large courtyard. In the courtyard were a few typical southwest style trees, and a few benches alongside a narrow walkway. A small fountain in the center was the focal point although Jack didn't know why anyone would want to sit out there in the blistering heat. It was still over one hundred degrees according to the gauge outside the office door.

The lady behind the counter was just finishing with a couple and their two children when he entered.

"I'll be with you in a moment Senior," she said as she looked up when he entered.

Jack nodded and waited. As the man turned, he noticed Jack and said.

"Warm enough for you?"

Jack smiled and replied. "Much too hot for me."

"Now sir," the lady said. "May I help you?" Jack saw she was middle aged and slightly overweight, but still displaying a trace of the beauty many Hispanic nationalities in the area possessed. She was typical of many people with apparent Spanish and Inca or other Indian ancestry living in the southwest. Her darker skin and facial features made it easy to tell her background. At least from his limited knowledge, he thought.

"Yes," he replied. "I'm hoping you have a room."

"Yes, Senor. You came in time. I expect soon we will be full."

Just then a young lady, probably in her late teens or perhaps maybe even early twenties entered from the doorway behind.

"Mama," he heard her say.

"What is it Maria?" the lady at the counter answered.

"You said you wanted me to go to the store? You mentioned it earlier." Her words did not sound like those typical of someone raised with a Spanish, Mexican or Indian background. Her command of English was better than most he remembered hearing. He also noticed that her facial features made her more beautiful than any lady of that ancestry he ever remembered seeing.

She was looking up at him as she spoke and her eyes never left his face.

"Wait until I finish here, Maria," the older lady, apparently her mother, said. "Room twelve Senior," she said as she handed him a key. He slid the card he'd filled out back across the counter along with his credit card.

Jack took one last look at young Maria and as he did, he thought he saw something in her eyes. Something he didn't want to see. Then she turned abruptly and disappeared.

A few minutes later he removed his luggage from his car now parked in front of room twelve. Inserting the key into the lock, he turned it, and opened the door. Stepping into the dark room and away from the brightness outside, he didn't notice her standing next to the bed. When he looked up and his eyes adjusted to the change, he was surprised to see her standing there.

"Hello Senior Dennison. Welcome to our motel," she said.

Looking at her now he knew she was even more beautiful than when he saw her minutes before in the office. But then the room was a bit darker than the office. Never the less, his mind remembered her earlier and he was certain less light in the room did not influence what she looked like. She was beautiful. No doubt about it.

"Hello Maria," he said calling her by the name the older lady used. "Is this the way you greet all your guests?"

"Only those who are special," she said in impeccable English.

"Really!" Jack replied. "And just what makes me special."

"Let's just say I can tell someone special when I see them." She took the few steps over to stand directly in front of him. She looked up into his face. She wasn't very tall, perhaps no more than five feet. That made her more than a foot shorter than him.

"I don't get to see many handsome men in Pecos. When I do, I need to take advantage of it." Then without stopping, she stepped forward a few more inches and asked. "Would you like to kiss me?"

"No," he replied. He could feel her inch even closer, until their bodies touched.

"Sure you do," she answered. "You think I'm beautiful don't you?"

"You're a very attractive young lady Maria," he replied.

"Then kiss me," she ordered as she raised up on tip toes and tilting her head back and raising her arms up as far as she could around his neck, she murmured again in a soft voice. "Kiss me."

Jack reached up and pulled her arms from around his neck and gently pushed her away.

"Maria. I'm too old for you.

"I'm nineteen," she replied.

"Are you really?" he asked.

"Yes," she replied. "I really am, and I can do whatever I want. Pecos is small and there aren't any men here that I like. I only stay because Mama needs me to help. When I see a handsome man like you, I can't let him get away. Make love to me Mr. Dennison." She stepped forward until she was touching him again.

She was beautiful. He knew that from the first time he saw her in the office. But she was only nineteen and half his age. Yet, if she was telling him the truth, he could understand if there were no men she liked in Pecos. It was a very small town and while he was sure there might be many young and old men who would desire her; if they were like the ones he'd seen, he understood why she didn't want a relationship with any of them.

Jack wondered how many other men traveling through Pecos had stopped here and been approached by her. Some must have been single or alone and certainly would not have turned her overtures down. Was she desperate enough that she felt her only chance at love was to latch on to any stranger passing through? Was her plight so bad that because she felt a need to help her mother, she was seeking this as the only possible way to leave?

He looked down as she reached up and placed her arms around him once more.

"Kiss me. Please," she said.

"No Maria," he replied pushing her away once more.

She looked up at him a moment and then unbuttoned her blouse and dropped it onto the floor. She was wearing nothing else under it. Stepping back to him and reaching her arms up around his neck once more, she said.

"Kiss me."

This time he reached down and picked up her blouse. Then handing it to her said.

"You'd better leave Maria. I'm not going to make love to you."

She took the blouse from his hands and put it back on. Then turning toward the door she said.

"I'm sorry. I shouldn't have done that. It's just that I want to find someone and there isn't anyone in Pecos."

He noticed a small amount of moisture forming in her eyes as she spoke. It looked like she was now going to cry. She stopped for a moment by the door and looked back at him.

"You're the best looking man to come here in some time. I was hoping." She stopped a moment, and then continued. "I was hoping if you liked me, you might take me with you. I thought if I let you make love to me, you'd take me with you. I want to help my mother, but I can't stay here. I need someone to love and who would love me. I came up from Mexico to help my mother hoping to find someone, but I've been here two years and there are no men here for me."

She had tried hard to lure him into a position that might get her out of this dry desolate town and his turning her down embarrassed her. Now this beautiful young lady who needed and wanted someone, was once again rejected by someone she considered the best person to take her away.

"I understand you wanting to find someone Maria. I do. I'm just not that person. Even if we made love, I couldn't take you with me. You need to talk to your mother. Tell her you want to help but you can't stay here."

Now the tears came. They could stay hidden no longer. She wiped them from her eyes and then turning once more, she said.

"I'm sorry Senior Dennison. You're a handsome man and for just a little while, I thought… I thought this might be my chance to leave."

She opened the door and disappeared into the heat and the last of the blazing sun, not yet gone.

It was much later, when he heard a soft knock on his room door. He opened it and there she stood in only the light from his room. The darkness outside did nothing to distract from her beauty.

"What is it Maria?" he asked.

"Can I come in? I'd like to talk to you."

He wasn't sure he really wanted her in his room, but there was something he sensed that she needed. Perhaps it was someone to talk too. Perhaps she was here for a more devious reason. For some reason, unknown, he opened the door wide and in she came.

"I can't talk to Mama," she started out. "I don't think she would understand. She's here and she will think I should be here with her."

"Have you tired?" he asked.

"No. I just know she wouldn't understand."

"You need to talk to her Maria. Until you do, you are not going to know how she will react or what she will say."

Maria changed the subject.

"Will you take me with you? I need to get away. Take me to where you live. It's a big city and there I can find a job and meet someone. Please!"

She sounded desperate. At least that was his first thought and it almost sounded like it.

"Where is your father?" he asked.

"He's in Mexico," she answered. He came here with Mama, and then awhile later he went back to get some things. He was supposed to come back in a week, but he never did. He has another woman there. When I learned he wasn't coming back to Mama, I came here to be with her. She got this job running this motel. I thought I could live here with her and perhaps find someone and stay. But there are no decent men in Pecos. Help me please Mr. Dennison."

"Maria. I want you to talk to your mother."

"I can't," she replied.

"Yes you can. You need to do it. Let's go do it now. I will go with you." He stood up.

"I can't," she repeated.

Jack stood up, slipped on his shoes and taking her by the hand, led her through the door and outside. Maria walked along side him seeming somewhat content holding his hand as if she was protected from anything bad that might happen.

He opened the door to the vacant office. A small bell rang and a moment later a lady appeared.

It was the lady who'd checked him in earlier and the one Maria called Mama.

She noticed her daughter with him and looked at him perhaps suspecting something bad.

"Maria wants to talk to you," Jack said.

She looked at her daughter, then at Jack and finally back at her daughter. "What is it Maria?" she asked.

Maria looked up at him before speaking, hesitated and then said.

"Mama. I can't stay here in Pecos any longer. I want to help you, but,…" she seemed unable to continue. Jack finished for her what she wanted to say.

"Maria wants to tell you that she is a young lady and she wants to find someone to be with. She tells me there is no one here in Pecos. She wants to be able to help you but she can't stay here."

Maria's mother turned to look at her daughter and walked around the counter and said as she took Maria's hands in hers.

"I know. I know you came here to help me Maria. But you must do what's right for you. I will be all right," she said in her broken English.

"Maria," Jack said. "When I get home, I might be able to help you. I know some people who might be willing to give you and your mother a job. Then perhaps you can find someone and perhaps your mother will be able to get a better job."

"You would do that for us?" Maria's mother asked.

"I'll try," Jack responded.

"I knew you were someone special," Maria said as she stepped forward to put an arm around him.

In the morning he stopped by the office to re affirm that he would see what he could do when he got home. Both Maria and her mother were there. Maria's mother thanked him, but Maria was more appreciative. She came forward to put her arms around to say her thank you. Walking him to his car in the morning heat, she said.

"If you do this for us, I promise you can make love to me when we get there."

Jack smiled down.

"You don't have to do that Maria."

CHAPTER FOUR
TWO LADIES AT THE GRAND CANYON

It wasn't long before he crossed the New Mexico border and came to the small town named "Loving." Perhaps appropriate considering what nearly happened back in Pecos. Jack checked into a small six unit motel that was nothing special, but it was convenient.

He slept a little uneasy that night. His mind kept going back to Maria and her mother and their situation, but he finally did manage some sleep. Awakened early by noise outside the motel, he peeked out his window to see what was happening. There was a New Mexico highway patrol car parked by the office. He watched, but in a few moments the Officer got in and drove away. Not knowing what that was all about, he decided to stay up as he wasn't sleeping well anyway. Jack put on the coffee pot provided in his room while he proceeded to get ready.

It was a very short drive to the Carlsbad Caverns so he knew he had plenty of time because they probably wouldn't open before 9 A.M. No one was visible when he left the tiny cabin and drove off to find a place to eat. It was only a short distance down the road before he found a place that was open so he stopped to eat. It wasn't crowded and the food did taste good. The coffee was much better than the cup from his cabin a few miles back. After eating, he was off to the Caverns. Jack arrived to find the parking lot already with quite a few cars. Many people were already lined up to purchase their tickets. Picking up some literature he started reading the information and after paying his entrance fee, followed the crowd to the entrance. It was a self guided tour he learned and the huge entrance was the same one used by the bats on their summer evening departures. The moderately steep paved trail wandered by a number of formations. Being underground and looking at the stalagmites and stalactites was something he'd never seen but only heard about. The area was lighted and the pathway allowed the visitors to follow it in easy manner. It was cool down there in spite of the hot temperatures rising above ground. He was glad he'd made it a point to stop. Jack also took advantage of going down the elevator to the "Big Room." The literature said it was 750 feet down to the cave's floor. Here he found a trail that was slightly over a mile long according to the literature. He saw the 42 foot high twin domes, the 62 foot high giant dome and the bottomless pit, now known to be 140 feet deep. At least that's what the booklet told him.

As he came to the end of the trail, Jack heard other talking about whether or not to go on the Ranger guided trip to the Slaughter Canyon Cave. Looking at his literature, he learned that it was not lighted, took three hours and he would need a flashlight. Besides reservations were required and he'd not made one.

It was mid afternoon when he returned to the surface and then looking at his watch, he decided to leave and drive north toward Santa Fe. He'd heard a lot about things to see there, and knew it was a 4 hour or more drive. With time running short he knew he'd not be able to spend the time in Santa Fe he wanted. Stopping at a tourist information location he saw coming into town, Jack gathered pamphlets and selected a few places he hoped to be able to see the next day. Those he wouldn't have time for this trip would have to wait until the next time he might come this way. After overnight in one of the large motel chains that was convenient, he toured all he could in one day and then was off again the following morning, heading toward Arizona and the Grand Canyon. He traveled south and then west crossing into Arizona and finally stopping in Winslow for the night. It would be a short distance the next day to Flagstaff and north to the canyon. Thoughts of Pecos began to fade. He hoped that Maria and her mother would be all right. He'd try and find someone who might be willing to take them in but in case he couldn't he hoped they would be okay.

Here too, he knew he'd have little time except to drive to the South and North Rim's, and see only a minimal amount of the beauty and then it would be back to San Bruno and home. There was only ten days left of his eight week vacation.

The drive north to the south canyon wall was made easier by the air conditioning in his car. He could never have made this trip without it. In fact the whole trip had been hot except for his journey to Switzerland. The higher elevation there made it a bit cooler and more enjoyable.

Walking around the rim of the canyon and looking down into its depths tired him and perspiration appeared on his forehead and other parts of his body. After spending time looking down into the great emptiness and being amazed at it all, he drove to the Grand Canyon Village. The parking lot was full with private cars and tour buses. People were everywhere in spite of the temperature. Once inside he ordered a drink and a sandwich at the hotel restaurant and then searching for someplace to sit and enjoy his food, he spotted a table that two couples were just leaving. Quickly he latched on to it. No sooner was he seated, than two ladies approached apparently looking for someplace to sit as well, and one of them asked?

"Would you mind sharing your table?" The taller one asked.

"No," he replied. "I don't mind at all."

"Thank you," the shorter lady said and then continued. "It's too hot to spend a lot of time outside."

"I noticed that," Jack replied laughing slightly.

"I'm Melinda and this is my friend Mary Lou."

"I'm Jack," he replied.

Jack noticed the taller lady, the one named Mary Lou, was indeed quite tall and slender. Probably about five ten he estimated and perhaps not more than a hundred fifty pound if that. The shorter of the two, really wasn't short, but perhaps only five foot five and he would guess her at being perhaps one thirty. Anyway it was just a guess. Both appeared to be in their early thirties, perhaps even late twenties. Not really very old he thought.

"We're here on a tour," Melinda continued. "It's our first visit to the Grand Canyon. We're part of a tour group from San Jose."

"Are you having a good time?" he responded to her burst of information.

"Yes pretty good," Melinda replied but most of the people are married couples. There aren't many singles.

"Where are your husband's?" he asked. "Two attractive ladies like the two of you certainly must be married."

They both laughed a bit and Melinda answered.

"Mary Lou is. I talked her into coming along with me anyway. Her husband said he didn't mind," and then without hesitation she asked him.

"Where is your wife, Jack? Are you alone?"

"I'm not married," he replied without explaining why.

"Really?" she answered surprised by his answer. Then without waiting she asked.

"Are you staying here at the lodge tonight?"

"I hadn't planned on it. I didn't make a reservation since I didn't know just when I might be arriving. Anyway I think they're probably full since this is their busy season. When I finish eating I was going to drive to the North Rim and then head home."

"You should check," Melinda said. "You can't see everything in just part of one day."

"I know, but I'm kind of in a hurry to get home and back to work."

Changing the subject, Melinda said. "Our tour has reservations here tonight and tomorrow and then we head toward Yosemite and home. It's too bad you're not going to be here. I'd invite you to join us at dinner tonight."

"Well thanks," Jack said with a smile. "But I can't stay."

"Where do you live Jack?" Mary Lou asked joining in the conversation.

"San Bruno," he replied. "And you said you're from San Jose?" he questioned in response.

"Yes," Melinda answered. "We both are."

"What do you do for a living Jack?" Mary Lou asked keeping the conversation going.

"I'm with the San Francisco Police Department,"

"Oh, really?" she answered. "That sounds interesting."

"Well, it can be at times," he replied.

"What brings you here Jack?" Melinda asked. "Vacation?"

"Yes. Sort of. I took a couple of months off work to see the country, but now I must get back. I've been gone six weeks, well actually almost seven already."

"Our tour actually ends next Saturday." Melinda said. "I'll be glad to get back. I've never taken a tour on a bus like this before, and I thought I'd try it and talked Mary Lou into coming with me. I just didn't know anyone else to ask so I convinced her to come. We've been best friends forever."

"No man in your life?" Jack asked.

"No. Not at the present time," Melinda responded.

"How come you're traveling alone Jack?" she asked.

"I just felt it was something I needed to do," he replied without offering an explanation.

"I'd sure like to take a motor trip like that with someone," she smiled, and then continued. "With a nice gentleman, hopefully."

Jack smiled. "Perhaps someday you'll get a chance to do that."

He took another bite from his sandwich and a drink from the paper cup.

"Excuse me," Mary Lou said. "I'll be right back." And with that she got up and disappeared.

She was back before Melinda and Jack finished their sandwiches with an announcement.

"I just talked to the room desk person and you're right. They are full. But I was thinking. If you would like to stay over another day so you can see more of the area, and since Melinda and I have separate rooms, we could double up and you could have one of our rooms. Besides, we'd like the company of someone not on the tour. If you wouldn't mind, the three of us could drive around and see everything. It would be a nice change."

"Yes, that is a great idea," Melinda said. "Then you can have dinner with us tonight and we could visit some more."

"That's nice of you to offer but I don't want you to have to do that," he replied. "Give up one of your rooms."

"Nonsense. We want to do it. We'd much rather get away from the tour for awhile. It's kind of boring. You have a car and if you wouldn't mind the three of us can drive around and get away from that crowd for awhile. It will be a nice change for us and it would give you a chance to see more. What do you say?

"Well, I don't know. I should be getting back to work." he replied thinking this was kind of sudden from two ladies he'd just met.

"Certainly you can spend one more day. When your vacation is over, it's going to be over and then when are you going to get another?"

He looked at the two of them, wondering why these two would think of trying to talk him into driving them around. Have they learned their bus trip was so boring that they needed to break away and decided to try and get him to help them?

"I really should be on my way," he repeated.

"Come on Jack," Melinda said. "Help us out here. We need to get away from that bunch for a bit. We know you would enjoy seeing more and now that we've met we'd sure enjoy having you along. It would be a pleasant break."

Jack was planning to keep on moving and really thought he would get home early and perhaps save one of his weeks of vacation, or at least a few days. He might need it later and if not, then so be it. As he was thinking, Melinda said.

"Do it Jack. Drive us around the Canyon. The three of us can have more fun together than alone."

"Well, okay. If you really want me to," he conceded. He wasn't sure why he said that. It just all of a sudden came out.

"We do."

Mary Lou handed a room key to Jack. "Here's the key to my room. I'll bunk with Melinda. Let's get my things out and yours in."

After making the exchange of rooms, the three of them got into Jack's car and he drove to places around the canyon listed in the information pamphlet that were not only on the tour bus schedule, but places that were not. Dinner that night was good. The ladies dinner was included in their tour price, but Jack had to pay for his and it wasn't cheap. After dinner drinks in the lounge added to his bill but the ladies did each paid for one round of drinks. The entertainment was not to his liking, but he stayed to keep them company. Finally at midnight the three of them walked up the stairs to their rooms. The rooms were located side by side as he'd learned earlier.

"Good night ladies." he said as he opened his door.

"Good night Jack," they each replied. "See you in the morning."

It didn't take him long to fall asleep.

It was much later. He didn't know how much, that he became aware of someone in his room. At first he thought he was dreaming, and in the darkness he wondered if his mind was playing tricks on him. Usually his senses were keen enough to be able to tell when someone was present or moving around in the darkened room. Whoever, was careful moving through the darkness. Then he felt the bed move. Jack reached over and clicked on the bedroom light.

It was Melinda.

"What are you doing here?" he asked the startled lady.

"I couldn't sleep over there. I thought I'd sleep better if I were here."

He sat up and noticed her in her robe sitting on the edge of the bed.

"I didn't like sleeping with her. If I was going to be in a crowded bed, I thought I'd like sleeping with you better.

"Why would you do that Melinda? You don't know me. Why would you take a chance coming over here? I could turn out to be... Well perhaps an undesirable person."

"I knew it would be okay. Besides I could just tell you were a decent person. I took classes in college on Psychology."

"Well, you could still be wrong."

"I don't think so," she replied.

"Melinda."

"What?" she answered.

"I think you should go back to the other room."

"Am I making you uncomfortable?" she asked.

"It's just that we don't know each other. We only met a few hours ago."

"I know, but I was sure the moment I saw you that I was going to like you."

"I still think you need to go back to the other room," he said. "By the way. How did you get in?

"We had two keys to each room. We only gave you one."

"So you were planning this?" he asked.

"Not really, but after she went to sleep and I couldn't, I decided to come here."

"I think you should go back to the other room." He said.

"I don't have anything on under my robe," she announced suddenly as she stood up.

"Go back to your room Melinda," he commanded.

"I just wanted to show you our appreciation for driving us around."

"Go back to the other room Melinda," he said again in a stern voice.

"And if I don't want to?" she asked.

"Then I'll have to get up and carry you," he replied.

She looked at his bare chest and asked.

"Do you sleep in the nude Jack?"

"Never mind. Now are you going, or do I get up and carry you?"

Melinda stood up facing him, fumbled with the belt of her robe as if starting to undo it and asked.

"What would you do if I took my robe off?"

She was teasing he thought, but one never really knows for sure. She had the courage to come here no doubt to sleep with him and if she'd do that, perhaps she have no qualms about standing naked in front of him hoping that it might cause him, to pull her down onto the bed. If so, she'd win this challenge.

Jack flipped back the covers and she could tell immediately whether he slept nude or not.

"Okay. I'm going," she said and turned toward the door cinching her robe tightly about herself.

"Give me the other room key," he ordered.

Gently she handed it to him. Stopping at the door she looked at him from head to toe.

"I'll bet you wouldn't have gotten out of bed if you had been naked," she said.

"Don't be so sure," he replied.

She was smiling as she opened the door.

"I'll bet I wouldn't be leaving now, if I'd taken off my robe either, would I Jack?"

He didn't answer but tried to keep a sober face. She was grinning broadly as she stepped out into the hall way.

He watched until she was inside the room next door and then closed his door and returned to bed.

All during breakfast the next morning, she was smiling at him as she remembered the night before. When they got into the car to drive to the places they hadn't seen the afternoon before Melinda turned to her friend and asked.

"Guess what I did last night?"

"I don't know." Mary Lou answered.

"I took the other key and went to Jack's room." Melinda said.

"She didn't stay," Jack said. "I sent her right back."

Mary Lou looked at her friend and smiled, but said nothing.

They were back for dinner and another stint in the entertainment lounge. It didn't sound any better to him this evening than it did last night.

After a couple of drinks and taking all of the music he could stand, he said.

"I'm going to turn in. I want to be on the road early. After spending more time here than I intended, I'd better get going."

As he stood up, Melinda stood with him.

"Where are you going?" He asked.

"With you. If you're going to turn in, then so am I."

"Fine," Jack said. "Look! I appreciate your arranging a room for me and I've enjoyed the time together, but you need to stay with Mary Lou."

"You won't change your mind? This is our last night here and I'd like to show our appreciation for giving us a break from the tour."

"Melinda, you don't need to do this. Besides, I need to get up early and I want a good night's sleep."

"I plan on going to sleep too." she replied with a smile on her face.

"Sure you do," he answered. "Good night ladies."

He was in bed and not quite asleep, when he heard a soft knock on his room door.

"If that's Melinda?- - -

Jack got up, undid the latch and opened the door slightly.

"I thought you might change your mind," she said.

"I'm not changing my mind," he replied.

"Come on Jack. I don't really want to sleep with her. I'd be more comfortable in here."

"I need to get a good night's sleep Melinda and you know neither of us would sleep if I let you in."

"Would that be so bad?" she said with a devilish smile on her face.

He opened the door wider, intending to escort her back to her room. She was quicker than he was prepared for. Melinda threw her arms around him and kissed him hard. Surprised by her actions, he at first returned her kiss, and then just as quickly, broke their connection, and grabbing her hand escorted her to the other room.

"Now, get in there and stay," he ordered.

"But Jack," she whined.

"Just get in there. We are not sleeping together, and he pushed her through the open door.

As Jack turned to head back to his room, he noticed a man about his age nearby, who apparently had seen what happened.

"I don't know about you," the man said. "But she's pretty nice looking. I don't know that I could have done that."

Jack smiled and answered. "I just met her a day ago. She's too young for me."

"I still don't think I could do that," the other man said and then opened the door across the hall and walked in closing it behind him.

The next morning he was up early and while getting breakfast down in the hotel eating area, she walked in.

"Why didn't you come and get me?"

"I thought you were probably still sleeping," he answered. "Besides, I wouldn't have left without saying goodbye."

Melissa sat down in the chair next to him and looking at him, said.

"Will I ever see you again?"

"I don't know," Jack answered.

"I want to ask you something." she said and after hesitating a moment. I was wondering if perhaps when we get back if,... if maybe I could see you?" She paused a moment before going on. "I'd like to know you better. I'm unattached and you said you were and San Jose isn't too far from San Bruno." She handed him a slip of paper. He glanced down at it and saw a phone number and her name.

"I'm flattered," Jack replied. "But you don't really know me Melinda and I really don't know you."

"We just spent two days together." she said, "That must count for something."

Jack looked at her and he knew she was really a very attractive lady. Before he could say anything, Melinda continued.

"I'm not really this forward Jack, but I admit I found myself attracted to you the first moment in the restaurant. The moment we sat down I knew I wanted to know you better. When you said you weren't attached I knew I had to see if you might be interested. I want to see you on a regular basis. I'd like to find out if you'd be interested in knowing me better." She didn't give him a chance to answer.

"Anyway I want to know you better. Perhaps we could meet when I get home. What do you say Jack? Will you call me?"

He looked at her. He couldn't ever remember another young lady being this forward before.

"I don't think so Melinda. We only just met. Besides I'm going to be pretty busy when I get back to work. I'll have to be catching up on things, and working a lot of extra hours. I'm sure a lot happened while I was gone."

He knew he should have told her there might be someone. After all Marian was coming in a few weeks and he thought it was unfair to say he was unattached, but then he didn't know what was going to happen.

"I know you might be busy when you get back to work, but I want to see you again. I knew right after we'd met that you were someone I wanted to know better. I could feel it. I need to find out. I do. Will you call me?" She asked again.

He really didn't want to start a relationship with her, but he had to admit he was intrigued by her forwardness and being so frank.

Looking down at his nearly empty plate and then at her, he hesitated a moment, and said.

"No. I'm not going to call you Melinda."

"I'd really like you too," She said. "Please. I really want to continue seeing you. Are you turned off because I was so forward? Was it because I tried to sleep with you? Is that it?"

"No. Right now I'm not thinking about having a lady friend. Let me tell you something."

She didn't know what he would say, but she did stay seated in the chair next to him. He went on to tell her about Jacquee and why he was on this journey. Then when he finished, she placed her hand on his and said.

"That's terrible. I'm so sorry. I can understand why you're not interested in another relationship at the moment. I really can." Melinda hesitated before going on, but finally said.

"I still want to see you. Do you think you might call me sometime?"

"I don't know. I don't want to promise anything. I think it's better if you just forget about me."

"I'll never forget these two days. It's the best part of this whole trip," she replied as she held onto his hand. He looked down at her hand for a few moments, and then said.

"I'd better get going."

They got up and walked back to his room, with her holding on to him all the way. He picked up his luggage and turned toward the door and she stopped him.

"At least you can kiss me good bye," she said. He did. Then afterwards, she walked with him to the car and as he turned to get in, she asked.

"Are you sure Jack? Are you sure about us?"

"I'm sure," he replied. "It's better if I don't make a promise I may not be able to keep."

He gave her one last kiss. It was one she did not want to end, but he finally ended it, pulling back. Then getting into his car he drove from the parking lot.

She stood watching until he was out of sight and then turned to find her friend.

Jack stopped again at the North Rim to take one more look and then headed north through Kanab Utah, and turned toward Bryce canyon. He thought about skipping the stop at Bryce Canyon because it would mean back tracking, but at the last moment decided to go there anyway. After leaving Bryce canyon he turned back south west toward Las Vegas. It seemed like the wrong way to go, but it was the only decent highway and in reality the best way. Deciding to stay overnight in Kanab after spending the whole day going to Bryce canyon seemed a bit out of the way but it was the best town and the closest. It would mean a bit of driving back over the same road, but he liked the looks of the early American style motel he'd seen coming through earlier. There were several other nice looking places to stay in Kanab, but he selected the one he'd seen on a curve as he came into town. After checking in he learned they offered a free movie and popcorn in an old barn on the property that evening, but he decided he was too tired to consider taking that offer. The next morning they gave him a free breakfast and while he thought of leaving much earlier, he'd slept longer than he intended, so he decided to take advantage of the food. He was finally on the road and again later than planned, but he was on his way. A couple more nights he thought and he'd be home. That would mean he'd arrive late Saturday afternoon or evening. Missing Yosemite and Death Valley this trip, was too bad, but they were close enough and he could catch them later.

Not staying long in Zion Park, which he liked better than Bryce, Jack drove on toward Las Vegas. Stopping only for gas and some food, he continued on crossing into California. Trying to roll up as many miles as possible, he finally arrived in Barstow and decided to call it a day.

The next morning as the sun was once again heading higher into the sky, he headed toward Bakersfield and up Highway 5. He thought again that he might even drive straight through, but after stopping to consult the map once more he decided against it. That would just be too much for one day. Cutting across just north of Wasco, he hit Paso Robles and then driving north on highway 101 he saw a sign directing people to the mission called San Miguel Archangel. Just beyond in the town of Bradley, he decided he'd come far enough for one day and stopped for what he knew would be his last night on the road. He found a nice looking place to stay decorated in Spanish architecture that appeared to be in good condition.

Looking into the bathroom mirror, he said out loud to the face looking back at him.

"It's been an interesting trip Jack old boy, but I know you'll be glad to get home. You didn't see all that you thought you might, but it was an enjoyable trip and you met some interesting people. Yes, very interesting."

He emptied his pockets and there on the table was the piece of paper from Melinda, the lady he'd met only days before. He starred down at it thinking about her.

"Melinda" he said. "You'll find someone to be happy with. It's not me," and he tossed the slip of paper into the waste paper basket.

THE RYMAN/ORVETT CASE

CHAPTER ONE
WORK LOOKS LIKE A STRANGE PLACE

It was the middle of Saturday afternoon when he drove down his street and turned into his driveway and then into the garage. Getting out, he dragged the luggage from his car and into the house. Everything looked the same, except she wasn't there.

I'd better get a shower and then head to the cemetery to let her know I'm back, but I guess I'll call Sarah first. She'd want to know I was back. He called and she was indeed happy to know he'd returned. She wanted to know all about his journey and how he was. They talked for about half an hour.

"Come over as soon as you can," she said.

He promised to come the next day.

He looked at the telephone answering machine. There were several calls backed up. Pushing the button, he learned the first few were not important. Then there was one from Marian. Then another unimportant call and then there was one from Don telling him the wedding was going to be in two weeks on Saturday.

Jack looked at the calendar and learned that the Saturday in question was next Saturday. He'd have to get up early and drive there. There were a couple of other unimportant calls and finally one more from Marian. It was yesterday and she wanted him to call when he arrived. She was anxious to fly over.

Getting back into the car again so soon, didn't seem very important, but going to visit his dear deceased wife was. First there was the stop at a local store to pick up some flowers.

He noticed when he arrived that apparently Sarah had been here recently. There was already a fresh pot of lovely flowers sitting on a corner of the headstone. He didn't know what kind they were, since that wasn't something he really knew anything about. Jack set his potted plant down on another corner of the headstone right next to the name of Jacquee Parker Dennison.

"Hello Love. I'm back," he said and stopped to brush some fallen leaves from her name. "It was a long, but enjoyable journey. I visited my sister and my friend Don. He's getting married. He met a lovely lady and he's going to stay in Walker after all. I guess we did the right thing in not selling his house. Anyway I drove east and I ran into a lady I knew from high school. She's running a motel near Reno. I saw Zeke and Gail. You remember them. They came to our wedding. While I was at Don's place, Marian showed up and talked me into going to visit her parents in Switzerland. That was nice but it took time from my car trip.

Anyway I'm glad to be back. I have to get to work Monday. I'm sure that will keep me quite busy. I sure miss you. We had such a short time together." He stayed for quite awhile cleaning the stone and pretending to make it look better. Finally after about an hour he bent over and kissed the stone, promising to return and then walked back to his car.

Shortly after he returned home Oscar and Doris Chapin came over.

"Welcome back stranger," Oscar said. "How was your trip?" While they talked outside, another neighbor saw him and came over.

"Welcome back Jack," Carl Everson said.

"Thanks Carl," Jack replied.

Doris invited him over for dinner. The next day he visited Sarah and stayed most of the afternoon. That evening he called Mike, his sergeant at work to see what was happening.

"Well, there's plenty. Someone's been taking shots at people walking down the street. Two people have been wounded. None killed. And we've got someone murdering young ladies. Jancee Ryman and Mary Orvett are the first two. I'll give you the details when you get here."

"I'll be in early," Jack said. "I guess I need to get caught up."

It was shortly after noon when Jack walked into the office and over to his desk. Right on top sat two files, one for the Orvett/Ryman case and the other on the street shootings. Apparently Mike had called in and told someone to place the files on his desk.

"Well, if it isn't Jack Dennison," one of the detectives said. "We thought you had retired."

"Sometimes I wish I did and it appears this might be one of those times," he replied.

They all asked how his trip went and was he glad to be back. There was the usual conversation about that and some about the activities during his absence.

Jack started going through the street shooting file first since it was smaller. A week ago last Wednesday during the lunch hour an older lady, one Gertrude Spader was shot in the upper shoulder while walking down the street in front of one of the large buildings on Market Street. It wasn't serious and she was doing well.

Then last Wednesday about the same time of the day, another lady was wounded when a bullet hit her in the side. She had just come out of a building a few blocks away from the first shooting. There were two shooting on the last two Wednesday's about the same time of the day. Both ladies were doing all right and neither wound was serious. Both shots apparently came from a high angle as determined from the investigation. No other information was available.

He sat the file back onto his desk and picked up the one on the Ryman/Orvett case.

Jancee Ryman, a young lady with no criminal background was twenty two years of age. She worked at a local insurance agency. She had been with them only eight months and had been a resident of the bay area all her life. She had an older brother and two younger sisters. Her parents lived across the Oakland Bay Bridge in Berkley. Her parents said she didn't have any special man in her life and didn't date very often. On the night of her disappearance she had gone with a girl friend to a movie. When the movie was over the two of them stopped for bite to eat and then they separated, each going home in their own cars. Jancee's car was found on the street in downtown San Francisco. Her body was found near the docks the morning after her disappearance. She had been strangled. There were no clues.

Discussions with people at her place of employment as well as friends, revealed no helpful information. However her mother said, when interviewed, that Jancee told her she had dated a man from work. When she found out he was married, she stopped seeing him.

Within ten days Mary Orvett's body was found in the same location. Her car was found in the water off the end of the dock close to where her body was found. She too, had been strangled.

Mary Orvett was working at the same insurance company, but she was upstairs in one of the executive offices. From the information gathered in interviews, the two did not know each other. She was divorced, and had no children nor did she have any known relatives.

When quizzed, other employees were unaware of her dating anyone from work or elsewhere.

Forensics had been unable to find any clue's pointing to anyone that could be responsible.

Mike, Jack's sergeant walked in a bit before three P.M.

"Welcome back Lieutenant," he said.

"Hi Mike."

"I'm glad you're here." Mike replied. "Now you can be responsible to solve these cases."

"I was just looking over the files and I'm not sure I want too. By the way, what's being done about the noon time shootings on Wednesday's the last couple of weeks?"

"Well, we've arranged to have more policemen on the street this Wednesday and there will be a helicopter in the air."

"Anything else?"

"No. We're a bit strapped for personnel and the budget the way it is, the Chief is reluctant to put men on overtime. We're hoping this will be enough."

"We won't use overtime. But I want to put some men on the roof tops with field glasses." Jack said. "Round up every available man from day shift here and I'll borrow what I can from adjoining precincts. We'll put a man on every other building on both sides of the street."

"Think that will work?" Mike asked.

"I don't know, but it's worth a try. We can't have someone taking shots at people on the street. One of these days he will kill someone."

"What I don't understand, if he's trying to kill someone he's not done a very good job. Is he just a bad shot or what? Both ladies were hit, but neither was hurt too badly. They're going to be okay."

"I don't know" Jack replied. "But if we don't catch him, he may very well kill someone, either by accident or on purpose. If he only wants to wound them, what's the point?"

"About the other case," Jack changed the subject. "Have we talked to everyone at the insurance company?"

"Yes. I talked to quite a few people myself."

"Anything at all. Did anyone say anything at all?"

"Not that I know of," Mike replied.

"I'd like to go back and talk to them all again. Be sure different detectives talk to different people. In other words, don't have our people talk to the same people they talked to before."

"That could take a lot of time. We've got a lot of other work to deal with." Mike replied.

"I know, but many times we've learned things by having our people talk to folks they didn't talk to before." Jack instructed. "People will say different things to different people. Right now we have nothing to go on. I hate to spend the man hours, but it's all we have."

"Okay. I'll get them started, but it may take awhile. We just can't stop everything else."

The afternoon went pretty fast. Captain Horace Beecham dropped by to welcome him back and to let him know he wasn't needed to help try to recruit new people for the department. The Chief decided he was too important right where he was to pull him off his regular assignment.

The drive home that evening was quiet and as he sat in his newly constructed living room, the phone rang.

"Who could that be?"

When he picked up the phone, he learned it was Marian.

"I know this was you first day back at work, but I'm anxious to come for a visit," she said.

"How much longer will I need to wait and do you still want me to come?"

"Yes of course you can come. Give me another week or so. At work today I learned there are two new rather difficult cases that will require a lot of my time I'm going in early each day and don't leave until midnight, so better figure on awhile longer."

"Okay," she replied. He could hear the disappointment in her voice. He knew she'd really like to come right away, but he needed to spend more time on the new cases and also get caught up on cases that were backlogged on his desk.

The next morning he woke up to a heavy rain shower. It surprised him since it was only September and usually weather was still good. After breakfast he finished taking care of all his accumulated mail from his seven week absence and was just putting things away when the door bell rang. He opened the door and there stood his neighbor Doris Chapin.

"Hi Doris. It's good the rain stopped or you would have gotten really wet walking over here."

"Yes, I waited for it to quit," she replied.

"What can I do for you?"

"I'm inviting some neighbors over this Saturday for a small gathering. One of my best friends from college is dropping by for a visit and I'd like everyone to meet her. She's an executive for a big company back east. We were very close in college and I haven't seen her in several years, so I thought I'd try and impress her. Can you come?"

"I think so Doris. What time?"

"Any time you want. We'll probably eat about 2."

"Okay. I should be able to make it."

After Doris left, Sarah called and wanted to talk. There was nothing special on her mind, but she couldn't help wondering how he was doing since the loss of her sister and his wife. Finally after she got off the phone, Jack thought he might as well go to work. There wasn't anything here to do anyway. Most of the mail was advertisements and he'd paid his bills in advance so he wouldn't have to worry about them while he was gone. There were also people requesting donations, but he had his own special charities, so each of those became one more item to discard. Tomorrow he was going to call a house cleaning service and hire them to take care of things he either didn't want to do inside or never had the time.

He no more than walked into his second floor work area, than who should he find waiting for him, but Julia Davis, the daughter of Police Captain Don Davis.

"Julia. What are you doing here?"

"I was down town and had just finished some errands, and I thought I'd drop by and say hello."

"Okay," he replied thinking it a bit strange. She'd never just dropped in before and he'd known her since she was small. Her father and he started at the same time and he'd been to their home many times. Jack knew she'd been divorced now for quite awhile and he thought it strange for her to be here.

Somehow he sensed she'd dropped in because she had a purpose, so he asked her if she wanted a cup of coffee, but she declined.

She looked at him, hesitating as if she wanted to say something and not quite sure how to say it. Then finally after a moment he noticed her take a deep breath.

"Jack I want to know if you would be my date Sunday at our company picnic. Everyone is bringing someone and I don't know anyone. I told my dad what I was thinking and he said to go ahead and ask you."

"I'm surprised an attractive lady such as you doesn't have anyone to ask for a date."

"I really haven't wanted to try and find someone after my divorce," she said. "I guess I have too many bitter memories."

"And you thought I'd be a safe date," he chuckled beneath his breath and continued. "You thought you wouldn't have to worry about beating me off. That I wouldn't try and take advantage of you."

She looked back in silence before speaking, but then said in a soft almost in too quiet a tone, and said.

"Perhaps I wouldn't try too hard to beat you off."

He heard and wasn't sure what to say, but she smiled and asked.

"Would you like to take me to my company party Sunday Jack? I'd appreciate it. I want to go and I don't want to go alone. Besides I'd like to show everyone that I do know a handsome man and I'm not just a wall flower. I think there are a couple of ladies in my office that are beginning to think I don't like men. That perhaps I prefer..." She didn't finish.

"Sure Julia. I'd love to be your escort Sunday.

Marian called again Tuesday and Wednesday. Preparations were put into place to prepare for the sniper of Market Street. By noon everyone was in place. Jack was on the roof of one building just about exactly between where the two previous shootings took place and Mike was two buildings down to his left. To his right was Detective Brennan and beyond him was Detective Spencer. Over the several block area there was a Police officer on every other building with binoculars. On the street below there were as many plain clothes officers as Jack could round up. There were the usual number of marked Police cars in the area and on the side streets there were a few more than might be normal.

Noon time came and all seemed normal. At about fifteen minutes past noon, a frantic call came over the radio.

"This is Ryan. A man with a gun just came onto my roof. When he saw me, he turned and ran. I took after him, but I tripped and fell. I'm chasing after him now."

Jack knew which building Ryan was on. It was just beyond the location of the last shooting. Quickly he notified units on the ground to surround the building and he hurried in that direction. Then he called all others to stay in place in case this wasn't the real shooter.

When he arrived a few minutes later, there were three patrol cars in front of the building in question, and so was detective Ryan.

"He got away Lieutenant. I never caught up with him."

"Did you recognize him?" Jack asked.

"No. It happened so fast, I never got a good look. All I know is that he was dressed in dark clothes and wore a dark wool cap, or what appeared to be a dark wool cap."

"We've not let anyone in or out of the building Lieutenant," one patrolman said.

Then turning to detective Ryan, Jack asked.

"Do you think you might recognize him if you saw him?"

"I don't know. Unless we found him dressed the same way, and then it's only a guess."

"Okay," then Jack turned to his portable radio and asked. "Anything going on anyone?"

Back came several calls telling him nothing happened. Then he told everyone to hold their positions until one P.M. or until he called them again. Then turning again to Ryan he said.

"Let's go up to the roof." Then to the Sergeant at the front of the building he said.

"Keep everyone in and don't let anyone out until I call you."

Jack and Detective Ryan exited the elevator on the top floor.

"It's this way Lieutenant. There are stairs to the roof."

After Jack inspected the roof top, he sent Ryan back to the street level and called the Sergeant on the street and told him that as soon as Detective Ryan arrived, it was okay to let people in and out but to stay in place and watch for anyone suspicious that fit the description He then called everyone on the lookout positions and on patrol and secured the watch. After returning to the street, Jack said to detective Ryan.

"Call forensics. Have them send a team over here. I want them to go over everything from the top floor up the stairs and onto the roof.

"Do you think they'll find something Lieutenant?"

"I don't know, but let's have them look. You stay here until they arrive."

Back at his desk sometime later and again looking over the two most important files, Captain Horace Beecham walked in.

"Did your efforts do any good Jack?"

"I don't think so. We saw one person that appeared to be holding a gun come onto the roof of one building. We had a detective there and he gave chase, but he tripped on a cable that was on the roof and the person got away."

"Too bad."

"One good thing. There was no one shot today so we think we might have thwarted the attempt."

"Yes that is good. Keep me posted," he said as he turned and walked away.

Just then Mike, his Sergeant, walked in.

"Want to go over to the Monkey Tree and get something to eat? Now that Annie is no longer there, you won't have to worry about her making a play for you."

Jack looked up with a smile. "No I won't."

"When's her trial? Do you know?"

"No. It will probably be awhile. Attorneys always take plenty of time in defending their clients and who knows. I might be retired by the time that trial comes about."

The lunch was uneventful and when he returned there was a familiar face waiting.

"Remember me Lieutenant?" Henry Mullins asked.

"Yes, Mr. Mullins, I do. I've got a couple of cases that I think might interest you."

"Good. Good. When can I see them?"

Jack arranged to meet him the next day before work and Henry promised to get right onto putting the material together and off to his publisher.

Marian called again the next day and the next. Forensics called Friday afternoon.

"Lieutenant," the voice of a lady said. "This is Ellen Wilson in forensics. We got some things to examine from the building but I don't know how soon we can help you? We're so busy and this is going to take a long time."

"I know, but if you concentrate on fingerprints first. I think that's our best chance to find this person."

"Well, maybe, but even that is a slow process."

"I know Ellen. But it's all we've got at the moment. We need to catch this person before he kills someone."

"I understand. I just wanted you to know it's not something we can give you an answer to quickly."

"I know Ellen. Just do what you can."

CHAPTER TWO
THE LADY FROM AKRON

It was a bit after one P.M. on Saturday, when Jack left his house to walk over to Doris and Oscar Chapin's house for the party she was giving for her college friend. It wasn't the warmest of days in what is usually a good September, but the weatherman did promise sun. Everyone knew he wasn't always right, but the clouds were scattered and no rain was predicted. Still the wind off the ocean kept the temperatures down a bit.

"Come in Jack," Doris said as she opened the front door. Several neighbors that Jack recognized were already there. The O'Toole's, Amanda's parents were present, and Carl and Trisha who lived next door to him, and several others he'd seen but didn't know too well.

"Jack," Doris said. "I want you to meet my special friend." She led him across the room to a tall attractive blonde dressed in a moderate blouse and skirt. She was wearing flat blue shoes with a beaded design on the upper front part. Her dark blue skirt ended just above the knee and had one pleat near the edge of each corner extending from the waist line to the hem.

A narrow light blue beaded belt ran around her waist and closed via a silver clasp.

The blouse seemed to match the belt in color, but it was perfectly plain except for two pockets that adorned the front.

Her hair was shoulder length with a slight wave and curled under just above her collar.

She was wearing small gold framed glasses and behind the lens's he could see the light brown alert eyes. His training to observe told him she was the most beautiful lady he'd ever seen except for his dear departed wife, and perhaps Maria he'd seen just recently while on the road.

"Jack, this is my friend Breanna," Doris said.

"Hello Jack," she said extending her hand. "I've heard a lot about you."

"Really?" he questioned. "Good I hope."

"Oh yes. Very good," she replied.

"I'm going to leave you two alone. I've got some other things to attend to." Doris said as she turned and left.

"What brings you to our part of the world?" Jack asked.

"Well, I could say I came just to meet you," she was smiling a broad smile as she continued. "But I know you wouldn't believe that, so I'll tell you I just came to get away for a week or so."

"Get away from what?" he asked.

"From my job."

"Tell me about your job. Is it stressful? Difficult, or are you just taking a vacation?"

"I manage an avionics company and we have been in negotiations for some time to provide parts for an aircraft company in Europe. We finally just came to an agreement and signed a long term contract. It will mean a lot for my company and provide many more jobs for quite awhile. It was very stressful and I just decided to take a break. In fact the board of directors insisted."

"Well, that surely sounds great for your company."

"Yes, I'm really pleased we were able to do it. Now tell me all about yourself. Doris told me you lost your wife a short time ago."

"Yes," he replied. "We'd only been married for a little over a year."

"How terrible," she answered.

"I took a few weeks off to get away. Actually about seven weeks. I drove around the country to see some things and to visit friends. I even flew to Switzerland to see some people I knew. Anyway I'm back at work now. For one whole week."

"San Francisco Police Department I understand," she stated.

Oscar showed up with a couple of drinks in hand for the two of them.

"Thought you might need this." Then turning to Breanna he said. "He's not giving you the third degree is he?" They all laughed slightly.

"No," she responded. "Not yet."

"Well, I just wanted to be sure. I can't have one of my guests being interrogated without council." They laughed again and Oscar turned and walked away.

"Well how did you get an important job like that?" Jack asked.

"Lucky, I guess. I went to school with Doris, but I was also in school with a young lady named Mary Ann. Her father just started a small company a few years before and was doing quite well. She took me to meet him a few times and I guess he liked me, so when I graduated Mary Ann and I took job offers from him. I think she put in a good word for me."

"That never hurts," Jack replied.

The World of Jack Dennison-Detective

"Well, I liked it and I just stayed. He must have liked my work, because as time went by I moved up the ladder and two years ago I was appointed to my present position."

"And your friend Mary Ann?"

"She got married and moved away."

"Did you ever marry? I should think there would have been a lot of men trying to convince you they were the right person for you."

She blushed a bit before responding. "No, I never did. I really got wrapped up in my work and I never dated much. I felt that some men I dated either thought it was a way to improve their position in life, or I was someone who could support them."

"I'd never do that," Jack said and then regretted his words.

"Really?" she questioned. "Maybe we should discuss it a bit more," she was laughing.

"Sorry," he said. "I didn't mean to say that."

"It's okay," she said reaching over and placing her hand on his arm. Tell me about your job Jack. Is it dangerous?

"It can be. I've had a few shots taken at me."

"I guess no one killed you since you're here."

"No, I've been lucky," he answered.

"Do you think you'll get married again?" she asked changing the subject.

"I don't know. Right now it's too soon to be thinking about that."

"Yes I guess so, sorry I mentioned it."

"Time to eat everyone." Doris announced sticking her head through the door.

The afternoon passed all too quickly. Jack and Brianna spent more time together, but he also took time to visit with other members of his neighborhood. Finally as the afternoon passed, a few people started to leave. Breanna and Doris were in the kitchen attending to the clean up. Jack and Oscar stayed in the living room with the few guests that were still there.

Finally Breanna and Doris put in an appearance and while Doris sat next to Oscar, Breanna took a chair near where Jack was seated instead of the vacant chair next to Doris even though Jack was across the room. Someone might think they were all couples seated together.

The group continued in a bit of chit chat for about a half hour and finally the remaining neighbors decided it was time to leave. Soon only Oscar, Doris, Breanna and Jack remained. With only the four of them left in the living room, Jack thought perhaps it was time for him to leave as well.

"I suppose I should go too," he said.

"You don't have to go Jack just because everyone else has." Doris said.

"No. Don't go." Breanna added. Wait. I have something to give you. She walked to the room provided her by friend Doris and returned and handed a small card to Jack. It was her business card. On it was the company address as well as her business phone number. As he looked down at it, she reached and turned the card over. There was another phone number. If you're ever in Akron, call me."

"I was just in Cleveland a few weeks ago," he said.

"I'm sorry I didn't know that," she said. He smiled and said nothing.

"I guess I'd better go too," Jack said.

"I'm going to walk Jack home." Breanna announced and she took Jack by the arm. Doris and Oscar looked at each other and after they disappeared through the door Doris turned to her husband and said.

"I didn't know Jack needed someone to show him the way home."

"I didn't either." They smiled at each other and turned to pick up the last few remaining items left from the afternoon gathering.

The next morning he was up early and after going to visit Jacquee's grave, Jack headed home to have something to eat. He knew he'd have to pick up Julia and take her to the company picnic as he'd promised. As he approached his house he saw there was a car in his driveway. He looked over to see it was Julia waiting patiently for his return.

"What are you doing here?" he asked when he got out of his car.

"I came over to take you to breakfast," she responded.

"What would you do if I'd already had breakfast?"

"I guess I'd have to go alone. Have you had breakfast?" she asked.

"No," he replied. "I've been to the cemetery."

"Oh," she answered. "Then how about breakfast?"

"Well, I do need to have something, but you don't have to take me. I can take you."

"Okay. I'll settle for that," she answered.

Across the street in the Chapin house a pair of eyes watched the two people in front of Jack's house. When she saw them go inside, she turned to Doris and asked.

"Does Jack have another lady in his life so soon after his wife's passing?"

"I don't think so dear, why?"

"I just saw him and a lady in his driveway. They just went inside. I was going over in a bit to see him again today. Looks like I won't be able to do that now."

"Maybe it's just a friend." Doris answered.

"On an early Sunday morning?" Breanna questioned. She sounded a bit perturbed as she walked back to the window to watch more.

It was only about twenty minutes later when Jack and Julia got into her car and drove away. Breanna was watching as they disappeared. She was still sitting in the chair by the window when Jack and Julia returned nearly two hours later and she noticed them go inside once more.

Breanna was talking with Doris an hour later when she saw Julia get into Jack's car and drive away once more. Finally turning to Doris, she said.

"I think I'll pack and leave today instead of Tuesday."

"Why Dear?" Doris asked. "Did we do something?"

"No. Her answer was curt. Then she turned and walked toward her room, put her things into her luggage before returning and when she did, she asked Doris, "Will you call me a taxi?

"You don't have to leave, dear."

"Yes I do." Her voice was a bit harsh.

As Breanna drove away in the taxi, Doris turned to her husband and said.

"Breanna seemed very upset. I think she was disturbed at seeing Jack with another lady this morning. I think she was really taken by him yesterday."

"Yes. I got that feeling too. They spent a lot of time together. Still after we put on that party for her yesterday, it wasn't very nice of her to just take off like this. I thought she was a good friend of yours."

"I thought so too. But now that I think of it, I do remember back in college, there were a few times when she showed a bit of a temper when things didn't go her way. Maybe she felt some attraction to Jack and then seeing him this morning with another lady perhaps that made her very upset.

"Maybe! Well we can't do anything about it. She's gone and that's the end it."

CHAPTER THREE
JULIA

It was about eight P.M. when Jack and Julia returned from her company picnic.

I had a really good time Jack. Thanks for taking me. Maybe now some of the people at work will realize that I do date men," she was laughing a bit and he joined in.

"Well, I never considered the possibility you didn't like men," he replied. She turned to him with a serious expression on her face.

"Jack, would you think it? Ah" ...she stopped a moment, before continuing. "Would you be uncomfortable knowing my dad and all, if we,...If we went out on a date? Or perhaps started seeing each other? I know it hasn't been long since you lost your wife, but...But I enjoy your company and I was wondering if perhaps,...perhaps we might go out again?"

Jack looked at her, not sure what to say. Certainly she was a lovely young lady. Don and his wife had produced a beautiful girl that had grown into a beautiful lady. Now here was that beautiful young lady sitting in his car and proposing that they start dating. What would her father and mother be thinking if he were to start seeing their daughter? Yes, Don had suggested it would be all right to ask him to take her to the company picnic, but what if their relationship was to go further? What then?

"Julia. I don't think I'm ready for another relationship yet. It's too soon for my mind to consider that. Besides what would your parents say if we started dating?"

"I think they'd be very happy that I was seeing someone they both liked and knew." She replied.

"I'm flattered Julia. Someone is going to very lucky one day. But I don't think that person is me."

"I like you a lot, Jack," she said. "I know my parents like you. I know you're a good person and I could do a lot worse. I really would like to start a relationship. I think I'm ready again. I enjoyed today very much and as I look at you, I just know I'd like to spend more time with you. Are you sure you won't consider it? Maybe if we dated a few times you might change your mind. You might find that I'm someone you enjoy being with."

He looked at her. She was very much trying to convince him they should see each other again.

She reached across the front seat and gave him a big kiss, much to his surprise. When she pulled back, she said.

"There. It's something to remember me by. There could be more." Julia opened the car door, got out and walked around and getting into her car, drove away.

He sat there a few moments, and then said out loud. "Don't even consider it, Jack, old boy."

There was a phone message from Marian asking him to call. He didn't, even though he knew it was tomorrow in Switzerland.

It was Monday again and the start of his second week back. Still there were the two big cases and so far no progress had been made in either. The Wednesday shooting had been prevented, but they couldn't continue doing what they did before, and as far as the other case was concerned, the department didn't have a clue about either lady's death.

Henry Mullins was waiting for him when he arrived.

"I've got the story written Jack," he said. "I'm sending it off to my publisher today. It will be in next month's edition which is due to hit the market in two weeks. You should see the results shortly after that. I think you'll be happy."

After Henry left Jack turned to the file on the deaths of Jancee Ryman and Mary Orvett. There just had to be something there. Veteran Detective Brennan was assigned to work on it but he'd been unable to turn up a clue.

Jack's phone rang. It was the forensics lab. "We didn't find anything in the hallway or stairs leading to the roof of last Wednesday's incident Jack. There were a few prints but they were from the maintenance man. A few others were from employees who work in the building. Sorry."

"Me too," he replied. "Thanks."

Detective Brennan came in a bit later. "We interviewed people again who knew Janice Ryman. We learned she had dated a man named John. Last name unknown. Funny, but when we talked to people who knew Mary Orvett, we were told by one of the office ladies, she was dating a man who she thought was named John. Neither knew any last name."

"Both ladies living quarters were gone over by forensics weren't they?" Jack asked.

"Yes," Brennan replied. "But no prints were found that led to anyone named John."

"Were there any photos in among either ladies belonging's we couldn't identify?"

"There was one as I recall," Brennan said.

"Was it from a photo studio or just a snap shot?"

"It was from Princeton's Photo Studio but we already checked there and they didn't have any record of who the person was in the photo. I talked to Maggie at the studio and she seemed to think they'd just made a copy for Jancee off another photo."

"The name Jerry is the signature on the photo," Jack said.

"Yes?" Brennan questioned as if waiting for Jack to say something else.

"It might be a nick name. It might be a relative. It might be a friend."

Brennan continued to wait thinking Jack was leading someplace. Finally he did.

"Are there any employees where they were working named Jerry?"

"I don't know. We talked to a lot of people, but I don't remember any Jerry."

"Check again. Let's rule that out and rule out anyone where they lived who might have been named Jerry."

Captain Horace Beecham walked in as Brennan left.

"Jack," he started. "Remember sometime ago we asked you to help the department in recruiting?"

"Yes."

"Well, you were gone when we started and so far it's been going quite well. Anyway I was wondering if you were still interested. We're going to expand our area for seeking recruits beyond our immediate area. In other words we want to send someone up north into Oregon and also into Nevada as well as Idaho and Utah. We're looking not only at people who have never considered Law enforcement, but Police people who might want to move up into better paying Police work. Salaries here are higher than in many smaller towns. It might interest some people."

"I thought you told me the Chief wanted me to stay where I was?" Jack asked.

"Well, yes he said that, but now that we are expanding our search area, I asked him if he wanted me to ask you again."

"I know that when asked before, I would have done it because it would have allowed me to be home evenings with my sick wife, and I would do it now if you really needed me, but I think my situation has changed and I'm really happy doing what I'm doing. So if you don't mind I'll stay right here."

"Okay Jack. I think you'd do a great job for us, but if that's what you prefer we'll leave it at that."

Later when Jack returned from lunch, Brennan was waiting.

"I've learned there are two Jerry's working at the insurance company. One of them, Jerry is his real first name. For the other John is his first name, but he prefers being called Jerry."

"Okay. Get a full background check on both," Jack ordered.

"I've already ordered it," Brennan replied. "Hopefully we'll know more by tomorrow or the next day."

When Jack got home he heard his phone ringing as he walked in from the garage. Quickly he hurried into the kitchen and picked it up. It was Marian.

"I didn't hear from you yesterday," she said sounding disappointed.

"I know," he replied. "I was invited out and by the time I got home, I was too tired to call."

She didn't waste any time in asking the question.

"When do you want me to come? I could leave tomorrow."

"I'm still in the middle of two difficult cases," he replied. "I've been going in early each day and working eleven or twelve hours or more. If you were here we wouldn't have much time. Unfortunately that's the way police work is sometimes."

"I know, but I'm anxious to be with you," she said hoping he'd respond with something saying he'd like her to be there also. But he didn't. Instead he said.

"I hope we can solve these two cases soon and things will return to a more normal routine. Then if you're here, I won't be gone so much. I just don't want you to be sitting here in a strange city alone."

"I wouldn't be alone. You'd be there most of the time."

"Well, just a bit more," he said. "I think were making some progress. We might be able to solve these cases soon or at least get to a point where I can keep regular hours."

He thought he could hear the disappointment in her voice, but they talked for awhile longer anyway. She told him about her friends and they were planning a skiing trip. Her dad was looking forward more all the time to his retirement.

Jack didn't really know if they were making progress and his hours would improve, but he was trying to put her off just a bit longer. It wasn't that he didn't want to see her; it's just that he was not only involved at work, but Jacquee was still on his mind. He knew Marian cared for him and he knew he cared for her, but it just wasn't the right time. If she came now and they were together he felt it wouldn't be right. He just needed more time. He still thought about Jacquee a lot when he wasn't working and he missed her. Having Marian here now while he still mourned the loss of his wife just didn't seem proper.

He was up early the next day and his first thought was what they would do this Wednesday about the shooter. They couldn't put all those men out there again. Still he didn't want anyone to be shot. Since he didn't feel like fixing his own breakfast, after his shower he drove to a nearby eating place to take care of his food needs and then on to the cemetery to visit his wife's grave. Somehow he just had that urge to go there this morning.

As he stood there looking down and missing her and thinking about her, he finally asked.

"Love, You remember Marian don't you? Well we've been talking. I think I told you she talked me into going to see her parents. Anyway she wants us to pick up our relationship again. She's a really lovely person and I was almost,...Almost persuaded to marry her. But as you know I chose you because I realized I loved you just too much.

Anyway, would you mind if she and I considered getting married one day? As I get older I realize more and more that I need someone in my life. Work just doesn't offer the fulfillment it once did. Besides, I'm beginning to think I'd like to have a child or perhaps two. I know I was happy when you and I learned you were expecting. Anyway I've been thinking about it more since losing you and I really want to find someone. I think it could be Marian."

He kissed the fingers on his right hand and pressed them against her name.

"I'll be back tomorrow. I love you."

He turned and walked back to his car and drove on to work, with Jacquee on his mind.

Arriving at about eleven A.M. he turned to his "IN" file box to see what was new since he went home the night before. There were a couple of shootings and a few traffic stops, a home break in, but nothing that involved his section. Picking up his coffee cup, he filled it and walked to his desk. Sitting down and taking a sip of coffee, still too hot, he sat it back down and thought.

"I guess we'll just scale it back a bit. I'll just have a few people on roof tops and no extra people on the street. Maybe that will work."

His phone rang. It was Henry Mullins.

"Dennison," he said.

"Just wanted to let you know" Henry said. "I've started another story using another of the cases you gave me. It will be out the following month. I'm going to put three stories in that issue."

"Okay Henry. Whatever you think?" Jack replied.

"By the way. The publisher has decided to send you an advance check based on this first issue. You should be receiving it in a few days."

After Henry hung up, Jack decided that would be nice getting a check from the publisher. Then wondered just how much it was going to be. A few hundred? A few thousand? Well, when it shows up, I guess I'll know he thought.

His phone rang and picking it up he said.

"Dennison."

"Lieutenant. The sniper just shot a lady over on Market Street."

"What? It's only Tuesday."

"I know, but I guess he changed days after he found us there last Wednesday. You'd better come over."

The lady was Lucinda Stevens. She was fifty two years old. The wound hit her in the left shoulder. Wasn't serious and she was going to be okay, but the shooter was still on the loose.

"I guess we don't have to worry about tomorrow now do we?" Mike asked Jack later.

"I'm just wondering," Jack replied.

"What?" Mike asked.

"I've been thinking. This shooting? I wonder if it could be just to make us think he was changing his days. Maybe he's still going to take a shot at someone again tomorrow and then be laughing at us for thinking he'd changed days."

"Do you really think he might do that?"

"It wouldn't surprise me," Jack answered. "In fact I think now I will double the number of people on the roof tops. Maybe we can outsmart him."

"And if he doesn't show, then what?"

"Well, I guess I will have wasted a lot of man hours. Let's round up everyone we can and we'll put someone on every building top that is ten stories or higher."

"Okay," Mike replied. "I'll get right on it."

Brennan came in during the middle of the afternoon.

"The two Jerry's at the insurance company. One of them has been with the company for more than twenty years. His name is Gerald, and everyone just calls him Jerry. He signs his name Gerald on almost everything including photos. I've seen some photo's that his friends and family members have. The other Jerry, well it's really a nick name. His real name is Jasper and he hates it."

"So we really didn't learn anything?"

"I'm not so sure. Jasper or Jerry has been employed only four years. Not married and has tried to date several of the ladies including some of the married ones. He's not too well liked. Oh, no one really hates him, but they just think he's a bit strange."

"Okay. Let's see what we can find out about him."

Wednesday arrived and after his morning visit to see Jacquee's grave again, Jack showed up at work. There weren't any new cases for him to be concerned about. He'd talked to Marian last night again and they'd decided she could come week after next. If he was going to be too busy, they'd try and find something to keep her occupied.

She told him she was going skiing with friends this week end and possibly next and would book her ticket for the Monday after. Expect her a week from Tuesday in San Francisco she said. Marian told him she was bringing most of her things as she was planning to stay for a long time.

Jack was pleased she was coming because he had to admit he really did care for this special lady. Even though he was still mourning the loss of his wife Jacquee, he felt it was all right to pick up his relationship with Marian. He'd almost married her once and it was very apparent she still wanted to marry him. If Jacquee wasn't going to be there, then there was no reason he shouldn't think about being married to Marian. After being single for a long time before Jacquee came into his life, the time with her convinced him that he really preferred being married. Since he could no longer be with her, then why not Marian? It almost was once anyway. Besides, he was confident

Jacquee would want him to be with someone that cared about him and that he cared for as well.

The Wednesday roof top trap that was set to try and snare the shooter, failed. He never showed up and again Jack was frustrated by the waste of hours and the fact the shooter had out witted him again.

On Thursday morning Julia called. It was early and Jack was once again getting ready to go to the cemetery.

"I thought maybe I could talk you into taking me to lunch," she said.

He hadn't talked to her since Sunday and hadn't even really thought about her. He wasn't sure he wanted to do that, but he thought perhaps it was a good opportunity to let her know he'd decided to re-kindle his relationship with Marian. It wasn't that he didn't like Julia, but he just didn't feel strongly about her. A beautiful young lady he knew she was, but with her being the daughter of his long time friend, it still made him feel a bit uneasy.

Anyway it was best if he talked to her in person, so he agreed. He met her at Pochino's, a rather high class eating establishment not far from where she worked.

"You picked a really classy place," he said as they met in the entry way.

She took hold of his arm as she answered. "I thought we deserved the best. It has a very good reputation."

"For what they charge, I sure hope so," he replied.

They were led to a lovely table near a window looking down from the second floor onto the street below.

Jack opened his menu and looked at the prices and thought to himself, I may have to work some overtime.

"I'm paying, Jack," she said, surprising him.

"You can't afford to do that. Can you?" He asked.

"No, but this is a special occasion."

"It is?"

"Yes. Very special," she replied.

"Okay. When do I find out what it is?"

"After we eat," she replied.

He didn't say anything about his plans to tell her about Marian, but they enjoyed the lunch, even though he kept thinking of the exorbitant prices. It almost took the great quality of the meal away from the enjoyment. When they finished and the dishes were removed, Jack looked across the table waiting for her to tell him what this special time was all about.

"Jack," she finally said. "I've decided something."

He waited a moment for her to continue. Then she did.

"I didn't want to wait any longer. I've made up my mind and I decided to make the first step."

He waited to hear what it was.

"Jack." she said without any hesitation. "I love you. Will you marry me?"

He was speechless. It was a shock and he wasn't expecting it. He thought it could be anything, but he never expected it to be that. He looked back across the table at her unable to come to grip with the words he'd just heard her say. Then she continued.

"I want to get married again and it all of a sudden hit me over the last few days, that you're the person I want to be married too. I talked to mom and dad, and they said to go for it. So here I am. Will you marry me?"

He was at a loss for words. Never in his mind did he think she was going to ask him that question. She was sitting across the table now waiting for his answer. He knew she'd want him to say yes, but he couldn't. He just couldn't. She was beautiful and really a nice person. He liked her and someone one day would be very lucky to be married to her.

But being married to a good friend's daughter? Well, he wasn't sure about that. Besides he was fifteen years older than her. He could even remember her when she was just a very small young lady. He'd met Don, her father when they both joined the Police Department. Don, her father is a few years older than he and was already married when the two of them met.

"Well?" he heard her say. "I love you Jack and I want us to get married."

He heard the words and still he just didn't believe it could be. She might think she loved him, but it couldn't be. A few years down the road she might realize that it was just infatuation and then what? Another divorce? That would surely be an uncomfortable situation.

No, he wasn't going to marry her. If she was going to be disappointed, then so be it. But in the end it would be for the best.

"Julia," he finally said.

"Yes," she answered in anticipation.

"I'm not going to marry you. You surprised me by asking, but it's really for the best. One day you'll realize that. For one, I'm too old for you and, two, it's too soon for me to consider getting married again. I like you a lot but I'm not in love with you. I'm sorry."

He saw a look of disappointment on her face as she turned away for a moment. Then looking back, she said. "I knew you would say no. I know all about the differences between us. The age, my family and we've really not had a relationship plus the fact that you've just lost your wife. But I'd be willing to wait until you're ready. If I thought that one day,...That one day perhaps it could be."

He reached across the table and took her hand and as he did the waiter arrived and asked.

"Will there be anything else sir?"

"No thank you," Jack replied.

The waiter left the bill in a leather folder and walked away. Jack picked it up.

"I'm paying," she said. "It was my idea to come here."

"I know," he replied. "But I'll take care of it."

"I'm sorry Julia. I like you a great deal. I always have."

"But you remember me as a little girl, and you can't think of me being your wife?" she replied. "That's it, isn't it?"

"That's not it. I just don't want any attachments right now."

"I said I'm willing to wait," she responded.

"I know you did," he answered. "I know you did. I just don't feel I can or want to make any commitments right now."

He knew that wasn't exactly true. At least not one hundred percent true. He was seeing Marian, sort of, but they had a relationship before and he'd almost married her or was at least considering it at one time.

He escorted her to her car and when they reached it, he looked at her and said.

"I'm sorry Julia. I like you a lot. I really do. But…"

"But you don't want to marry me," she said.

"I'm sorry," he repeated.

"It's okay Jack. Somehow I knew it would end this way, but I had to give it a shot. I love you and always will." She smiled up at him, squeezed his hand and got into her car. He watched as she drove away. He was feeling bad about the whole situation, but he knew it was for the best. He was certain she was going to be just fine.

CHAPTER FOUR
OFF TO MIAMI

"I've learned from talking to several people at the insurance company where Ryman and Orvett worked that they think this Jerry is a bit strange," Brennan said.

"How so?" Jack asked.

"It's nothing they can put a finger on, except why does he sometimes ask married women out when he knows they are married?" Anyway I'm looking into his background. We know he worked at a machine shop across the bay before he was hired here as a gofer."

"A gofer?" Jack questioned.

"Yeah," Brennan replied. "You know. Someone who runs errands for anyone who need something so they don't have to do it themselves."

"You mean like my detectives do for me?" Jack said laughing.

'Exactly," Brennan replied with a smile.

"He's been there four years and that's still all he does?"

"Apparently."

"Let's get a warrant and search his place."

"On what grounds?" Brennan asked.

"Let's just say suspicion of theft."

"Theft of what Lieutenant?"

"I don't know. There must be something missing at the insurance company. Make something up. You're a good Detective Brennan. Use your imagination."

Thursday ended and Marian called again when he got home. She learned it was a good time to call him late at night his time since it was mid day the next day where she was.

Again she reminded him she was skiing this weekend with friends. Her plane would arrive in San Francisco Tuesday afternoon, a week from next Tuesday. Could he pick her up? He would he told her, and if he couldn't he'd make sure someone would.

Friday morning he prepared for work as usual and again as usual thought he would arrive early. First however he needed a trip to the store to get groceries and a few other assorted things. Since he'd been back from his trip, he'd been to the store only once and that was just to pick up a few of the most necessary things. He really needed a much larger shopping spree. Everywhere he looked, he could see he was out of whatever he needed.

He also knew that tomorrow he'd be driving north to Don's wedding. He was happy for his friend. Perhaps one day, he too would get married again.

Friday turned out to be a very dull day at work. Brennan succeeded in getting a warrant to look at Jerry's apartment. There wasn't much found except that Jerry seemed to be a gun nut. Several magazines about weapons of all kinds were present, and located in a few places around his residence, were four rifles and two pistols. Each one different from the other.

Jerry Evans was unhappy at his guns being taken for investigation. Detective Brennan was pretty sure only one of them had been fired recently and it was the same caliber as the weapon used to recently wound three ladies. Ballistics would try and determine if it might be matched to the shootings.

Saturday morning, Jack was off to the wedding. It was small by comparison to most weddings. At least the ones he knew about or been too. Most of the small town of Walker attended as both Margaret and Don were known to both of them. Weather was good and after the wedding the outside tables were filled with food provided by many of the local residents.

"Where are the two of you going?" Jack asked his friend.

"I'm taking her to New York to see her sister. They haven't seen each other in more than a dozen years. Then we are flying to the Bahamas for a week of sun."

"I'll bet she'll like that."

"She doesn't know yet. I'll tell her at the airport. She'll know we are going to New York when we get there. I'll tell her about the second part after we are visiting with her sister."

"I'll bet she'll be surprised," Jack said.

"I hope so," Don answered and then asked. "How are you doing?"

"I'm okay. I had a great trip. Went to see Marian and her folks, as you know, and I saw some other people I knew. Met some interesting people on my drive around the country and now I'm busy back at work. I'm doing okay. Marian is coming for a visit soon."

"Are you two going to get together?" Don asked.

"I don't know for sure what will happen there. I'm certain she'd like to get married and we almost did, so perhaps in time we will."

"Well, that will be good for you," Don said.
"Yes, perhaps so. But it's too soon."
"Yes. Maybe," Don replied.

Don and his new bride left later in the day, and as the crowd started to leave, Jack got back into his car thinking he'd drive all the way home, but part way down the road he became too tired, and changed his mind, so he started looking for a place to spend the night.

He pulled into one of the well known chain motels about half way from Walker to his home in San Bruno. After checking in, he decided to walk to the small all night store he'd seen a short distance from his motel. The afternoon meal at the wedding was good, but it was later now, and he felt the need for something to top himself off for the night. A full meal would be too much, so he thought he'd just get something to snack on.

As he walked across the open area that separated the motel from the store, he could see two men and a clerk inside. As he got a bit closer he noticed the two men had guns and the clerk standing behind counter was busily putting money into a bag. It looked to be a robbery in progress. Quickly drawing his service revolver he looked for someplace in the empty parking lot that might offer some protection. There was one car at the corner of the lot that looked to be the only spot, but all of a sudden the two men finished inside and they moved quickly toward the door. There wasn't time to find a spot that might offer him a place of protection, so getting down on one knee a mere fifteen feet from the front door, Jack waited until they both stepped outside. Neither saw him and pointing his service revolver in their direction, he yelled.

"Police. Drop your guns."

"They hesitated a moment and looked up. Not having seen him before in their haste to leave, and seeing him now a mere fifteen feet away, one of them raised his weapon and started to point it in Jack's direction. Jack fired one shot from his service revolver. He apparently hit the person closest to the store door, and the one who'd started to raise his gun. He gunman dropped his weapon and grabbed his leg falling backwards against the store wall. The second gunman, casting a glance at his partner, then raised his weapon and fired one shot in Jack's direction. As he did, Jack fired twice more hitting him and knocking him to the ground.

The man hit by his first shot reached out and picked up his gun from the walkway and fired one shot in Jack's direction. His shot missed. Jack fired a second time and hit his target once more causing the man to slump to the ground dropping his gun once more on the walkway. Rushing forward from his kneeling position, Jack kicked the revolver away from the man lying on the ground. The second man now sitting against the wall with blood on his leg and upper body did not move. Jack also kicked his gun away beyond his reach.

Just then the store clerk appeared through the slightly open door of the store.

"Call the Police," Jack ordered and the clerk disappeared back inside.

The robber sitting against the store wall said.

"Call an ambulance. I'm bleeding."

Jack said nothing but walked over to the second man lying on the ground with blood on his chest, and also bleeding badly. He wasn't saying a word but was just lying on the ground looking up. His gun lay several feet away, but he made no attempt to reach it. Both were still alive but badly hurt from their wounds.

It was only minutes before two Police cars arrived and minutes after came the ambulance.

"Nice shooting, Lieutenant." One officer said after Jack identified himself. Soon after the ambulance left and Jack gave all necessary information that was needed to the local police, he returned to his motel room no longer interested in getting something to eat.

Leaving early Sunday morning, he stopped for breakfast some miles down the road and arrived home easily before noon. His telephone answering machine was blinking. It was the Chief of Police.

"Jack. This is Chief Polanski. Call me immediately as soon as you get this call."

He wondered about the urgency of the call, so a few minutes later, after dialing the home number of the San Francisco Police Chief, he said.

"Dennison here."

"Jack. Glad you got my call. Remember Enrico Del Carlo from about a dozen years ago? You were a new detective then as I recall."

"Oh Yes," Jack replied. "I remember him well."

"Well, the Miami Police have arrested him and are holding him for us to talk too. He tried to get back into the country because I'm told he needed medical attention. He's not well."

"Too bad." Jack said a bit sarcastically.

"The Feds were going to prosecute him on drug charges, but Del Carlo doesn't want to spend his remaining days in jail so he's willing to tell us where the remains of the five bodies are that we couldn't find years ago and couldn't prosecute him for. In exchange for this information we let him live his remaining days out of Jail."

"Are the Feds willing to not prosecute him on the drug charges?"

"Yes." The Chief answered. "Since they are convinced he wouldn't live to get through the trial, they didn't want to waste the time and money. Anyway he is willing to tell us where the bodies are so we can wrap up the case. I want you to fly to Miami immediately to interview him. Call us with the information and we will check it out. You stay there until we can verify the information and in case it's not accurate you may need to talk to him a second time. You probably won't be there more than a few days."

"Why doesn't he just tell the Feds and they can tell us?"

"For some reason he remembers you as the young detective on his case all those years ago. He wants to talk only to you. Anyway I've arranged for you to fly there as soon as I could reach you."

"Okay Chief. I'll get a flight this afternoon."

After the Chief hung up, Jack started to get some things together when he realized Marian would be arriving Tuesday and he might not be here.

"I'd better call her." Then he stopped mid sentence, hesitated a moment and said. "No! No! It's next Tuesday she's coming. Not this Tuesday."

The flight put him in Miami after midnight, so he checked into a convenient airport hotel. In the morning he called Captain Sundquist of the Miami Police who sent a car to pick him up.

When Enrico Del Carlo was ushered into the small interview room, Jack noticed right away he appeared to have aged a great deal. There were many more wrinkles in his face than Jack remembered and he was walking with the assistance of a cane and bent over slightly as he made his way to the chair. More than twelve years had passed since Jack saw him last. His hair was white, not long and black as Jack remembered.

"Hello Jack Dennison," he said looking up and greeting Jack. His voice was weak and not as Jack remembered it from many years ago.

"Long time no see. They tell me you've made Lieutenant." He eased himself gently into a chair. It appeared difficult for him.

"Yes." Jack answered.

"I always liked you Jack even though we seemed to have our differences. That's why when I told them I'd be willing to tell them where the bodies were, I wanted it to be you I'd tell. Only you! I don't have much time left as I'm sure you can tell. My body is giving out and I'm probably going to spend eternity in hell, but I thought I'd do one decent thing before I go. I think the families would like to know where the bodies are. I decided I'd tell you and you can tell the families. The Feds decided I wasn't going to live long enough to try and put me on trial, so I made a deal with them."

He stopped to take a drink of the water from the glass that was placed on the table.

"Anyway Jack. How has the world been treating you?"

"I've been okay," Jack replied.

"I heard you lost your wife."

"Yes," Jack replied.

"Too bad! Too bad!" he replied. "I always wish I'd had a son Jack. If I did, I'd want him to be just like you and not like me. Instead I had two daughters. Silvia died a few years ago at age twenty three in a car accident and my older daughter, Alogia who changed her name to Alexis is an attorney in New York. The last I heard she is doing just fine. I haven't talked to her in years. I think she is trying to forget where she came from. Anyway I'm very proud of her."

Enrico stopped and coughed a few times and then after taking another drink of water, went on.

"Jack. Would you look her up and tell her I'm sorry. That in the end, I tried to do the right thing?"

"Sure Enrico. I'll do that."

"Thanks Jack. I'd appreciate it."

He coughed again and then said.

"Anyway I'd better tell you what you want to know."

After explaining to Jack where the bodies were located, they talked a minute more and Enrico, coughing again, decided he needed to rest. The guards got him onto his feet and assisted him back to his holding area.

Jack immediately called his Chief with the information he'd received from Del Carlo and then after a tour of Miami, compliments of the local Police department, he returned to his motel late in the day.

Tuesday afternoon Jack learned they found all but one body they were looking for, so a return visit to talk to Del Carlo was necessary on Wednesday morning.

"I'm sure it must be there Jack," Del Carlo told him when they met Wednesday morning. He repeated all the information again he'd given Jack on Monday when they first talked.

"They told me they checked the area carefully Enrico," Jack said.

"I don't understand," Enrico answered. "I'm sure they were all there close together. It was off cemetery road, near the old church."

"You say they found only four?" he asked.

"That's what they told me." Jack answered.

Del Carlo sat in his chair thinking, and rubbing his whiskers a bit trying to remember if he'd forgotten anything. Finally, looking up he said.

"Tell them to look across the road Jack. For some reason I seem to keep thinking about a small house across the road. There's something about that house. I don't know what. It keeps popping into my mind. I guess my memory is going. Anyway for some reason I keep thinking about that house across the road. Have them look near the back of that house," he said rubbing his whiskers once more. "I remember there were newly planted flowers in front. When we couldn't put the fifth body where we put the others; I think we may have put it across the street in the back of that house. My mind keeps telling me that's what we did. Tell them to check around the back of that house. I think we didn't want to disturb all the newly planted flowers in front. Tell them to check Jack."

"Do you know where in the back?" Jack asked.

"I'm not sure, but I seem to remember there was a driveway going around the house. Maybe it was near the driveway. I'm just not sure."

Jack called the information to his Chief and was told to stay put until they checked.

The next morning Jack's hotel phone rang.

"I knew you'd be up Jack," the Chief said. "It's only six A.M. here but I wanted to call you right away. Anyway we looked until late last night and he was right. We did quite a bit of digging but we found it. For some reason they must have buried one across the street. We've got what we want, so you can come home. Come and see me as soon as you get in."

"I've got to go to New York first Chief. Del Carlo made me promise to tell his daughter he was sorry and tried to do the right thing in the end."

"Okay Jack. I'll see you on Monday then. Take a few days to visit New York as long as your there."

His flight to New York wasn't long and he looked up the name Alexis Del Carlo, but there wasn't any attorney's by that name listed in the phone book. Then he thought that if she changed her first name, she might have also changed her last name. There were three Attorneys whose first names were Alexis in the New York directory. Each had a different last name, but the first one was Alexis Carlson, so he called that one first.

The young voice that answered the phone told him it wasn't her but just an office girl.

"This is Lieutenant Jack Dennison," he said. I'm not sure I have the right person, but how old is Ms. Carlson?" Jack knew from talking to Enrico that his older daughter was thirty one years of age.

"I believe she's about thirty or so," the young lady on the other end of the line said.

"Is she in?" Jack asked.

"No. She's in court. She said she'd be back about four."

"Thank you," Jack replied and hung up the phone. He'd decided he'd go to her office and wait. Better to talk to her in person.

He was seated in her outer office with the young office girl across the room, when the door opened. It was ten after four p.m. Jack looked up to see a beautiful lady, olive colored skin, very dark shoulder length hair and perhaps weighing about one hundred twenty pounds. She was dressed in a navy blue business suit with white trim around the Jacket collar and the single pocket. But what struck him most was the fact that she could have passed for his deceased wife Jacquee's twin sister. He was stunned and awe struck. He looked up at her speechless.

She glanced down at him in the chair, stopped at the desk a moment to ask the clerk a question and then turned toward him.

"Lieutenant Dennison?" she asked.

He was almost speechless, but a moment later managed to answer. "Yes."

"What can I do for you?" she asked.

Jack managed to stand and look down at her. Being closer now he could see a difference between her and his deceased wife, but the difference was slight and unless someone really knew Jacquee well, they'd swear it was her.

"I need to talk to you about your father Enrico," he said.

"My father is dead," she replied.

"It's important that I have a few minutes of your time Ms. Carlson."

"Very well. Come in," she replied seeming a bit hostile.

He followed her into her office, closing the door behind him. She put her brief case on the desk and then turning toward him asked.

"What is this about my dead father?"

Jack looked down at her desk and noticed her name plate. She'd apparently not changed her name entirely because on that name plate was, Alexis Del Carlo Carlson. She'd kept her last name as a middle name.

"I just talked to him this morning in Miami. He's here in the U.S. for medical reasons and wanted to see me. I flew to Miami from San Francisco at his request. He asked me to come and see you and tell you he was sorry for a lot of things in his past and he was trying to do a few things right in his remaining days."

"And just why should I believe you Lieutenant Dennison?" she asked.

"You don't have to believe me Ms. Del Carlo."

She interrupted him.

"It's Carlson Lieutenant."

"Sorry. Ms. Carlson," he corrected himself. "Anyway he asked me to come here and tell you in person he was sorry he wasn't a better father. He was trying to clear up a few things from his past. I met him many years ago when I was a young detective out west. For some reason he took a liking to me and now he wanted to talk directly to me. That's why I came east."

"And did he clear up some things Lieutenant Dennison?"

"Yes he did, Jack replied. "Anyway I came here to tell you. I figured I could do that for him. I don't think he has much time left. The Feds aren't even going to prosecute him because they are sure he won't live long enough to last through a trial.

"Well, he was right," she said. "He wasn't a very good father. He caused a lot of grief for me and my mother. She'd still be alive today if it wasn't for him."

"What do you mean?" Jack asked.

"Mom was a very sensitive person and he always badgered her about everything. She was under a lot of stress because of him and his associates. Anyway I blame him for her early death. I've hated him every since."

"I'm sorry things were bad for you and your mother. Anyway I felt obligated to deliver the message for him and I have."

She changed the subject at this point and asked.

"When I came into the office a few minutes ago, you looked at me like you'd seen a ghost. Why?"

"Well, I did think I saw a ghost," Jack replied. "You bear such a striking resemblance to my recently deceased wife that I was stunned. Same skin color and hair and you're about the same weight and height. Almost the same age. I was very startled when you walked in. She passed away only a few months ago."

Alexis paused a few moments before answering and then said.

"I'm sorry Lieutenant. I really am. I can understand your reaction now."

After a moment she walked around from behind the desk and said.

"Are you headed back to San Francisco now that you have delivered your message?"

"Not tonight. If I had gone directly from Miami, I'd be home now, but since I came here, I think I'll find a room and stay through the week end. My Chief told me as long as I was here, I might as well see the city."

"For whatever reason you felt it necessary to come here, I appreciate it. If I seemed a bit like I didn't care,... well, I don't really, but thank you anyway. It was considerate of you to do that."

"I guess I'd better be going," Jack said. "I need to find a room."

"Ah... Lieutenant," she said.

"Yes," he replied.

"Jack," she replied using his first name for the first time. May I buy you dinner? I appreciate what you did even if I don't care. It was a nice gesture. And I know someone who is manager of one of the airport hotels. I'm sure I can arrange for you to get a room. What do you say? May I buy you dinner?"

Jack wasn't sure. All of a sudden her attitude seemed to have changed. Should he consider having dinner with her? What would it be like sitting across the table from someone who resembled his wife so closely? Would he be uncomfortable?

Finally after a moment's thought, he answered.

"I think that would be very nice."

She took him to a very nice place in Queens. She ordered a bottle of wine for dinner, and when the food arrived he discovered it was excellent.

Their conversation was good. Alexis told him more about herself. She asked many questions about him which he answered even though he usually didn't like talking about himself much. She told him she'd never been to the West Coast, but hoped one day to go there.

"When you do, look me up and I'll give you the grand tour," he said.

"I may just do that," she replied and then asked.

"You said you're staying a couple of days?"

"Yes. The Chief said I might as well take the opportunity to see New York."

"I'd like to show you around our city, if you'd like," she said. "Then when I come west you can return the gesture. What do you say?"

"I think that would be really nice. I'd appreciate that a lot."

When dinner ended, she made a phone call and arranged a place for him to stay.

"I called my friend at a local hotel. If you're staying a couple of days, you're better off being right in town. It's more convenient for me to pick you up than having to drive all the way out to the airport."

She drove him to his hotel and dropped him off in front.

"Good night Jack," she said.

"Good night Alexis. Thanks for dinner and for the hotel arrangements."

She drove away and he watched still amazed at how close her resemblance was to that of his wife Jacquee. Even some of her mannerism, he noticed at dinner, reminded him of her.

The two days were very enjoyable. She took him to all the notable places, including the Empire State building, Central Park, Times Square, Rockefeller Center, and Saint Patrick's Cathedral. They took the Station Island ferry to Station Island and then back across the Verrazano Bridge to Brooklyn. She drove him out on Long Island where they had dinner.

Finally on Sunday, Alexis drove him to the airport for his trip back to San Francisco.

"Thanks Alexis," he said. "I really appreciate your taking the time to show me around. I'm sure I saw much more with you taking me than I would have seen on my own."

"It was a pleasure doing it," she replied. I don't ever get a chance to act like a tourist, so it was fun for me also. It was like a vacation."

He watched again as she drove away. Spending two days with her, a lady who looked so much like his deceased wife and at times even acted like her with so many of the same mannerisms, made him think that Jacquee could have been a part of that family.

Since Jacquee was adopted and no one knew anything about her past, wouldn't it be something if she really was a part of the Del Carlo family he thought as he carried his luggage into the terminal.

Detective Mike was waiting for him at the airport when he arrived.

"What are you doing here Mike?" he asked when he spotted him.

"The Chief sent me to pick you up. He wants to see you right away."

"Why? What's up?"

"He'll tell you. I'm to take you directly to his home."

Jack wondered during the drive what could be so important that the Chief would send Mike to pick him up and bring him directly to his house.

"Come in Jack," the Chief said when they arrived. "How was your flight?"

"A drag. I must be getting old. I don't care for those long flights much. Why do you want to see me?"

"I'll wait in the other room." Mike said.

The Chief cleared his throat and then said.

"Jack I asked you to come and see me as soon as you arrived because I have something I must tell you. I know you've had some tragedy in your life with the loss of your wife after such a short marriage, and I know you are still trying to get over that. I also have been told that a young lady named Marian Johnson who you almost married at one time, has once more been in your life."

"Yes," Jack replied not sure where this was going.

"I didn't want to tell you this while you were in New York, but we received word late last night, that Marian Johnson, daughter of the American

Ambassador to Switzerland was killed in a skiing accident in the Swiss Alps. I thought I'd wait until you were here to tell you. There wasn't anything you could do anyway."

Jack thought his hearing had suddenly deserted him. The Chief just told him Marian was dead. He knew that couldn't be. She was coming here in a few days. They were going to see if perhaps they might consider getting married.

"What?" he questioned in disbelief. "Marian killed. What are you talking about?"

"Yes Jack. We got a phone call directly from the Swiss embassy in Switzerland. The call never even went through their embassy here. They called my office directly wanting to talk to you."

All the breath and energy left his body. He collapsed into a chair without moving or saying anything. It was like a nightmare. It couldn't be true. It just couldn't be he thought. He looked up at the Chief who was watching from behind his desk.

"What can I do Jack?" he asked.

"I don't know," he said. "Nothing I guess." Then after a brief pause he said.

"I need to call her parents. Did they say how it happened?"

"Only thing I know is that it was a skiing accident."

"Use my phone," the Chief said. "I'll be in the other room." He got up and left to give Jack some privacy.

Jack spent half hour on the phone and finally opened the door to let the Chief back into his office.

"They're taking it pretty hard," he told the Chief. "She was their only child. They always wished she and I had gotten married. I told them just now that I thought we might. She was supposed to be coming here. If I hadn't put off having her wait until I got caught up at work, she'd have been here and not skiing."

His shoulders slumped and he looked as though the weight of the world had just been placed on his back. The Chief placed his arm around him and asked.

"I'm sorry Jack. Did they say how it happened?

"She was with three friends. She'd stopped to adjust her boots straps while they skied ahead. On the way down she took a short cut trying to catch up and fell in some soft snow. She slid over the side of a small cliff. There was a lot of new snow and apparently she didn't know she was close to the edge. Anyway they said it caused a small avalanche. By the time they got to where they thought she was located, all they found one ski sticking up out of the snow. They told her parents the dug as fast as they could, but by the time they found her, it was too late. They tried to revive her and when help arrived, the medic's tried also without any success."

"The funeral is a week from Wednesday in Virginia. I need to go."

"Of course," the Chief replied. "Take what time you need. I'm truly sorry Jack."

Mike drove him home. Not much was said between them. It was late into the night before he managed to get to sleep and almost noon before he awakened the next day.

The week was a nightmare. He couldn't concentrate on anything. The sniper did not make an attempt for some reason this week. No more ladies were killed. Friday came and went and during the week end he tried to keep busy, but his mind always haunted him that she'd be alive if only he'd let her come when she wanted. He knew her death was his fault and he had trouble living with that on his mind.

Monday he was back at work once more trying to help solve his two most important cases. They checked everything they could. None of the guns could be traced to the sniper and were returned to their owner.

On Tuesday, Jack boarded a plane that would take him to Virginia. A taxi took him from the airport to the Ambassador's house. The Butler greeted him at the door and he was shown inside. Soon the Ambassador and his wife appeared. She walked right over to him and gave him a hug.

"I'm so sorry Evelyn," he said. "It's my fault. I shouldn't have put off having her come. It's my fault. It would have been okay if she'd come early. I was just concern that I'd be busy and she'd be alone."

"You couldn't know Jack. We don't blame you," she replied.

"I'm sorry, Sir." Jack said addressing the ambassador.

The ambassador put his arm around Jack's shoulders and asked.

"Can I get you a drink Jack?"

"No sir. No drink can make me feel any better."

"You're staying here with us of course Jack," Evelyn said.

The evening was somber but cordial. The ambassador asked about his work, and how things were working with Henry Mullins. The conversation touched on many things but not on Marian's death.

Jack made an excuse to turn in early as sitting there with her parents made him feel uneasy.

The loss of two ladies so close, was almost too much to bear.

The next day Jack rode in the family car to the church and afterwards to the cemetery. He stayed with them all day and the next and the next as well. Then on Saturday, he took a plane back to the city by the bay and his house. His mood was somber and he visited Jacquee's grave Sunday as usual. Afterward he spent time with Sarah and her husband Dennis and Sunday evening he took time to open all his backed up mail from the last week.

The check Henry Mullins said the publisher would be sending was there. Thirty five thousand dollars. It was a real shock, but somehow he no longer cared about the money. He paid all the bills and went to bed. Early Monday morning he was awakened by the phone.

"Hello," he said.

"Jack," the voice said.

"Yes," he replied.

"We've got another strangled lady who worked for the insurance company.

CHAPTER FIVE

GUESS WHAT JACK?

"Okay," Jack answered. "I'll be in early. Thanks." He got up, took a shower, got dressed, went to eat before going to the bank to deposit the check and then on to work. It was nearly noon when he finally arrived.

"She was found in her car down near where the last body was. Her name is Lillian Lathrop. She's a divorcee and has been at the Insurance Company only two years."

"We have detectives interviewing people she worked with," Detective Brennan said. "Lieutenant Sharp is leading the investigation. He's over at the insurance company office now. The company president promised to do anything we want to try and solve this."

"Okay. Thanks," Jack said and then he glanced at what happened from over the week end and seeing nothing that was unusual walked over to the coffee stand to get himself a cup.

Just then, Mike, his sergeant, walked in and Jack stopped what he was doing and said.

"I'm sorry Mike. I've had so many things on my mind I forgot to ask how your wife was doing."

"Pretty good," he responded "She's no worse off now than she was before. It's pretty much we just wait and see how treatment goes."

"Well, Don Perry got past his, so maybe she will too."

Then changing the subject he asked. "What do you think we should do about the roof top shooter? He changed to Tuesday and tomorrow is Tuesday again."

"I was thinking Lieutenant. How about if we have the building superintendents lock access to the roofs. We can put a helicopter or two up and see what happens. We just can't keep putting large groups of people out on the street."

"Okay. Let's try that. I'll arrange to get the boys in the air tomorrow, and you start calling the supers."

Jack turned back to his desk when a uniformed officer came in.

"Lieutenant," he said. "I didn't know you were here already. There's a lady waiting down stairs to see you. I told her you weren't due in until three, but she said she'd just wait."

"Did she give you a name?" Jack asked.

"Yes, but I don't remember it now," he answered.

"Okay. Send her up."

He walked back to his desk to wait and a few minutes later she walked in behind the uniformed officer. He recognized her immediately.

"Bunny," he said. "What are you doing here?" Jack came out from behind his desk to meet her.

"Hello Jack," she replied. "I came to see you."

"Really? What a pleasant surprise. Anything important?" he asked.

"Yes I think so," she answered.

"All right. Let's go into the office," he pointed toward the corner. She followed him in and he closed the door.

"Can I get you some coffee? He asked.

"No thanks," she replied.

"Okay then what brings you all the way here to the big city to see me?"

"Well I could say I just came just because I wanted to see you, but it's really more than that."

He looked at her waiting, and then, not wasting any more time, she got right to the point.

"I came to tell you that I'm pregnant."

"Pregnant?" he questioned.

"Yes. I'm pregnant with <u>our</u> baby."

He stood there looking at her not knowing quite what to say and finally asked. "Our baby?"

"Yes. I'm sure it's ours. I've not been with anyone else so I'm sure."

He still wasn't sure what to say, but she went on.

"I felt you should know, so I drove over from my place to tell you in person."

"Oh Bunny. I don't know what to say. It's such a surprise. And shock."

"You might consider saying you're happy and give me a kiss," she replied.

"You're sure?" He asked.

"Oh yes," she replied. "And it has to be ours my dear."

"What do you want me to do?" he asked still shocked at her statement.

"I didn't come here to tell you that you have to marry me, but you should know that I'd be very pleased if you did. I'm going to have our baby honey," she said. "And raise it just like I raised my boys. I am capable of taking care of another baby, but I thought you might want to know about it. When we know if it's a boy or girl, you and I can both decide on a name. And even if we never get married, I'll always have a part of the man I love, forever."

Jack sat down in one of the chairs and said.

"I'm stunned. I just never thought…"

She walked over next to him, and leaning over said.

"If you're not going to kiss me, then I'll kiss you," and she did.

"Bunny, I never meant for this to happen," he said not responding to the kiss.

"Well, my darling," she said. "It did happen. Anyway I'm not very far along, but far enough."

He looked up. "Bunny, if I can do anything, financially, or otherwise. Anything at all? Just let me know."

She looked down at him and then said.

"You could marry the mother," she suggested.

He looked up at her a few moments before answering and before he could, she went on.

"I know you just lost your wife. I'm not trying to pressure you into anything Jack." She didn't know anything about the most recent tragedy to Marian. Marian's death was also on his mind and still it wasn't very long since Jacquee's passing. He didn't want to tell her about Marian because if he did, then she'd know he was considering getting married again and it wasn't to her. Instead he remained silent.

"Anyway I felt you needed to know. I want you to know that I'm very happy about it. Whenever you want, you are welcome to come and visit. Even if you and I never have each other, I would never keep you from knowing your child."

"I don't know what to say. I never expected anything like this."

She pulled up a chair next to his and sat down. He looked across and into her eyes thinking it might not be so bad if he were married to her. After all that happened lately, he just was not ready to think about it.

"Bunny," he said. She was listening.

"How about if I come over to see you as soon as I can, and we talk about this in more detail? I believe you when you say the child is ours and I will try and do the right thing. I will be responsible. Right now I have too much going on to think about it. Do you understand?"

"It's okay Jack," she said. "We can talk any time you want. I just came because I wanted to tell you in person. I'm going home tomorrow. You know my phone number and you know where I live. Come anytime."

"What time do you leave tomorrow?" He asked.

"As early as I possibly can. I need to get back," she replied.

"How about we have breakfast before you leave?"

"Sure. I'd like that," she answered.

He got to the office early again after having breakfast with Bunny and seeing her off. They didn't talk specific's about the baby, but just in general terms. Jack promised to come for a visit as soon as possible and they'd talk more.

After she left, he went straight to work. Bunny and the baby crowded his mind and Marian's death still lingered there making it difficult to concentrate on matters at hand.

It was Tuesday and the roof top sniper might be out there someplace.

"Everything in place Mike?" Jack asked when Mike arrived shortly before noon.

"Yes. We're as ready as we can be."

"Okay. Let's you and me drive down to the area now."

Again the noon hour came and went and nothing happened. When Jack and Mike returned to the office Lieutenant Stark was waiting.

"Jack. I wanted to update you on the latest killing of the Insurance Company employee."

"Thanks Leo."

"Lillian Lathrop was a pretty new employee. Just two years. We learned she had been dating several of the single men in the building. We spoke to all we knew about. No one said anything negative about her. The night of her disappearance she had been on a date with Jim Watland. He said they had gone to dinner, seen a stage play and had a couple of drinks after. He took her home about one A.M.

She lives in one of those apartments with a lock on the outside door to the building. He said she opened the door and went in. He left her there and that's the last he saw of her. He said he made sure she was inside the building before he left. He felt bad, but he said he didn't know what else he could have done."

"Does he remember anyone watching them?"

"No. We don't have anything yet from our team going over the apartment."

"Did this Jim Watland date either of the other two ladies?" Jack asked.

"Actually he said he dated both of them."

"Has anyone else dated all three?"

"Not that we know of. We talked to those we know who dated Jancee and Mary and none of them dated Lillian."

"So at this point we have no common connections between any of the women and the men they dated?"

"That's right."

"Okay Leo. Let me know if anything else comes up."

Jack's phone rang right after Leo left.

"Dennison," he said after picking it up.

"Jack," The voice said.

"Yes." He replied.

"This is Madeline." There was a slight pause as if the person was waiting to see if he remembered her. He did but it took a second for it to register.

"Do you remember me?" the voice asked.

"Of course I do," he replied. "How have you been?"

"I'm better now that I've found you again. I'm very upset that you left me at the altar Jack. I thought we were supposed to be getting married."

His thoughts drifted back to a time right after his first wife's divorce. He'd gone away to Mexico for a few days. A few days that he wanted to forget. He'd met Madeline in some little honky tonk south of the border and they'd partied for several days. Somewhere along the way they decided to get married while in one of their intoxicated stupors. Fortunately they both fell asleep before it happened. He hadn't really left her at the Altar, as she put it, but almost.

Anyway, he'd awakened before she did and wondering where he was, he'd gotten up and came back across the border. He thought nothing more about it since. Now here she was. She'd found him somehow and now he wondered what she wanted.

"Madeline," he said. "How did you find me?"

"Quite by accident," she replied. "I was in a jail cell in L.A."

"You were in jail?" he questioned. "What for?"

"I was in a bar having a few and a fight started. It got a bit rowdy and I hit some guy and, well finally the police came and a lot of us got arrested. Anyway while I was in jail waiting to see a judge, I met this lady named Ramona. I don't remember her last name. Anyway we got to talking and I told her about you. She said she knew you."

"Must have been Romona Gonzalez." Jack said.

"Yes." Madeline replied. "That's it. Anyway she told me where you were."

"So you're out now?" he asked.

"Yes. A couple of days later the judge let me off on probation because I had no record and he thought I was just in the wrong place at the wrong time."

"So why are you calling me Madeline? That Mexico thing was a long time ago."

"I was thinking we might pick up where we left off. You were going to marry me remember? You're not married are you Jack?"

"No. I'm not married."

"All right. Then how about it?"

Well, he remembered her all right, but he'd had a "few" to many that night and when he sobered up he was glad that it never happened. He never thought he'd ever see her again.

"I'm engaged Ramona," he lied hoping to get rid of her.

"Oh! Jack baby! It should be you and me. Break off the engagement. Meet me for dinner and when you see me again, I'll make you forget everyone else. You'll know when you see me that it should be just you and me."

He was sure he'd remember her all right. She wasn't someone you'd forget easily. She really stood out in a crowd.

"Madeline, I've got to go. It was nice hearing from you, but things have changed and I'm very busy here at work."

"How about just one drink for old time's sake?" She asked.

"There is no old times' sake Madeline?"

"Can I come to your office to see you in person?"

"No. Don't come. We have nothing in common."

"Please Jack. I want to see you."

"I've got to go Madeline. I'm busy. Goodbye," he hung up the phone.

I don't know what I was doing down there, he thought. My marriage had just ended. I don't know if I was celebrating or was sorry. I took off and went down there for a few days and ran into her right away in some bar. She'd latched on to me like a drowning, desperate person at sea. After a few drinks, I thought she even looked good. By then he'd had almost as much to drink as her and that was much more than his normal capacity. He didn't remember much of those three days, except, except she was always with him day and night. He didn't remember saying he'd marry her, but she must have thought so.

The next day came and went without any progress on the two major cases Jack was involved in. Madeline never called again or tried to come to the station and see him. He was glad. Finally on late Friday afternoon the desk sergeant from the first floor called and said there was a lady wanting to see him. It was concerning the insurance company murders. A few minutes later she arrived escorted by a uniformed patrol officer.

"Are you Lieutenant Dennison?" she asked.

"Yes," he replied. "I understand you have information on the insurance company murders?"

"Yes. I think so."

"Okay. Tell me what it is."

"My name is Debbie Thorton. I work there and knew the three ladies who were murdered. I knew one of them better than the rest. Jancee Ryman. I'd been to her place a few times. Anyway I knew she was dating one of the salesmen at the company. She showed me the necklace he'd given her. It was beautiful and she was very impressed. I got the impression she was getting serious about him."

"Who is this man?" Jack asked.

"His name is Don Borman. Anyway he asked me out a couple of times and last night after our date, he gave me a present."

She took out the small jewelry box, opened the lid for Jack to see. There was a beautiful necklace, perfectly displayed inside on the soft purple felt looking material.

"This is the same necklace that Jancee showed me."

"Are you sure?" Jack asked. "Sometimes different jewelry pieces can look pretty much alike."

"Oh no! I'm absolutely positive. It's the same."

Jack picked up his phone and dialed a number.

"Stark," he said. "Do we have a list of Jancee Ryman's jewelry?"

"We do? Good. Are there any pictures? Good. Bring them over. I may have something on the case," he hung up.

"Do you know where he bought this Ms. Thorton? It doesn't say in the box."

"No I don't," she replied.

"That's okay. We can find out. The box has the maker's name. Other than the fact he gave you this necklace, was there anything about Mr. Borman that would make you suspicious of him?

"No. Not really. He was very nice the two times we were out. He was never out of line. I'm supposed to go out with him again tomorrow night. Do you think I should? I'm a bit afraid now."

"I think you should tell him you're sick and can't go. In the meantime, we will check on him and the necklace. I will need to keep it for a bit."

"Okay, but what if he wants to come over and wants to see it?"

"Don't let him come over. If he does, call me."

Then Jack turned to Detective Ryan.

"Ryan I need you to check on this. As soon as Stark gets here with the photo's so we can check them against this piece, go to Feldman's jewelry and talk to Sid Feldman. Tell him I need to verify the manufacturer and see if he can find out exactly where this piece was purchased. Then go there and find out the date this particular item was purchased and how many others just like it have been sold. We need to know if other jewelry stores have sold this particular item, and find out who bought them and how many. I need to know that as fast as possible."

"Okay Lieutenant."

"What should I do?" Debbie asked.

"Go home. Call him tomorrow afternoon and tell him you're sick and can't go out with him. I'll be in touch as soon as I can. If anything comes up, remember, call me."

Jack gave her a receipt for the necklace, escorted her out before returning to his desk.

Stark showed up a few minutes later with pictures and a description list of the Jewelry. They both agreed the necklace in the box was the same one in the photo. The written description seemed to match as well.

"What does this prove?" Stark asked.

"If this is the same piece Borman gave Ryman and she was wearing it her last night, then how did he get it back unless he killed her and took it?"

"We don't know she was wearing it." Stark said.

"No, but the odds are that she was. Would not a lady wear a necklace when dating the man who gave it to her?"

"Yes. I guess she would."

"Exactly! Okay Ryan. Here, take it to Sid Feldman and see what he can tell us."

CHAPTER SIX
MADELINE'S NEAR TRAGEDY

Saturday morning came and as he was taking his shower he heard the phone ring but he knew the answering machine would catch it, so he didn't hurry. After he dressed and got a cup of coffee, he thought he would see who might be calling.

Much to his surprise, it was Breanna, Doris Chapin's friend. "Call me Jack. Please! I need to talk to you. My number is 555-233-5575."

I wonder what she wants he thought. She left rather abruptly the day after we'd had a pretty nice day together. I got the impression that she wanted to continue visiting, but the next day after I returned from the picnic, I learned she'd left. Well I'll call her after I go to the cemetery. He started to fix some breakfast and planned to read the morning paper before heading out to visit his deceased wife, and as he was about to sit down in front of his eggs, bacon and toast, the phone rang once more.

"Hello," he said after leaving the kitchen table to answer the ringing of the phone.

"Jack, its Breanna."

"I was going to call you in a bit," he replied.

"Jack, I'm sorry I left so abruptly. I need to apologize. I saw you Sunday morning with that other lady and I'm afraid I rushed to conclusions. I thought we were going to be able to spend the day together. Then you left with someone else. I'm afraid I let my temper get the best of me."

"I had an appointment to take a friend to a company picnic," Jack said. "I didn't know you wanted us to spend Sunday together or I would have told you I'd be busy."

"I guess I just assumed that we would be able to see each other after we had such a wonderful Saturday. It never even crossed my mind that you might have other plans. I knew you'd lost your wife and I guess I just assumed you were alone and I thought maybe I might enjoy the day with you. It never occurred to me that you might have someone else."

"She's only a friend. I don't have someone else. I was just doing her a favor."

"I'm sorry. I guess I jumped to conclusions. I am really sorry."

"It's okay Breanna. Don't worry about it. If you're out this way again sometime, let me know and if I get back your way, I'll call you."

"Well, the thing is," she replied. I could get away right now. If you'd like, I'll fly back out there tomorrow. Perhaps we could spend a whole week together."

He wasn't sure he wanted to spend a week with her. Especially if she had a temper. If she was going to be upset so easily, then it's perhaps better if she wasn't here.

"The thing is Breanna, right now I don't have a lot of time. I'm in the middle of two very important cases and I'm working very long hours every day. In fact, even though this is Saturday, I'm going to work in just a bit."

"Oh Jack. I do so want to see you. Can't you take some time off for me?"

"I just came back from eight weeks off from work, Breanna. I can't take any more time. If you want to come, perhaps another time would be better."

"I could visit Doris while you're at work and see you when you're home."

"I don't think that would work, Breanna. By the time I work twelve hours or so and get some sleep, there wouldn't be much time for us to visit. I think another time might be better."

"Oh Jack, do you really have to work all those hours?"

"I really do right now," he replied.

"Are you sure you don't want me to come?" she asked.

He thought he noticed a bit of sarcasm in her voice as if she didn't believe him.

"You really don't want to see me do you? It's just an excuse."

"It's not an excuse," he said. "I really am very busy. Until things here get back on an even keel, and I get caught up, I'm not even thinking of another relationship with anyone. It would be nice to see you, but this is just a bad time."

"I really want to see you Jack," she said pleading her case. "I know I acted in haste by leaving and I'm sorry, but I want to see you. I sensed something between us and I want very much to find out if there's something more than just my feelings. I've decided that it's time for me to find someone. Up until now I've been too busy in my career to think about it. Until I met you that is! Please Jack. Let me come out again. Even if we only have a few hours together each day."

He didn't want her to come out. Everything he told her was true. He wasn't going to have much time to see anyone and if she was there waiting each day for him to come home, then he'd feel an obligation to make time for her and that could just get in the way and perhaps hamper his efforts at work and other things. Besides he didn't know her very well and really wasn't ready to consider starting a relationship. Their one day together was very nice, but it was just one day. It wasn't enough to know if he'd want to spend more time with her. Especially when she was in the middle of the country and he was out here. Even if it clicked, it would be a long distance relationship and that never works well.

"Breanna. Don't come," he said. "I'm sorry but I'm just too busy right now. I really enjoyed our day together, but another time would be better."

There was silence on the other end of the line for a moment and then she said.

"Okay," the line went dead.

Jack stared at the phone in his hand and the silence coming from it.

"She hung up," he said out loud. "Interesting!"

He placed the phone back down and returned to his now cold breakfast.

He'd taken only a few bites of the food in front of him when the phone rang again. Thinking it was her calling back, he hesitated to answer it, but finally after it rang the third time, Jack decided it might be something more important. Picking up the phone one more time, he said.

"Hello."

It was a male voice on the other end of the line.

"Lieutenant Dennison?" the voice questioned.

"Yes," Jack replied.

"This is Lieutenant Schaefer of the Fire Department. We're on the Oakland Bay Bridge. There is a lady out on one of the bridge supports and every time one of our people tries to go out there and rescue her, she backs away closer to the edge. She won't let us near her. She said she wants only you to help her down."

"Me? What's her name?" Jack asked.

"Madeline. She says her name is Madeline."

"Madeline." Jack said shocked at hearing her name. Then thinking to himself what is she doing up there?

"Okay. I'll be right there," he answered.

It didn't take long to drive from his home in San Bruno to the bay bridge. Highway 101 all the way provided a fast means of transportation, but it was still about fifteen miles. He wondered how could she last up there in the cold high above the water. Maybe by the time he would get there, they wouldn't need him. Either she'd have fallen or they would have somehow managed to get her down.

"She won't come down Lieutenant. She wants you to rescue her." Lieutenant Schaffer said when he arrived.

"Me?" Jack questioned.

"That's what she said. Have you ever been up high like that before Lieutenant?"

"No." Jack replied.

"We can instruct you if you want to try and save her."

Jack looked up toward the spot where she was perched. She was nearly at the end of one of the cross supports with her arms wrapped around the beam.

"Okay. I'll try," he said apprehensive about the whole thing.

The placed the safety belt around him.

"Two of my men will follow you up. Remember when you get up there; hook yourself onto the eye hooks with these snaps that are attached to your belt. As you ease yourself out toward her, move your hooks out with you. Don't leave any slack between you and the bridge supports. When you get close to her, try and put this other belt on her and then hook her onto one or more of the eye hooks. Watch out, because in cases like this, she may try to grab you. If you and she are not attached to the bridge supports, one or both of you could fall into the water below.

As you ease yourselves back toward the center, be sure to re-hook yourselves each time. When you get her back close enough, my men will take over. Any questions?"

"I don't think so."

"Okay good luck."

Jack looked up one more time at the lonely figure near the end of the beam high above the water. Two firemen were already up the structure not far from the beam Madeline was hanging onto.

"Good luck, Lieutenant. Any last minute questions?" one of the fireman asked when he reached the beam level.

"I don't think so," he responded.

"Remember" the fireman said. "These nylon cords will each support five thousand pounds. Even if the two of you fall, they will keep you from falling all the way."

"Okay," Jack replied. "I hope I don't have to find out if they really will support us."

As he eased himself forward, he dare not look down the hundreds of feet to the water below, now filled with white caps from the morning breeze off the ocean.

He hooked his safety harness onto one clasp and then another as he moved forward. Finally he was within reach of her.

"I'm sorry Jack," she said. "Help me. I don't want to die," she said begging.

"Hang on Madeline. Now don't let go. I'm going to put this harness on you and snap this clasp onto a hook here so you can't fall."

"I'm cold. I can't hold on much longer," she replied.

"Hang on," he said. Gently he tried to place the belt around her. She was bigger than he remembered from many years ago. He had to get close and as he did she started to let go and grab him.

"Don't let go," he yelled. She grabbed the steel bar once more as he snapped the safety belt together around her and then took the safety snap attached to the belt and pulled it to hook it to the steel bridge support. No sooner than he snapped it into place, then she let go of the beam and grabbed him with both hands. Her unbalanced weight pulled him and her toward the side and they started to fall.

"Grab the beam," he yelled once more.

She reached for it with one hand, her weight still pulling her toward the edge. Jack reached for her other arm, missing it twice before finally managing to get his hand around it and pull her up just a bit. Letting go of the beam with his other hand, he took the one remaining safety hook on her belt and snapped it onto the support beam. Then with a super effort, he managed to get her upright.

"Okay Madeline," he said with a sigh of relief. "Now I'm going to ease myself back a bit. I'll unhook and re-hook each time. Then I'll do the same to you. Okay? Do you understand?"

She didn't say anything, but nodded her head. Gradually he eased the two of them toward the center where the two firemen were waiting. When he finally got the two of them close, one of the Firemen said.

"We'll take her now Lieutenant."

Jack, cold from his short time above, climbed slowly down to the deck below.

"Nice going, Lieutenant. You did a good job up there. If we need any help in the future, I'll know who to call," he laughed.

"No thanks. I wouldn't do that again for a million dollars."

The firemen brought her down and as they placed her in the car he could see the wet clothes she was wearing. He noticed they were partly torn. A portion of one breast was uncovered and looking at her he could tell she had indeed put on a bit of weight from the time he remembered her a dozen years ago.

"We're taking her to the hospital. They need to examine her and check her mentally," the fire Lieutenant said.

"Jack" she called from inside the car.

"What is it, Madeline?"

"Come and see me. I'm sorry."

"I will," he answered. "I will Madeline."

They took her away and Jack returned to his car, exhausted. The cold now started to show its effects as all of a sudden he began to shiver. He turned on his car heater to provide some warmth from the cold outside that had almost chilled his body too much. After sitting there a few minutes to absorb a bit of heat, he turned his car around and drove to the cemetery. Jack spent some time visiting his deceased wife's grave and then drove home to the breakfast still sitting on the kitchen table. He'd already put in a day with more excitement than usual. It was only a bit after the noon hour and more had happened in this short time than usually happens in several full days.

The remains of his less than half eaten breakfast still sat on the table. He picked up the few pieces of remaining bacon and ate them and then tossed the cold eggs and toast into the trash.

A hot shower removed the rest of the cold from his bones and hunger pangs began to find their way into his being. He was suddenly beginning to feel hungry now that things were once again normal.

I could fix myself another meal, but as sure as I do, the phone will ring and someone will want me. I guess I'll go out and no one will find me until I have a nice quiet meal.

It was October now and Halloween decorations were beginning to show everywhere. As he drove by the local supermarket and its decorations, he remembered there was a small restaurant attached to the store. He'd never been there although he'd often thought about stopping. Maybe today would be the right time. It would sure be different and he was sure no one would look to find him there.

Once inside, he ordered lunch and when it came he was able to enjoy it undisturbed. As he sat back enjoying one more cup of coffee and looking out the front window, he noticed a police car stopping a vehicle across the street. It was something that happened often and this was no different from all the other ones he'd seen before. He was only half way interested until he noticed the officer draw his weapon and fire it. Other shots were fired and Jack jumped from his chair and rushed out the door toward the street. He noticed as he approached the police office had apparently been hit by one of the bullets being fired from the other car and was on the ground.

"I'm a police officer." Jack called out as he approached. "Where are you hit?"

"Just in the leg," the officer on the ground answered.

"Did you get a license number? Jack asked after calling in for assistance.

"A partial, but I know the make and color and I believe I can describe them."

Several Police cars arrived in moments and an ambulance arrived minutes later.

When he finally returned home there was a call from Detective Ryan on his answering machine. Jack called him back, and learned that Sid Friedman said the necklace in question was purchased at Sorby's Jewelry across town. Ryan checked there and they confirmed that Don Broman had purchased this particular item.

"We can be pretty sure she was wearing it on her last date with Borman," Jack said to Ryan. "Since he gave it to her, she would have been wearing it. If we assume he killed her for whatever reason, he wouldn't have spent the money on it and then not taken it back off the dead body. Let's pick him up and see what he has to say."

Borman was arrested at his apartment Saturday night and booked into jail on suspicion of murder.

Jack spent some time with Sarah and her husband, but otherwise stayed at home for one of the quiet days he hadn't seen in some time.

A warrant was issued Monday morning to inspect Borman's living quarters and he was questioned by day shift detectives before Jack arrived at work.

"What did we learn from the questioning?" Jack asked.

"Not much. He swears he's innocent. His attorney says we don't have enough evidence to convict him. The necklace doesn't prove he killed her. There's no proof she was wearing it the night she died. The attorney, who did all the talking, said his client took her home after their date, but he left her a bit after midnight. He doesn't remember if she was wearing the necklace or not."

"Did the coroner ever determine the time of death?"

"The body was found about eight a.m., and as near as the coroner can determine, she'd been dead from four to six hours. Maybe a bit longer."

"And we didn't find anything in her apartment?" Jack asked.

"No," answered the day shift detective.

"Well, the attorney may be right about us having enough evidence. Let's see what an inspection of his apartment tells us. And be sure we check his car. And one more thing," Jack said. "If she was wearing the necklace, I'm sure he would have noticed."

"I think so too," answered the detective.

"Lieutenant," Sergeant Mike said about an hour later. "Look at this photo. It's of Mary Orvett. Notice what is around her neck?"

"It's the necklace." Jack said.

"Right! I was just going through the file again. It appears that after Borman got it back from Jancee Ryman, then he gave it to Mary Orvett. I wonder if he also gave it to Lillian Lathrop. Ms. Thorton brought it in saying he gave it to her. If he killed the others, was he planning to kill her also?"

"It seems strange that four different ladies, well at least three that were sure of, received this necklace and three of them are dead. Let's see if we can find anything that tells us he gave it to Lillian Lathrop. If we can, then we may have something because if he gave it to all three, how would he have gotten it back each time?"

"Easy." Mike answered. "After he strangled them, he removed it from their necks."

"Right. Check the Lathrop file and talk to her sister again. See if her sister remembers being told about Lillian getting a necklace."

"And what are we going to do about the shooter? It's another week."

"I'm not sure Mike. Did ballistics confirm the rifle might be the one that shot the ladies?"

"No. They couldn't give us positive information." Mike replied. "Which bring us to the question, what are we going to do this week?"

"I don't know. Have someone call the building supers and be sure the roof top doors on all the buildings along the area are locked. Maybe that will keep the shooter from getting up there."

Jack's phone rang about an hour later while he was putting away several case files that had been solved.

"Dennison," he answered.

"Jack?" the voice on the other end said. He didn't recognize it.

"This is Alexis. Alexis Carlson. Remember me?"

"Oh! Yes of course," he replied.

"I'm flying out tomorrow to San Francisco. I have a case that I need to get some information on out there and I was wondering if we might have lunch?"

"Sure. What time are you getting in? I'll meet your plane."

He saw her immediately. She would have been hard to miss in any crowd. He noticed two other well dressed attractive model type ladies walking nearby, but they paled by comparison to her. The dark blue suit, her skin color and very dark hair, along with watching her walk, just made her stand out from everyone. She reminded him so much of Jacquee. He noticed several men look in her direction and when she walked up to him, they turned and looked at him to see who that lucky guy was.

"Hello Alexis," he said.

She walked directly up to him and gave him a big hug, much to his surprise, but much to his pleasure.

"Hello Jack."

"What brings you clear out here?" he asked.

"I could say I came just to see you, but I don't think you'd believe me."

"No, probably not."

"I've taken a case and some of the information I need has to be researched out here."

"There are people here who would do that for you, so you didn't have to make the trip," he replied.

"Yes, I know. Let's just say I wanted to do it myself," she was smiling and he knew she wasn't exactly telling the truth.

"Okay! If you say so," he replied.

"Where are you taking me for lunch?" she asked changing the subject.

It was a great place overlooking the water and they could see the bridge. Well, just barely. The day wasn't the best, especially for this late in the year, but he thought he'd try and impress her a bit, especially since she'd come this far. (He knew she hadn't come this far just to gather information on a case he thought, but perhaps to gather some information about something or someone else. He was, after all, a detective he reminded himself.)

"I went to see my father," she said all of a sudden.

"You did?" he asked.

"Yes. I hadn't spoken to him in years. He said he was glad to see me and apologized for how he treated mom years ago. He hoped I was doing well. He even said he thought I should come to see you."

"Really?" Jack questioned. "Why?"

"He said I should find someone. He thought I should meet you. I told him you came by my office."

"And?" Jack asked.

"He wanted to know what I thought of you. I told him I took you to lunch."

"What did he say to that?"

She smiled across the table and answered.

"He told me not to let you get away," she laughed once more. Then changing the subject she asked.

"Can you drop me off at the prosecutor's office?"

"Sure," he replied. "By the way. Are you staying overnight or are you catching a flight back right away?"

"Well, I don't know. It depends," she was looking across the table into his eyes.

He noticed just as a good detective might that she was fishing for just the right answer.

"When will you know?" he asked.

She didn't answer right away as if thinking it over, and before she could answer, he went on.

"I was just thinking. I have a spare bedroom at my place. I'd be happy to have you stay and then I could take you to the airport tomorrow."

"That would be nice. I'd appreciate that. Would you have time to show me around too?"

"Of course," he replied.

He dropped her off at the prosecutor's office with instructions to call him when she was ready. He drove on to his office and was no more seated at his desk, when his phone rang.

"It's me," the voice said.

"Done already? That didn't take long."

"No," she replied. "Can you come and get me?"

"I'll be gone the rest of the day, Mike," Jack said as he walked out of his office.

The sights around San Francisco this fall day made it difficult to view anything from any distance, but he did his best to show her all that his city had to offer. After dinner, they drove to his home in San Bruno.

"You have a very nice home Jack," she said as she looked around. "A person could be really comfortable here."

"I've enjoyed it for the time I've been here. It's a bit of a drive to work, but I don't mind that."

He led her into the hall and toward the front of the house to the new guest bedroom. The one that had been completely re-done after the blast that destroyed it some months before.

"This is the guest bedroom," he said walking into the front of the house and turning on the light to show a double bed, night stand, dresser and two chairs. "My room is at the other end of the hall. The bathroom is here in the middle and a smaller third bedroom is also here between the bathroom and the guest bedroom."

"And this is where you want me to sleep?" she asked.

He looked at her but didn't answer her question, but did ask.

"Would you like a drink?"

"Sure. Can I have bourbon and seven up or if you don't have that bourbon and coke?"

"I think I can manage that," he replied and turned toward the kitchen. She in turn walked down the hall to see where he slept. She turned on the light. It was larger than either of the other two bedrooms, and tastefully decorated. The large oversized bed along with a night stand on both sides sat along the inside wall. A large dresser was placed against the wall beyond and a smaller matching version was against the wall next to the large walk in closet. A good sized window occupied the wall opposite the bed. Inside the closet she saw his clothes hanging on one side and opposite his and occupying all of one side and the entire back wall were ladies clothing of a wide variety. Many at first glance looked very expensive. Alexis stopped short not expecting to find what she now realized was his deceased wife's clothing. She turned away and back toward the bed and night stand. There her eyes caught the large eight by ten color photo of an attractive lady that looked very much like herself.

She stopped short at seeing it. Her first thought was, where did he get a color picture of me. Quickly she knew it was a photo of his deceased wife. Alexis picked up the photo to look more closely and as she did, she learned Jacquee looked so much like herself, it was almost spooky.

"We could almost be twins," she said softly. "I know now why I struck him so when he first saw me in New York. He thought for a moment I was her."

"Here you are," he said walking into the bedroom. He noticed her holding a photo of Jacquee, and said. "That's Jacquee, my wife." He hesitated a moment and continued, "my deceased wife."

Alexis put the photo down and said. "She's beautiful Jack."

"Yes," he answered.

"I'm sorry. I just wanted to see where you slept."

"Well, this is it," he said.

Alexis took a drink from the glass he'd given her, took a step toward the door, stopped, turned back toward him and asked.

"Jack. Will you take me to the airport? I think I'd like to catch a flight back tonight."

He looked at her mystified for a moment, and then said.

"Sure if you want. Did I do something?"

"No. You didn't do anything. I just think I'd better go home," she answered.

She was seated in her first class seat looking out into the night sky as the aircraft buzzed its way east, and thinking. It wouldn't work. It just wouldn't. Sure Alexis, you came out here just to try and seduce him and make him feel he needed you, but when you saw her photo and saw he still had all her clothes, well, you know it just wouldn't work. Every time he made love to you he'd be thinking of her. You look too much like her and he's not gotten over her yet. Perhaps he never will. It's too bad Alexis my dear. He's one man you thought you could be happy with, but it just wouldn't work. You know it wouldn't.

She slept most of the way to New York, not waking until the wheels of the plane hit the runway.

Once she reached her apartment, Alexis walked into her bathroom and looked at the face in the mirror.

"Why do you have to look so much like her?

CHAPTER SEVEN
TWO SOLVED CASES

"What did Borman say about how he got the necklace back? Jack asked.

"He said on their last date she gave it back because she didn't want to see him anymore." Brennan replied.

"Well, that's a convenient excuse."

"Yes it is. I talked to Debbie Thorton again," Brennan said. "I asked if she could identify any more of Jancee's jewelry."

"And what did she say."

"Only that there was one bracelet she'd seen among Jancee's things that she really liked. She thought she might recognize it if she saw it again."

"Okay, then let her see all the jewelry," Jack said.

"Oh, I already did. I had her look at the photos, but she couldn't tell, so I had her see it all in person."

"And?"

"She saw it immediately among the items in Borman's apartment."

"So he took it, but when? I doubt he would take it while she was around. I suspect he went back after he killed her and took it then."

"You may be right Lieutenant, but how do we prove it?"

Just then Jack's phone rang.

"Dennison," he answered.

"Lieutenant. This is Molly in forensics."

"Yes, Molly. What is it?"

"I was going through some of Jancee Ryman's things and I looked at her diary."

"Yes. And what?"

"On her last entry which was partially scratched out, was written, *I'm breaking off with Don tonight and giving him back his necklace. I'm not comfort-*

able dating him. It was partly scratched off and written below were the words, *are you sorry now babe?"*

"Thanks Molly. If you find anything more let me know."

Then Jack turned to detective Brennan.

"Let's get a handwriting sample from Borman and compare it with the writing Molly in forensics found in Ryman's diary."

Just then Sergeant Mike walked in.

"What are we doing about the shooter? Tomorrow is Wednesday."

"The gun we got from Jerry's place doesn't match with the recovered bullet we got from the first shooting does it?"

"No. We can't prove he was the shooter or any of the weapons we found in his apartment had anything to do with the shootings."

"Okay. I guess we have to return them."

Just then a detective across the room hung up his phone and called over.

"Lieutenant. There's been a shooting on Market Street near where the other shootings were. A lady was wounded walking down the street. A man was seen running away. A patrol car in the area was stopped as it passed by and told about it. A civilian also just phoned it in."

At that moment a uniformed office stuck his head in the door.

"Lieutenant. There's been a shooting on Market Street."

"Yes, we just heard," Jack replied.

"Okay. Come on Ryan! Let's get over there," Jack said.

Witnesses said a man was seen running away after the shot and someone gave chase but lost him. The only description was that it was a male about five feet ten, slender and wearing a dark coat.

"That's not much to go on," Jack said.

"No and now that he can't get up on the roof tops, he's apparently come down to street level."

"How's the lady?" Jack asked.

"She's going to be okay Lieutenant" one of the officers said. "The ambulance took her away."

"How old was she?" Jack asked.

"I don't know, but I'd guess about fifty or so," the officer replied.

"He seems to be targeting ladies in the fifty plus age group. Why I wonder?"

"I don't know." Ryan replied. "We aren't going to know until we catch him."

"Okay, let's get back to the office."

They no more than returned to the office when the front desk officer, a floor below, called him.

"Lieutenant! There's a man here who says he knows who killed that city council lady a couple of years ago."

"Really? Okay. Bring him up," Jack replied.

When an officer came in escorting an older gentleman, Jack asked him.

"What's your name sir?"

"John Grievy," he answered.

"And you say you know who killed Bertha Bergstrom a couple of years ago?"

"Yes I do."

"And just who might that be?" Jack asked.

"It was Councilman Michael McKillory."

"How do you know this Mr. Grievy?" Jack asked.

"I had a dream. This voice told me I had to let the police know."

"You had a dream?" Jack asked.

"Yes," he answered.

"Do you have any other information about this case?" Jack asked.

"Yes. The dream woke me up, and there at the foot of my bed I saw this ghostly figure. It scared me out of my wits."

"Go on," Jack said.

"Well, this figure told me, and these are the exact words. It said, *"Michael McKillory killed me."* I didn't know who the ghost was and I asked and it said. *"I'm Bertha Bergstrom. You must tell the police."*

"And then what happened?" Jack asked.

"The ghost disappeared. I was afraid to go back to sleep, so after thinking about it all day, I decided to come here."

"And so you're saying that Bertha Bergstrom appeared in your dream as a ghost at the foot of your bed to tell you Michael McKillory killed her?"

"Yes sir," he replied.

"Where do you work Mr. Grievy?"

"I work at the city office building as a janitor. Why?"

"So you saw Mr. McKillory and Ms. Bergstrom many times during your work?"

"Yes, many times."

"How did they treat you? Did you ever talk to them?"

"I talked to Ms. Bergstrom many times. She was ever so nice. Mr. McKillory wasn't very nice. Whenever I'd say hello, he'd never answer or he'd give me a look as though I wasn't important enough to talk to. It was like he couldn't take the time to even say hello. He'd just keep on going. Ms. Bergstrom would always stop to talk to me. She was very nice."

"Well Mr. Grievy I'll look at the case file to see what I can find and if you learn any more, let me know."

When John Grievy left, Jack turned to detective Ryan, who was nearby listening and said.

"Bring me the file on the Bergstrom case."

"You don't really believe that, do you Lieutenant?"

"Well, it does sound a bit goofy, but why don't you get me the file and then check into Mr. Grievy. Let's see what we can find out about him."

"A ghost at the foot of his bed?" Ryan said. "I know we get a lot of gooneys in here and I think we just got another."

"The file Ryan," Jack said.

"Yes sir."

The next morning was Thursday and there wasn't anything special on Jack's morning agenda, so he wasn't in any hurry to get up. He lay in bed wondering why Alexis left so suddenly, but finally it occurred to him that she must have felt uncomfortable after looking at Jacquee's picture and discovered how much they looked alike.

"I wonder if they could be related?" he mumbled. "That would be strange."

Jack's phone rang while he was eating the breakfast he'd fixed for himself. It was a day shift detective.

"Lieutenant. There is a Mr. Grievy here. He said to tell you he had that dream again last night. He said you'd know what he was talking about."

"Yes I do. Thanks. Tell him I'm looking in to it. Find out if he knows anything new."

Arriving at work at his usual time was a little different. It was the first time since returning from his long vacation that he'd done that. Sergeant Mike was already at his desk.

"I was looking at this file on Ms. Bergstrom," he said. "There isn't anything here that I can see pointing toward McKillory."

"No and I didn't yesterday when I looked at it."

"You think this Grievy character is a bit off his rocker?"

"I'm having Ryan check on him. Why don't you talk in private to all the other members of the city council? Let's see if they know anything. Like what do they think about McKillory."

"Don't you think something might have come out after Bergstrom's death?" Mike asked.

"We can't be sure. From the file it sounds like very little questioning took place with other city council members. And remember one person on the council at that time is no longer on the council. Anyway why don't you talk to all of them?"

"Okay. I will." Mike answered.

Just then Detective Brennan walked in.

"Lieutenant. I had the sample of Borman's handwriting and the note in Ms. Ryman's diary compared by an expert and he said it looked the same. He's checking more closely and will let me know tomorrow."

"Okay. Good. If it's a match, I think we may have enough to turn it over to the prosecutor.

The rest of the day was quiet and Jack spent some time thinking about Marian and how he should have let her come sooner. If he'd done that, she'd still be alive. He really felt bad, but at the time it seemed like the right thing to do.

The day ended without any unusual things going on. It was pretty quiet evening and soon he was on his way to his home in San Bruno. He knew the house would be quiet and empty. He'd just gotten used to her being there and now he was back to being alone once more. Until he'd married Jacquee, he'd become used to living alone, but for the short time they were together he knew he liked having her there. He liked coming home to someone. Now he was alone again and he knew he didn't like it at all.

Should he get married again he wondered? Inside his brain he was sure he would have married Marian. He almost did once and it seemed like that might happen again before the tragedy. But it wasn't to be. Now what? There was Alexis who seemed interested, but she left not thinking she could compete with Jacquee's ghost. There was Breanna, but he didn't really know her and she seemed a bit temperamental. Of course if he wanted to get married, there was Julia Davis. After all she had proposed to him. And there was Bunny. He should probably marry her. After all, she was pregnant with their child. That would be the right thing to do. But he didn't really know her very well. Yes, they had a few days together. She had her memories from the past and was influenced by his showing up one day. He had no excuse for letting what happen between them, happen. He could blame the three or four drinks and her enthusiasm at seeing him again, but it was still no excuse.

As he pulled into his driveway he could see a few of his neighbors were still awake. It was just after midnight and lights were still on at several houses, but he didn't worry about that. He didn't feel tired, so once inside and after looking at the mail, he tried to read, but couldn't concentrate. Tomorrow was Friday and then the week end was again upon him. What was he going to do? He didn't have any plans.

I wonder if I should drive over to see Bunny, he thought. I told her I would come. It would take a half a day to get there, but when he did what could he tell her? Could he tell her he'd decided to marry her and take care of her and the baby? While he figured he probably was responsible, still he didn't know her very well. After all they'd only seen each other a few days since high school and he didn't know her then. Could they be happy? If they did marry and she came here, at least there would be someone home when he arrived each night. He'd like that.

Then he promised to visit Madeline. A few days had passed since he'd managed to rescue her and he did promise to visit. Perhaps he should do that.

Just then his phone rang.

Who could that be at this hour?"

"Hello,"

"Jack," the voice said.

"Yes," he replied.

"Chief Polanski here. I hope I didn't wake you, but I needed to get hold of you right away."

"It's okay Chief. I was still awake. What's up?"

"My granddaughter's husband has just been arrested along with two of his friends for a mini market robbery. Drugs were also found in the car I understand. She called me after he called her. They were driving her car. I know this young man and I was shocked. It just doesn't seem like something he'd do. I'd appreciate it if you'd look into it personally."

"Sure Chief. I can go down there right now if you'd like."

"No. Wait until morning. He'll be okay until then. I know you've been up all day. Let me know what you find. Call me anytime, night or day Jack."

"Okay Chief. I'll be down there first thing in the morning."

Jack arrived at the lock up shortly after eight. They brought him into the small room used to question prisoners. He was a bit shorter than Jack, slender, blond bushy hair, but pretty well built. Must be about one hundred ninety pounds he thought. He looked down at the floor as he walked in.

"Sit down," Jack ordered.

"You're Gary Winters?"

"Yes sir," he answered.

"Why don't you tell me what happened in your own words?"

"It's in the report," he replied. "Don't you know?"

"Yes, but I want to hear it in your words."

"I was out with some friends I knew from high school. I hadn't seen them in a few years. We visited for awhile and then they wanted to go to a store and pick up some cigarettes. I was driving Roxanne's car because mine wasn't running. We stopped at this all night Mini Mart and they both went in while I waited. Pretty soon they came out and we drove off. I was told a man came running out of the store as we drove off, but I didn't see him. The Police report said he did, but I didn't see him. Anyway we got stopped by a patrol car a bit later. I had no idea why we were stopped.

They found the cigarettes and they searched the car and found drugs. I don't know how they got there. Neither Roxanne nor I use drugs. These friends said they didn't know anything about it. They said since it was my car the drugs must be mine. They claimed they were only along for a ride. I heard the store clerk identified my so called friends, but since I was in the car I was arrested also."

"And you didn't know they robbed the store?" Jack asked.

"No. I thought they just went in to buy cigarettes."

"Gary, I hope you're telling the total truth."

"I am," he replied.

"Do you have an attorney?"

"No. Do I need one?"

"Yes. It would be a good idea. There is a process that you will have to go through and an attorney can get you bail. If you are not involved he can help get through the process. I know someone who might help. I'm going to check more into this. In the meantime behave yourself while you're here."

Jack left, went on to his office, called the Chief to give him his version and then called his friend Attorney Christian Welp.

"Sure Jack. What is it?"

After he finished talking to his friend he all of a sudden realized it was nearly noon and he'd not even had breakfast. The Monkey Tree restaurant was across the street from his office and it was a good place, so he went there. As he walked through the door, who should he spot sitting alone at a nearby table, but Angela Cunningham, the most beautiful attorney in all of California. At least he thought so. She was about his age, never married as far as he knew. She was too busy she'd told him last time they talked.

"May I join you?" he asked.

"Well," she said looking up. "If it isn't Jack Dennison, my favorite and most handsome detective. What brings you in here?"

"I just had some early work, and I all of a sudden discovered I hadn't eaten yet today."

"How are you doing?" she asked. "I heard about your wife awhile ago. I'm so sorry Jack," she said reaching across the table to place her hand on his.

"I'm surviving. Keeping busy," he replied. "What brings you down this way?"

"I had to come down here to your station to pick up some things and as long as I was here, thought I'd get a bite to eat. I have to be in court this afternoon and this seemed like the best time to have something."

She hesitated a moment before going on, but then asked.

"What are you doing week after next?"

"I don't know. Why?" he asked.

"I have to attend a conference of the leading attorney's from across the country in Los Angeles and I was wondering if maybe you'd like to go with me?"

He looked across at her a bit surprised by her suggestion. He imagined she might be nice to be with, but he wondered why she would ask him now. He'd thought about asking her out before he met Jacquee, but never did. Jack always felt she was too involved in her work to date much, but perhaps now that she was getting older, she felt maybe it was time to be looking for someone.

"I'd never be able to get away even if I wanted. Too many things going on at work and I've taken a lot of time off recently, so I don't have any more time available."

"I can talk to the Chief," she replied.

"You think you can get me off to go with you?"

"I'll bet I can. I can be pretty persuasive," she replied.

Jack laughed and said. "Well if anyone can, I'd bet it would be you. Sorry Angela, but I've got some cases that need my attention. I'd better not plan on it."

"There's always a lot of free time at these events," she said. "I can't think of anyone I'd rather enjoy spending some of it with."

"Thank you," he replied. "And I don't know of anyone I'd rather be with than you, but not this time."

"Darn Jack. I was hoping you'd say yes. It would make the time away from the meetings so much more interesting."

"I'll bet it would," he answered.

"I could use a vacation," she said. "Could we plan one together some day?"

"Sure. Why not? I'll save my vacation and hope I get another opportunity."

Angela laughed. "You never know." She picked up her papers off the table and announced. "Well, I'd better be going. Nice talking to you, even if you don't like me well enough to go with me."

"Oh, but I do like you well enough," he replied. "It's just a bad time."

"Bye Jack," she said as she walked away.

He finished eating and when he returned to work, he was met by Detective Ryan.

"Lieutenant, this Mr. Grievy is some kind of nut. A few years ago he reported the same kind of thing. It was on his next door neighbor. He filed a police report that he dreamed she was trying to kill him."

"What happened?" Jack asked.

"Nothing was ever proved that the lady next door did anything. The case was dropped."

"So he's done something like this before."

"So it appears," Ryan said.

"Well, there's nothing we have to go on, so I guess there's nothing we can do."

Just then Sergeant Mike walked in and announced.

"I just turned the Borman case over to the prosecutor. He's going to look it over and let us know if he thinks there is enough information to get a conviction."

"Okay. Now if we can just find the shooter. Have you started talking to the council members yet?"

"No." Mike replied. Several of them are out of town. I'll wait until Monday."

The weekend was here again. The sun was peeking through his bedroom curtain when he opened his eyes. Glancing across the room at the clock, Jack learned it was nearly six a.m. As he lay there a few moments, the sudden urge to get up and drive to talk to Bunny seemed too strong to resist. He rolled out of bed and headed to the shower.

"I might as well get this over with. I don't know what I'm going to say, but I told her I'd come so no use putting it off."

She was out front when he pulled up to the motel office. He could tell she didn't recognize him or his car at first. When he turned off the engine and eased himself from the front seat, she immediately became aware it was him. Bunny dropped the broom she was holding and ran to him.

"Jack," she called as she ran the few feet and threw her arms around him.

"I thought I'd better come so we can talk," he said.

"I'm so glad to see you," she replied not responding to his statement. "Are you hungry? Its lunch time and I was going to fix something for the boys in a few minutes anyway."

"Sure," he replied. "I decided to come so we can talk," he said once more.

"Let's eat first," she said.

They didn't talk about anything in particular during lunch. The two boys remembered him from his earlier visit and now he was back. Jack was sure they must be wondering if he was going to be staying. It was evident their mother seemed to be very interested in him. Even at their ages they could tell.

Then as they were almost finished eating, Jeffery looked at Jack and asked.

"Are you going to be our daddy?"

The question caught him off guard. He wasn't expecting to be asked that and wasn't sure just what to say. Turning toward the boys, he finally said.

"Jeffery. Michael. I don't know. Would you like to have me be your daddy?"

"Yes." Jeffery said. "Mama says you're a very nice person and we think it would be nice to have a daddy."

Bunny was sitting across the table, a big smile on her face.

"Well, Michael, Jeffery, I'm going to talk to your mother today and we'll see."

Just then Michael, who was the quiet one, jumped in and said.

"Did you know Mama is going to have a baby? Maybe it will be a little girl. Then we can have a sister."

Jack didn't know if the boys knew whether or not Bunny had confided in them, but he knew now.

"Yes," Jack answered. "I knew that."

"Boys," Bunny jumped in. "Why don't you go play since you're finished eating. Jack and mommy want to talk."

They promptly got up and left. When there were out of sight, she looked across the table at him and asked.

"What do you want to tell me Jack? That you don't want to marry me. Its okay you know. I understand you just lost your wife and that maybe you're not ready. Besides we hardly know each other and what happened was just as much my fault as anyone's. I guess my emotions just ran away from me at seeing you again after all this time and I didn't use very good judgment. So if you don't want to marry me, it's okay. Really it is."

"I didn't know you told the boys."

"Yes," she replied. "I thought they should know. Pretty soon they would be able to see that I look different."

"What did they say?" he asked.

"Oh, they seemed happy. But then at their ages one never knows if they will like the idea or not."

"Anyway Bunny. I don't know about anything else yet. I will support the child and help in any way I can. I'm just not mentally ready to take the step of being married again. At least at the moment. The right thing would be to marry you I guess, but I'm just not ready."

"It's okay Jack. I'll be okay and I appreciate your willingness to help. I've had to be pretty self sufficient after my husband's death. I've had to take care of the boys and run this place and I know I can handle having another child. Besides I've always wanted a girl and maybe this one will be a girl. Besides I know this child is part yours and to me that is special.

He reached across the table and took her hand before saying.

"I believe that Bunny. I know you would," he hesitated a moment before going on. "I know you would be okay. I came because I said I would and I wanted to reassure you that I will be there. I believe you when you say the baby you're going to have is ours. I feel responsible for the situation as much as anyone. I should have never let it happen, but it did and I came to let you know that I will be there as much as I can."

"Thank you Jack. Thank you for saying that."

"When I get home, I'm going to start putting some money aside in a fund to help educate him or her and to support him or her. I'll put both our names on it, so either of us can get it when it becomes necessary. In my line of work, one never knows when something might happen and I just want you to know. I'll send you a check each month to pay for whatever you need. If there is anything else you need just let me know."

She grabbed his hand back.

"I love you Jack," she said.

He didn't know what to say in response so she continued.

"If someday you decide you would like to marry me, I just want to let you know my answer is yes," Bunny was smiling broadly. "If you don't that's okay. I'll understand and you should know you can see our child anytime you want."

He still didn't know what to say.

"You're going to stay overnight aren't you?" She asked changing the subject.

"I guess I'd better. I don't really want to drive back tonight. Do you have a room I can rent?"

Bunny smiled back at him.

"Oh Jack. You know where you are sleeping tonight and it's not for rent."

She got up and walked to his side of the table.

"Bunny, I don't." That's as far as he got as she bent down to kiss him.

Jack drove back the two hundred plus miles on Monday morning. He pulled into his driveway shortly after noon and into the garage just in time to miss the deluge of rain that seemed to be following him the last few miles.

There was a call on the answering machine from Sarah, wondering where he was. There was another call from Breanna wanting to talk and asking him to call. The house was cool because he was gone for a couple days and the area had been experiencing cool weather, but he knew he'd have to get ready for work so as he prepared for that, the phone rang once more.

"Jack," the voice said.

"Yes," he answered.

"It's Ryan. We just had another lady shot on Market Street."

"It's only Monday," Jack replied.

"I know, but anyway the shooter apparently isn't sticking to any particular day. I understand the lady is going to be okay. The good part is that two officers and another man caught the shooter. I thought you'd want to know."

"How did they catch him?"

"A man was nearby and witnessed the shooting. He took chase and as the shooter ran around the corner, who should he run into but two police officers who were on their way to lunch. They saw the rifle in his hand and stopped him just as the man chasing him was about to latch onto him. Anyway he's in custody now and is being questioned. I don't know any more at the moment."

"Okay Ryan. I just got home, so I'll be there in awhile."

THE UNWILLING RECRUIT

CHAPTER ONE
GETTING MARIA A JOB

"Here's what we know," Ryan said when Jack arrived at work. "From what the shooter told the detectives who questioned him, he was angry at women in their fifties or older because his mother and her sister treated him badly all his life. He said they were always nagging and picking on him and nothing he would do satisfied them. He said he was criticized for everything even though he was helping support them. They were after him all the time and finally he just had enough."

"Were those his words?"

"So I understand. I wasn't in on the questioning, but that's what I was told."

"Did he say why he was picking on women in general?"

"I was told he said he developed a hatred for all women over fifty. He thought they were all that way. He thought they were just all nasty and liked picking on men."

"Did he say why he was only wounding them and not killing them?" Jack asked.

"Yes. He only wanted to make them suffer. He figured that was more punishment than killing them. He said if he killed them they wouldn't suffer and he thought they should."

"Well, he's in custody and I guess we can let the prosecutor determine if he's mentally disturbed or not."

"I suppose so," Ryan answered.

Just then Detective Brennan walked in.

"Lieutenant. On the Bergstrom case. I talked to three of the council people and so far the only thing I've learned was that there were some bad feelings between McKillory and Bergstrom. I understand she once dated his cousin for quite some time and then broke up with him. The cousin felt they might get married and then all of a sudden she dumped him."

"That doesn't sound like much of a reason to kill her if indeed he did."

"I'm still going to talk to the other council people, but that's what I've learned so far."

"Okay Brennan. Keep me posted."

"Lieutenant." Sergeant Mike said as Brennan walked away. "I need some time off. The Doctor's said they think my wife's condition is not getting any better. She's depressed over her health and wants to visit her sister in Colorado. I think she feels her days are numbered. The Doctors haven't actually said that, but she feels it because this has been going on so long and she's not getting better."

"I'm sorry Mike. Of course you can take time off. I'll arrange it. When do you want to leave?"

"As soon as possible," he replied. "I've got a month's vacation coming. I thought I'd drive her back to visit her sister. I told the Doctor and he said he would arrange to have her take treatments in Denver."

Jack walked around from behind his desk to put his arm around him and said.

"Do what you need to do Mike. We all hope she's going to get better, but you need to do what you have to."

"Thanks Lieutenant. I'd like to leave now if you don't mind."

"Of course," Jack replied.

As soon as Mike left Jack noticed Detective Octovio Jones, the newest detective on his shift, come into the office.

"Hey Jones," he called out. "How are things going? Is your wife adjusting to your being on afternoons better?"

"Yes Lieutenant. Now that she has someone to talk to and visit with, it's much better. She understands I need to be working other shifts if I'm going to get ahead."

"Good. I'd hate to lose you."

"Yes sir. I'd hate to have to go back to patrol again."

"Are you having any problems?"

"No sir. Harris and Spencer, as well as some of the others, have been very helpful."

"Good," Jack replied. "I'm glad."

Tuesday morning Jack decided he must go see Madeline. He'd promised he would visit her after her rescue and so far he'd not made it. It was important that he go see her since her attempt to jump because he knew she needed someone and apparently it was him. Why she climbed up on the bridge he might never know, but she did and now he knew he'd have to go talk to her and see if he might help. She was evidently a person who needed help.

The mental health facility staff brought her to him in a small visitor's waiting room. She was dressed in the usual drab gray colored gown issued to all those staying there undergoing treatment.

When Madeline saw him, she hung her head down in embarrassment.

"Hello Madeline," he said.

"Hello Jack," she answered. Her voice was soft and barely audible.

Jack took her hand and as he did she looked up slightly and said in the same soft voice.

"I'm sorry."

"It's all right," he said. "It's over now. Let's look forward to better things. You've got a lot of years ahead of you."

"I've made such a mess of my life. I was out there just trying to have a good time. Drinking too much, going to parties all the time and who knows how many men"

She stopped there as he squeezed her hand. Tears were now running down her cheeks. He handed her his handkerchief. Madeline took it and wiped the moisture.

"Now is the time to start over Madeline. I know you can do it."

"No I can't. Look at me. I'm big and fat and ugly. No one would want me." She started to sob and the tears started again. She tried to wipe them as she lay her head down on her hands. Then all of a sudden she raised her head again, red from crying, and said.

"Of all the men I've been with, you're the only one I remember. You're the only one who ever treated me decently. My life could have been so different if I'd just been smart enough to realize that. I'm so sorry that I made you climb up on that bridge. I almost killed us both."

"It's all right Madeline. It's over now and this is a new starting point. You're still young and I just know there is someone out there that will make you happy."

"No there isn't" she sobbed.

"Yes there is," Jack replied. "I'm going to help you get started."

"You are?"

"Yes I am. You concentrate on the treatment here and when you get out, I'll help you get a job, an apartment and then you can start a new life. Put everything else behind you and things in the future will be much better. I promise."

"Oh Jack!" she squeezed his hand. "I don't know if I can do it."

"Yes you can," he said. "I know you can. Just put your past behind you and we'll get you a fresh start. Promise me you'll try and let me arrange the rest. Promise me Madeline."

She looked across the table, his handkerchief crumpled in her hand wet from the tears. He face was red from the crying as she looked at him.

"Why Jack? Why are you doing this? I'm not important to you. You hardly know me. All we ever had was a few days in Mexico years ago and that was a drunken binge. Why do you even care?"

"Because I owe you Madeline."

"You owe me?" she questioned, mystified at his statement.

"Yes. I owe you. I was young and down there trying to get over my marriage break up and I took advantage of you. I woke up that morning and suddenly I knew I had to move on with my life. I knew what I was doing was not what I wanted to do. I got dressed while you slept and I left you there to look out for yourself. At that moment I wasn't thinking about you at all. I was just thinking about myself."

"It wasn't your fault Jack. I was just trying to have a good time with anyone I could find. You weren't the first or the last. I've just made a mess of my life." She started to sob once more.

"Stop it Madeline. Stop it. We're going to get you a fresh start and I'm going to help you. Now dry those tears and let's get you going on a new life."

She looked up at him across the table. He was still holding one of her hands while she dabbed at the tears with her other hand and his handkerchief.

"Oh why couldn't I find someone like you?" she said squeezing his hands.

"Now," he said. "Are you going to let me help you?" She didn't answer immediately as she looked across the table at him. "Are you?" he asked once more.

"Yes," she answered meekly.

"Okay," he replied. "Then you finish the treatment here, and when you're ready, I'll have a place for you and I'll try and find you a job. It will be a new start. Your new beginning starts right now."

She walked out looking back at him, still seated at the table, but with hope in her eyes looking forward to a new start.

Jack got up when she was gone, wondering if he'd promised too much. Somehow he felt an obligation to help her, even if their relationship was many years ago and only a few days long. But he'd clearly, at least in his mind, taken advantage of her. The fact that they had both been drinking too much didn't enter into the picture. Thinking back, he knew she was a young wild lady out having a good time and not caring where she went or what she did as long as she was having a good time. Well, he'd shown poor judgment taking advantage of the situation and now he felt he needed to help her get a new start.

Jack walked out of the building, got into his car and drove home and prepared for another day at work.

Detective Brennan was waiting for him when he arrived with an announcement.

"The judge ruled this morning that Borman should be held over for trail. The attorney for the defense wanted a dismissal of all charges, but the judge said there was enough evidence for it to go to trial."

"Did the judge grant any bail?" Jack asked.

"Yes, but Borman doesn't have the ten percent required."

"What was the bail?"

"He'd need to come up with ten thousand." Brennan said.

"Well, unless he can, I guess he will remain locked up. Assuming he's guilty, I guess that will keep more young ladies alive."

Jack's phone rang at that moment.

"Dennison," he answered.

"Lieutenant, there's a young lady down here who wants to see you," the voice said.

"Who is it?" he asked.

"She said her name is Maria Hernandez."

"I don't know anyone by that name," Jack replied. "Did she say what she wanted?"

There was a slight pause on the phone line and then the downstairs officer said.

"She said to tell you she's from Pecos, New Mexico."

Jack was startled at hearing the name Pecos, New Mexico. All he could remember for a moment was the beautiful young lady partially naked in his room.

"Oh yes," Jack replied. "I know her. Send her up."

I wonder what she wants he mumbled in his mind. And what is she doing here?

It only took a couple of minutes before she entered accompanied by a uniformed officer.

"Hello Jack," she said using his first name. "I'll bet you're surprised to see me."

Her command of the English language was impeccable. Better than most of the people he knew or worked with.

"Well, yes I am," he replied. He wondered what she wanted coming here all the way from Pecos. He was almost afraid to find out.

He couldn't help notice that she was even more beautiful than when he remembered her before. Now she was dressed in a very smart ladies business suit and looked older than her nineteen years. Back in Pecos she was wearing jeans and what appeared to be an un-ironed blouse. They didn't do her justice, but here all dressed in very neat fitting clothing, she was even more attractive than he remembered. The eyes of every detective in the room were glued on her. Jacquee and Alexis were the only ladies he'd ever known who might be more beautiful than Maria.

"I came here looking for a job and to go to school," she announced.

"I thought your mother needed you at the motel."

"Well, she does, but I told her I had to leave Pecos. There was no future there for me. Finally she gave me some money for new clothes and then she asked where I would go. I told her I was coming to San Francisco to see that very nice man who stayed with us. She told me to be careful and not to worry about her because she would be fine. So here I am."

Jack was puzzled as why Maria would select him. From all the people who must have stopped at her mother's motel, why would she come and ask him to help her?

"Why did you select me to help you Maria?" he asked. "And what made you think I would or could?"

"I just had a feeling Jack," she said. "For some reason, the first time I saw you in the motel office in Pecos, I knew you were an honest, dependable person. I felt an attraction to you."

"And you came to my room to test me by trying to get me to seduce you. Was that it?"

Maria didn't hesitate one bit, and responded.

"I wouldn't have let you take advantage of me. I just wanted to be sure you were a decent person. And when I took off my blouse and you simply picked it up and handed it back to me, I knew you were someone I could trust. Most other men wouldn't have done that."

"You're sure about that are you?"

"Yes. I'm sure. Anyway, I plan on going to school. Perhaps I will meet a nice man one day. I've always wanted to see San Francisco and I knew you were here, so I thought I'd come by and perhaps you'd help me get started. Do you know where I can get a job?"

"Well, I have no doubt that you will meet a lot of men Maria."

She laughed again and said. "By the way Jack, I really am nineteen," she laughed once more and after a moment's hesitation he did as well. Maria went on.

"Mama wanted me to be sure and thank you for helping me and if you could help her by finding her a job also, she would be forever grateful. I think she'd like to get out of Pecos."

"I'll see what I can do Maria. Where are you staying for now?" he asked.

"I'm at the ladies Y.W.C.A. until I can find a job and an apartment."

"Okay. I'll talk to a few people I know and I'll let you know what I find out."

"Thank you. I'd better go Jack," she said finally. "I know you've got work to do and I don't want to take anymore of your time."

"Call me tomorrow," he said. I may know where there is a job for you."

She left after thanking him again and he returned to the pile of cases on his desk that never seemed to grow smaller.

Detective Brennan came in awhile later to report he's spoken to all of the city council members about the Bergstrom/McKillory case.

"There was sure some friction between them," Brennan said. "They were in the best of terms until she broke off the relationship with his cousin. Several members recalled seeing them in heated conversations."

"Yes, but would that have been enough for him to kill her?"

"I don't know. It certainly isn't sufficient cause for the prosecutor to charge him with murder."

"No it isn't. I take it that nothing any of them said indicated he might act violently."

"No," Brennan replied.

"I want you to talk to some of his other friends and relatives. See what kind of disposition he has. Is he prone to be quickly upset and do irrational things? Does he have a temper and has he ever done anything in the past of a violent nature."

"Isn't Ryan doing that?"

"Yes, but I want you to do it also. Maybe we can get a different slant on things."

"Do we need to bring him in for questioning Lieutenant?" Brennan asked.

"Not yet. I'd rather he didn't know we are investigating him, though we may not be able to avoid him finding out. Someone is probably going to let him know we are asking questions."

Brennan had no sooner left than Jack's phone rang. It was Chief Polanski.

"Just wanted to let you know Jack that Enrico Del Carlo died a few hours ago. I got a call from the Chief in Miami telling me. I guess we got our answers from him just in time."

"I guess so Chief."

"I wanted to let you know."

"Appreciate it. Thanks."

Friday afternoon Detective Ryan came in to announce he'd talked to several friends and relatives of councilman Mike McKillory and most of them agreed he did at times show signs of having a temper. Mostly, however, he had a pretty even personality and managed to keep whatever temper he had under control. When they were asked if he'd ever displayed an uncontrolled temper, one relative said when they were teens he'd remembered one time when Michael got so upset at missing a shot while deer hunting, that he fired ten or more shots wildly into the woods and then threw his gun onto the ground and stormed off to the car. That ended their deer hunting trip until the following season.

"Okay, he does show uncontrolled temper," Jack said.

"Well, one time doesn't prove anything."

"No, but that doesn't mean it couldn't flare up again. People who show a temper once may well show it again. Even if it never shows for years and years, it could take only one small thing to cause them to lose control."

"As I remember," Ryan said. "She was found shot in her apartment."

"Yes," Jack replied. "There were many fingerprints including Councilman McKillory in her apartment. But then that's not unusual. The council often met there. In fact we found several council people's fingerprints. And as far as we know he doesn't own a gun."

"Isn't that a bit unusual?" Ryan asked.

"Why?" Jack replied.

"Well, if he was a deer hunter as a youth, and had a gun, it just seems to me that he would own a gun now. Even if he no longer hunted, people who own guns early in their life, usually have them forever. Sometimes they never use them, but they always have them."

"Did you check records to see?"

"No," Ryan replied. "But I'm going to now."

Hours later, Ryan returned to inform Jack that records indicated that Councilman Mike McKillory did not own a gun.

"In fact," he said, "I had to go back ten years to find a gun registered in his name. That was three years prior to Bergstrom's death. Since we require guns to be registered every two years, either he didn't register it or no longer had one."

"Unless he forgot."

"Yes, unless he forgot. By the way, have you spoken to the man Bergstrom was seeing?"

"No I haven't." Ryan replied. "I was concerned that since he was related to McKillory word might get back to the councilman that we were looking into the case again."

"I think it's time to talk to him and let the chips fall where they may."

Jack spent his Saturday at leisure. It was a day with nothing special on his calendar. He paid a visit to his deceased wife's sister Sarah and her husband Dennis. Their baby was almost due and they were excited about the event. On Sunday he visited his wife Jacquee's grave as usual, had lunch at his favorite seafood place by the water and then drove home. He noticed a blinking light on his phone answering machine. It was Detective Ryan so Jack called him back.

"I just talked to Rod Collier." Ryan said when Jack got him on the phone. "The man Bergstrom was seeing. He doesn't know why she broke off their relationship. He told me they'd had a very nice weekend together and he planned on asking her to marry him the next weekend, but before that weekend arrived she called and said she didn't want to see him any longer. She wouldn't give him any reason. He was very upset and told Michael."

"And?" Jack asked.

"Collier told me Mike said he would talk to her. That's all he knew. Then all of a sudden he learned she was dead. Someone had shot and killed her. He got very upset and emotional when he was telling me."

"Okay. That's not much help, but at least we know his side of the situation. By the way Ryan, what are you doing working on Sunday?"

"It was the only time I could talk to Collier. I'd called earlier and he wasn't in town. He's leaving again tomorrow on a business trip, so I had to catch him while I could."

"Okay. I'll see you tomorrow."

Monday morning Jack called Maria at the Y.W.C.A., to tell her he might have a job for her. He'd talked to the owner of the Monkey Tree Restaurant across the street from his work station, and the owner agreed to interview her. When Jack dropped by for a late afternoon lunch before walking across the street to work, he was spotted immediately by owner Gilbert Prolofski.

"Thanks Jack. I hired that young lady you sent here."

"That's great Gil. I hope she works out for you."

"Well, she's a beautiful young lady and I'm sure my customers will like that even if they don't like the food." Gilbert was laughing. "Anyway she starts tomorrow afternoon. I sent her to get some uniforms today. Nancy will be working with her for awhile so she can learn where everything is. She told me she is going to school in the morning so the hours will work out best for her."

"Thanks Gil. I appreciate your giving her a chance."

CHAPTER TWO
THE COUNCILMAN

When Jack arrived at work Councilman Michael McKillory was waiting for him.

"Lieutenant Dennison?" he asked.

"Yes," Jack answered.

"I understand you've reopened the Bertha Bergstrom case."

"Yes, we have."

"May I ask why?"

"It's an unsolved case Councilman and we have new evidence to consider, so we are taking another look at it. We always do that in an effort to solve a case. They are never really closed until they are solved."

"What kind of evidence do you have?"

"I'm not at liberty to say," Jack replied.

"Well, I've learned that you have been questioning council members as well as my cousin. Is that true?"

"Yes it is."

"And you've been asking a lot of questions about me. You think I might be responsible for her death?"

"I don't know. We are just checking all angles and trying not to overlook anything."

"Well, you're wasting your time. If you think I had anything to do with her death, you're sadly mistaken. I want you to stop wasting tax payer's money on this Lieutenant and get on to solving some of this city's more important problems."

"I can't do that Councilman. My job is to investigate all unsolved cases, especially when new evidence comes to light."

"I want to know what kind of evidence you have." McKillory said. His voice spoke as if he were used to demanding compliance from those around him.

"The only thing I can tell you is that a man came in to tell us he thought we should look into it again."

"Why? What did he say? What evidence did he give you?" He asked. Again his voice sounded as that of someone used to getting what he wanted.

"I can't tell you that, Councilman."

"And why not? I'm in charge of the City Council and as such, I should know what is going on."

"Not when it comes to a case under investigation Councilman. I'm not required to tell anyone except my superiors, should they ask, about any case under investigation."

"Well, we'll see about that. I'll see what the Chief has to say about it. Remember, Lieutenant, the council determines the budget for the Police department. We'll just see about that." He turned and walked away dissatisfied and in an angry mood.

Jack chuckled to himself at the councilman's threat.

Detective Ryan arrived on the scene near the end of the conservation between Jack and McKillory. He stood off to the side and when the councilman left, he looked at Jack and then back at the departing councilman and turning to Jack said.

"He doesn't seem too happy that we're looking into the case."

"No and it makes me wonder why he's so concerned. What is he hiding? I should think he'd want us to solve all our cases."

A couple hours later Jack's phone rang. It was the Chief of Police.

"Jack," he said. "I just had a visit from Councilman McKillory. He's concerned about the Bergstrom case and why we are wasting time on it. What do you have that's new?

Jack explained about Mr. Grievy and his dream or whatever he was having and the Chief asked.

"Do you really think there is anything to it, Jack"

"I don't know, Chief. All we are doing is taking another look and asking some questions that weren't asked before to people we may not have talked to before. I think it's interesting that the councilman is so concerned. What is he trying to hide? I've been in this business for quite awhile and it's been my experience that when an innocent person or a person who seems innocent is so concerned about a case, I start to think there might be something more there."

"I see what you mean Jack. Do you have anything that points to the councilman?"

"Nothing yet sir, but we're still looking."

"And you think Mr. Grievy's dream is worth considering?"

"I don't know that either. All I want to do is go over the evidence and do some more checking."

"Well, I don't want you to worry about him or his threats. I trust your judgment Jack. Let me know if you find anything."

"I will sir."

The next morning while Jack was having breakfast at home, his phone rang. It was detective Ryan.

"Hope I didn't wake you Lieutenant."

"No. What's up?"

"I just met with Councilman John Miller. I'd talked to him earlier and didn't learn anything, but he called me late last night and I met with him again this morning. He told me he overheard a conversation between Councilman McKillory and Rod Collier, his cousin. Remember Collier's the man Bergstrom was seeing, right before Bergstrom's death."

"Yes, I remember."

"Anyway Miller told me he overheard McKillory telling Collier he could stop being upset. He'd made Bergstrom sorry she dumped him."

"What were the exact words he said?" Jack asked.

"According to Miller, McKillory exact words were, *"she made me so angry, I lost my temper and I pulled out my gun and shot her."*"

"What did Collier say?" Jack asked.

"Miller said that Collier was silent for a moment and then simply said, *"you shot her?"*"

"And McKillory answered." Ryan continued, *"yes. I lost my temper. Don't tell anyone Rod. No one needs to know. Just go on with your business and pretend you're saddened by the event and pretty soon it will all be over."*"

"And then what?" Jack asked again.

"According to Miller, McKillory just turned and walked away." Ryan answered.

"Did Miller say why he didn't tell us about this earlier?"

"Yes. I asked him and he said that most of the council is bullied by McKillory all the time. He told me he was ready to resign because they don't get a lot done unless he (McKillory) wanted it done."

"Did he say he would testify?"

"Yes. He said he had to get it off his chest. He couldn't keep it quiet any longer. He was glad we were re-opening the case."

"Okay Ryan, Good job. I'll be in there in a while. Keep this information under wraps until I get there. We need to find out more before we let this get out. And now we know McKillory has a gun even if it's not registered.

CHAPTER THREE
BREANNA RETURNS

Jack was delayed getting to work. When he finished his breakfast and was about to take his car in for its new car check up, a taxi pulled up in front of his house. A lady he would recognize got out and walked to his front door and rang the bell. When he opened it, he was surprised by who was there.

"Breanna!" he exclaimed.

"Hello Jack. May I come in?"

"Sure," he replied and she turned and waved the taxi away.

"I had to come and talk. I needed to explain my behavior."

"No you don't," he answered.

"Yes I do. I behaved badly and I've let my temper get in my way. I have resolved not to let that happen again and now that I've decided to settle down with the man I love, I'm going to be a different person."

He was taken aback by her statement but said nothing as she continued.

"I decided last night that I needed to change, so early this morning I got on a plane and flew out here to ask you to marry me. If you say yes, I'll resign my job in Akron and move out here and I promise not to be a jerk and let my temper get in the way of my happiness ever again."

Jack looked at her and wondered what he should say. It was obvious that he was the object of her intentions and he didn't really know her very well. Besides he wasn't ready to settle down. There was a lot going on in his life and to consider making a commitment to a lady, beautiful as she was, just didn't seem like the right thing to do.

"Jack," she said. "Will you marry me?"

She was standing only a foot away now having moved a bit closer and her voice was soft and sincere sounding. Her eyes were looking into his and on her face was a smile of anticipation.

He looked down slightly at her, noting that she was indeed very attractive, but then he already knew that from their earlier encounter.

"Breanna."

"Yes," she answered looking for a positive response to her question.

"Breanna," he started once more. "I don't know what to say. I hardly know you. I'm not sure I'm even ready to be married again."

"You could say yes, and it wouldn't have to be something we'd need to do right away."

"You don't really know me Breanna."

"I've always been someone who knew what they wanted and I was sure the moment I saw you at Doris' house that I wanted you. I promise I won't let my temper get in the way no matter what. I can be a different person from the one who worked her way up to become the executive in a growing company. I'd give that all up just to be your wife."

It all sounded sincere to his ears and perhaps it was. At least at the moment it was. But then she was a woman who was used to getting what she wanted and at the moment he was what she wanted. He couldn't be sure and her behavior up until this time gave him cause for concern.

"Breanna, it's all too soon for me. I'm just not ready to embark on another relationship. In my mind there are too many obstacles. I'm flattered to think that you might love me, but I don't believe you can be sure. And I don't really know you well enough. Besides you're living in Akron and with me out here, it just doesn't lend itself to our becoming better acquainted."

"I could be here every weekend and on vacations and we could get to know each other better."

"It just wouldn't work Breanna."

She could tell he wasn't convinced she was sincere. Perhaps it was too soon for him to make a commitment to her, but it was the first time ever that any single male had moved her to consider such a definite and positive change in direction. Up until now, she was always motivated only to promote her career and move up in the corporate ladder to a position of importance. She'd always wanted to be someone others looked up to. She liked knowing that others had to come to her and she liked making important decisions. Decisions that made companies go from being small and unimportant to large dynamic national businesses.

She'd reached that pinnacle where she was now, and there was hope other large national companies would notice and encourage her to come work for them. It was always her drive and desire to be in the spotlight nationwide that propelled her to her present position. She knew she could do it, yet here for the first time in her life, a man was standing in the way. Yet in spite of her plans, he was now someone she was willing to give it all up to be with.

"Jack, I love you and want to be with you. If you say yes, I'll quit my job and move here tomorrow."

He looked at her knowing that she appeared to be sincere, but still he could not be certain. She had the drive and desire to obtain what she wanted, but was that really enough.

"Breanna. Go back to Akron," he said. "I want you to wait awhile and think about it. Getting married to me may not really be in your plans. I want you to think about it for six months or longer. You're making too rash a decision right now. I know you don't do that running your business. It takes a lot of research before you commit to something that might be lifelong. And marriage is a lifelong commitment. Go back to Akron."

"But I've made up my mind. I don't need to wait."

"Yes you do," he replied. "I need more time and so do you."

She stepped back and he could see the redness creep into her cheeks. Her temper was starting to show its ugly head and she was fighting to keep it under control. He sensed deep down that she was always going to have a problem with her temper and one day it might very well be her undoing.

"Breanna. Marriage is not like the business world. Marriage is a joint agreement that two people enter into and it's where they agree on things together. It's not like the business world at all. You've become used to giving orders and having them followed. In a marriage you can't expect to do that and have it last. I'm not sure you really are ready to give up the business world and all its perks. There is a bright future ahead of you and if you give that up now and get married and settle down, one day you're going to look back and think about all you've missed. You're going to see other ladies advancing in the business world and think it could have been you, and you're going to be unhappy. That doesn't lend to a successful marriage.

I think you need to give this more thought. You don't look like the kind of person who makes rash decisions and while I don't know you very well, I don't think you're ready to give up the business world and settle down.

Go back to Akron and your job. Wait awhile and stay involved in the business and see how you feel six months from now."

"You don't love me, do you?" She asked.

He looked down at the lady standing in his living room, the lady who'd traveled across country to propose to him. He wondered if she'd become so desperate all of a sudden that she'd flown here because he was the first man she knew could control her? Was that what she really needed? Did she need someone to control her life? Was she fearful that the possibility of having a family was going to pass her by? She was about his age and perhaps there was more to her decision than being in love with him. Maybe! Just maybe she all of a sudden realized if she was ever going to have a family she needed to do it now and the only man she might consider having a family with was here.

"No, Breanna I don't. Doesn't mean I couldn't but we really don't know each other well enough to reach that conclusion. Go back to Akron. Go back to your job and take some more time to think about this. I'm not ready and I don't think you really are either."

He took her to the airport and put her on a plane heading east. They talked more on the way and while she was disappointed at leaving and not getting his commitment, she managed to keep her temper under control.

His car appointment would have to be another day.

He arrived at work a bit early to be greeted by Henry Mullins, the man who was writing the detective stories for a national magazine.

"Hello Mr. Mullins. What brings you here today?"

"I'm here to see if you have any additional stories I might start putting together for my magazine."

"I might have a few. When do you need them?"

"The sooner the better," he replied. "That way I don't have to hurry. You should know the issues with your stories are selling really well in this country as well as overseas. You should be getting your commission check pretty soon. I think you'll be surprised."

"Maybe I'll be able to retire early," Jack said half smiling.

"You just never know," Henry answered. "You just might."

"Check with me on Friday," Jack said. "Give me a couple of days."

No sooner had Henry Mullins left, than Attorney Christian Welp called to tell him the Chief's granddaughter's husband was being released. Enough evidence in the case showed up to convince the prosecutor that he was just an innocent victim. The store owner didn't recognize him, but did identify the other two. Besides both the other two had a couple of encounters with authorities before.

Detective Ryan came in shortly after and they discussed the McKillory case.

"We need to be sure Miller will take the stand and testify, because if he doesn't then we have no case. I want you to talk to all the other councilmen again. We need to find out if any of them are willing to talk about anything concerning McKillory. His behavior and especially his control of the council would be helpful. Perhaps someone else will know something and come forward. We need to know if any of them knew he had a gun. In other words we need to give the prosecutor as much evidence as possible."

"Are we going to have Grievy testify?" Ryan asked.

"That's up to the prosecutor, but given how Grievy got the information, I don't think he'd want to bring that up. The jury, if there is a jury trial, might look at that a little suspiciously. Anyway, that's not up to us.

Jack went over to the Monkey Tree for dinner and found Maria working along with another lady.

"Hello Jack," she said when she saw him. "Thanks for getting me this job."

"It's okay Maria. I'm glad I could help. How are things going?"

"Just fine," she replied. "I called Mama and told her you found me a job. She said to thank you."

"That's okay. When does school start?" he asked.

"Next week. I'm taking Business Administration and Accounting."

"That's too much for me," Jack replied. "I'm not smart enough for that."

Maria laughed and replied.

"I don't believe that for a minute."

His lunch was good and his day finished without incident. Friday rolled around and on Saturday morning after a visit to Jacquee's grave, he drove the few hundred miles to see Bunny and talk more with her to reassure her he would help as much as possible when the baby arrived.

She was most happy at seeing him and to her it was an indication that he was interested not only in the arrival of their baby, but also interested in seeing her. Whether or not Jack thought of it that way didn't cross her mind but she was most happy to see him under any condition.

His drive home on Monday morning was tiring. He hadn't meant to get such a late start. Bunny wasn't anxious to have him leave, but finally she had to get up and attend to her boys, so he was able to extricate himself from the bed. Of course she insisted on fixing breakfast, so his departure was further delayed.

Her final words were, "Come anytime darling."

When he arrived home, the street in front of his house was filled with fire trucks. Parking at the corner he walked toward his house only to learn that Carl and Trisha's house had suffered a severe fire. Since they lived next door, some of the heat from the fire caused damage to the side of his house. It appeared to him, that maybe only the siding of his house was damaged, but he wasn't sure.

Oscar his neighbor and a member of the fire department, was there and spotted him.

"Hi Jack," he said. "We couldn't keep the fire from causing some damage to your place. By the time we got here, it was pretty much going full force."

"Do you know what caused it?"

"Not yet. After it cools some more, we'll take a look."

"Where are Trisha and Carl and their kids?"

"They are over at my house," Oscar replied.

"Can I get into my place? I need to get ready for work."

"Oh sure! You might as well call your insurance company to let them know. I'm sure Trisha and Carl have insurance so it will probably cover any damage to your place as well, but you should let your company know."

It looked to him like Carl and Trisha would be living someplace else for awhile. Jack looked at the side of his house and it didn't appear to be too badly damaged. Mostly the damage was to the siding and he suspected it would all need to be replaced.

When he was ready for work, Jack took time to walk over to talk to Carl and Trisha for a few minutes and learned they were going to move into an apartment near Trisha's sister in Oakland. When he finished visiting with them, he drove on to start his day at work. On his desk, when he arrived, was a list of all the crimes in the area that took place over the weekend, but it didn't appear to be any worse than any other weekend.

CHAPTER FOUR
JACK IS AN UNWILLING RECRUIT

At dinner time Jack walked downstairs on his way to the Monkey Tree. He reached the corner and stood waiting for the light to change so he could cross the street, when all of a sudden he felt something in his back and a voice said.

"Just walk straight ahead Lieutenant. Don't try anything funny. I could shoot you right here."

He didn't know who it was, but he did walk straight ahead as instructed and past where he would turn if he were going to the Monkey Tree. Whoever was behind him stayed very close, not saying anything until they were half way to the next corner.

"Stop here," the man behind ordered and then he reached inside Jack's coat and removed his service revolver.

Just then the back door of a large dark colored vehicle with tinted windows parked next to the curb, swung open.

"Get in," the man ordered.

Inside, Jack saw an older man, who he guessed to be in his seventies, perhaps more. As Jack bent down to climb in, the man behind gave him a push and he stumbled forward. Then his abductor got in putting Jack between the old man and the one with the gun who escorted him from the corner.

"Go," the old man ordered and the driver pulled away.

Jack didn't recognize any of the three people, but he kept quiet as he expected that at some point they would tell him why they were abducting him.

The car headed south down Highway 101, past the airport, Millbrae, Sunnyvale and off onto Highway One. It was dark outside now and still not a word from either of his abductors. He couldn't help wondering who these people were and where they were taking him and what they had in mind. He was sure he didn't know any of them. Jack was sure they were taking him to see someone else. But who would that be? I guess I'll find out in due time, he thought to himself.

Jack caught a glimpse of a road sign that said Santa Cruz so he knew they were heading to the coast and toward Castroville. Were they going that far and if so, just where would it be? He knew just south was Monterey and Pebble Beach. It was an area he liked a whole lot and thought if he'd ever had enough money, would like to live near there. Was that where they were going? They'd been on the road for the best part of an hour and still not a word was spoken by any of the three.

Jack wondered if anyone at his work place would wonder where he was. They knew he'd gone to eat, so they wouldn't worry for awhile. In his position as Lieutenant, he was pretty much free to come and go as he saw fit. Even if he never came back tonight, they might not miss him. If he failed to show up tomorrow, then maybe it would be another matter. He also knew he would find out sooner or later where they were taking him. This certainly wouldn't go on indefinitely.

It wasn't long before they turned off the main highway and when they did the older man finally spoke.

"Ricky is going to put a blindfold on you now. The boss doesn't want you to see where you are. It's only a few minutes away."

With that, the other man in the back seat, the one that must be Ricky, took a cloth from his pocket and proceeded to cover his eyes. A few minutes after the blindfold was in place, the car slowed and came to a stop. The man called Ricky took his hand and helped him from the car.

"This way." Ricky ordered as he escorted Jack along some kind of walkway. A few moments later Jack could tell they were headed down a sloping walk. He could also tell there were narrow boards across the walk. It reminded him of a wooden ramp leading to a dock. Then they were again on a flat surface again and from the motion he was sure it was some kind of floating platform.

"This way," Ricky said again as he pulled him forward. They walked about twenty steps and stopped. Jack felt another person take hold of his other hand.

"Step down," the voice said. It was easy to tell from the rocking motion that he was on a boat. The second man led him a few feet and then said.

"Sit down."

As soon as he did, a motor started and a moment later Jack could feel the boat move. Slowly at first, and minutes later it picked up more speed and finally a few moments after, a great deal more speed. No doubt it was now outside the bounds of whatever yacht facility they were in. They traveled for what seemed to him to be about seven or eight minutes. He timed the minutes in his head by counting the seconds. Jack knew he could do that pretty well. The ride was pretty comfortable, even though there were bumps as the boat hit some small waves. Either they were in a sheltered area away from the ocean or the ocean was exceptionally calm. He knew it wasn't often that the ocean water was this calm, so it figured they must never have left whatever harbor they were in.

Shortly, the motor slowed and he could feel the backing sound of the motor as if it were positioning itself alongside another, perhaps larger vessel. Then the motor stopped all together. There was a slight bump as if hitting against something.

"Stand up," the same voice said. "Step up and take hold of the hand rail on your right and walk up the steps."

Jack climbed several steps, blind fold still in place. Suddenly two sets of hands, one each grabbing hold of an arm, guided him onto the deck.

"This way," another voice said as they led him several steps and into a doorway. Someone pushed his head down, he assumed to keep it from hitting a low entry way. He heard the door close behind and then after being led a few more steps, the voice spoke once more.

"Sit down."

Jack did and learned that what he was now sitting on was very soft and comfortable. His blindfold was removed and as his eyes blinked a few times, he could see a very tastefully decorated cabin. The walls appeared to be teakwood. There was a thick carpet on the floor and in front of him a big desk. Seated behind the desk was a large sized man with very dark skin. Jack was sure he wasn't Negro, but someone from perhaps a part of the world where their skin usually was quite dark. He was seated in the shadows and his features were not totally distinguishable. A light was shining in Jack's direction making it hard to see very much.

"Thank you for coming," the man behind the desk said. His voice had the sound of someone having been raised in one of the Caribbean islands. It had that slight English accent.

"Did I have a choice?" Jack replied.

The man laughed and replied. "No, I guess not. I'm sure you are wondering why you are here. Well, I'll get right to the point.

"I need someone who is totally outside of my organization to do me a favor. I would be most grateful in return. My daughter Viola is being held prisoner by drug dealers in Mexico. They want me to use my large group of ships to help them transport their goods. I have told them no. I don't want to have anything to do with their drugs. Well, they hoped to persuade me by taking my daughter captive and threatening her harm if I do not cooperate. If I don't cooperate, they have said they intend to kill her."

"Why me?" Jack asked. "I don't have any way to deal with the drug dealers in Mexico."

"Why you?" the man asked. "Well, I know your reputation and I know that no one would suspect you of doing something like trying to deal with these people. Besides if you can't do it yourself, I think you might know someone who could."

"You give me a lot of credit. What if I can't?"

"If I am convinced of that, then I will look for someone else and my men will return you home safely. But I've checked into you and your background. I learned that when you were at the F.B.I. school in Bethesda, you met a government man who was, shall we say, not quite the government man we tend to think of as," he hesitated a moment and then went on. "Let's just say he's part of the government that does things behind the scenes. Things that never gets out in public. They have a reputation of getting things done when no one else can."

Jack knew he must be speaking of Rocky. That was the only name Jack knew him by and even that probably wasn't his real name. Zeke and he met Rocky one night in a local bar on one of their evenings out. The only thing Jack ever learned was that Rocky also worked for the government. He'd told Zeke and Jack if he ever needed anything, he was to call. Rocky had given each of them a card with a phone number and cautioned them to never call unless it was absolutely urgent and beyond the scope of their ability to deal with. Rocky instructed them to tell no one. As far as they were concerned, he did not exist.

Jack had almost forgotten about it, but he knew he'd filed the card away at home. Whether or not Rocky could help, was anyone's guess, but he knew he had no way of dealing with a drug group in Mexico. He didn't know anyone down there and he didn't know of anyone in the department here who did. But then of course, he didn't know all that might be going on.

Now this person, whoever he was, seemed convinced that Jack knew someone with the ability to resolve this problem.

"I don't know if I can help," Jack said. "I will try. That's all I can do."

"You're a very resourceful man Jack Dennison. I know a bit about your work and that's why I selected you at this time. If you are helpful and I get my daughter back, I will not forget."

"If I can help, I will." Jack repeated. "That's all I can do."

The man in shadows responded by saying.

"The person you are looking for in the murder of Bertha Bergstrom is indeed Mike McKillory."

Jack was startled by this *'out of the blue'* statement.

"How do you know about that?" Jack asked.

"I know, because he came to one of my people to get a gun. He wanted one that could not be traced. This is the gun that killed her." With that he handed a small package to one of his assistants, who in turn handed it to Jack. Jack took the package and looking down at the small item, said.

"If this is really the gun, that's a big help. Thanks."

"Let's just say it's a token of my appreciation for whatever you can do. Someone will contact you and he will testify that McKillory asked him for the gun and then returned it a few days later."

The man in the shadows motioned to a man nearby and nothing more was said. They put the blindfold back on him and transported him back to shore and then into the car for the drive back. Part way there, they removed his blindfold and he saw they were not going back to the police station, but were headed for his home in San Bruno. The big black car finally stopped in front of his house and he got out. As soon as he was outside the car, it drove away. Jack turned and noticed his car in the driveway. Someone had returned it to his home.

"They even returned my car. I wonder how they got it out of the police lot?" he said in a soft out loud voice.

Jack went inside and after a few minutes, found the card Rocky gave him. After dialing the number on the card, a voice answered.

"Yes?" was all it said. He couldn't tell anything from that one word.

"I need to talk to Rocky."

"He'll call you," the voice said and the connection ended.

It was several hours later, when Jack's phone rang, waking him from a sound sleep.

"Hello."

"Rocky here," the voice said.

"This is Jack Dennison," he answered.

Jack then went on to tell him what happened a few hours earlier and Rocky responded.

"We've been working on that group in Mexico. We didn't know they had captured a lady. I don't know what we can do, but I'll look into it. I've got to go."

The line went dead. Jack lay awake for some time wondering what that was all about.

The next morning after a quick breakfast, Jack hurried to work with the small package he'd acquired the night before. Taking it directly to ballistics he spoke to his favorite person, Molly and asked if they could hurry it along.

"You're always in a hurry Lieutenant," she said.

"Yes, I guess I am, but that's the nature of this business," he answered smiling.

It was too early to go to work, so he got back into his car and drove to see how Madeline was doing. According to her and the staff, she was doing very well and expected to be released in a week. Jack knew he'd promised her a job and a place to stay, so that was the next project on his agenda.

Returning to work he found detective Ryan waiting for him.

"Where did you go last night Lieutenant? I was looking for you."

"I was working on the McKillory case," he answered without giving an explanation.

"The prosecutor doesn't think we have enough to hold him." Ryan said.

"We do now," Jack replied. "I believe I have the gun that killed Bertha. It's in ballistics now for verification and I have a witness who will testify that McKillory got the gun from him."

"How'd you do that?" Ryan asked amazed by the statement.

"Let's just say someone contacted me and gave me the gun."

"That's terrific Lieutenant. Shall I call the prosecutor?"

"No. I'll do that. You might just get on to your other cases. I'm sure you have a few of them."

The rest of the week was slow. Ballistics confirmed the gun was the one that fired the shot killing Bertha Bergstrom and the prosecutor charged Michael McKillory with the crime. A witness that Police knew and who was also known to provide things for a price, came forward as promised, to testify he gave the gun to McKillory and took it back afterwards.

Jack never heard anything from Rocky or anything from anyone else concerning Viola, the daughter of the person who asked him for help. Jack still didn't know who this unknown man on the boat was. His only clue was that he was a person who owned quite a few ships of one size or another and sounded like someone who had been raised in the islands of the Caribbean. But that might be several people and not someone whose vessels were registered in the U.S. Checking vessel registrations didn't shed any light on the subject, so Jack decided to just forget about the matter. There was enough to do without being concerned about that matter as well.

CHAPTER FIVE
JACK GETS SHOT

Saturday morning while washing his car in the front yard of his home on a day that turned out to be sunny and warm, Jack noticed a classy sports car drive by slowly in front of his house. He could tell there were two occupants behind the darkened windows and it appeared they were looking in his direction. He admired the car and as it drove away he returned to his efforts to get the dirt and grime off his new vehicle. Jack always liked his car to be clean looking but his job didn't always allow time to spend taking care of it as he once did. He noticed as he got older that his desire in that direction became less and less important to him.

A few minutes later as he bent down trying to clean the rear tail lights, the flashy car came by once more. He noticed it out of the corner of his eye as it slowed in front of his house. Jack straightened up to look again and as he did, the darkened window on the passenger side slid quickly down and a flurry of bullets from a semi-automatic weapon sent him diving for cover. But it was too late.

Several bullets hit him, knocking him to the ground. One grazed his head, two others struck him in the chest, another hit his shoulder and one hit him in the leg. Several others hit his car breaking the rear window, the tail lights, and causing one tire to go flat. A few others punctured the rear and the side of his car and several more found their way into his open garage striking a number of different items.

The dark colored sports car sped away, ties screeching on the pavement. Jack lay on the ground next to his car, blood flowing from several parts of his body. He lay there, not moving.

Ray Murphy, a neighbor from across the street that Jack didn't know very well, was looking out his front window and witnessed the whole event. He quickly came running across the street to find Jack conscious, but bleeding.

"Call an ambulance," Jack ordered, his voice was weak. Another neighbor who was in his front yard and heard the shots also came running across the street. While Ray Murphy ran to call for help, the second neighbor tried to assist. Calling to his wife who had come out front at hearing the shots, he yelled.

"Bring the first aid kit." Turning to Jack, he said. "Lay still. Help is coming."

The second neighbor's wife came running moments later with the first aid kit.

Ray Murphy returned his home, first aid kit in hand to announce. "Help is on the way."

It seemed like it took the ambulance and police forever to arrive but actually it was only minutes.

While waiting, the neighbor's wife determined the head wound was minor. It was only a crease with just a small amount of blood. The chest wounds were bleeding profusely and Jack had already lost a lot of blood. His shirt was soaked with his blood. She used her talent as a former first aid instructor and doctor's assistant to stem the bleeding. Opening his shirt immediately and using the limited items from the home first aid kit, she worked on stopping the bleeding of the wound that looked the worst. The second wound, while bad and still bleeding, did not appear to be as serious.

She handed Ray Murphy a package of gauze and said.

"Hold this firmly on the wound. See if you can stop the bleeding while I deal with this one."

Her husband meanwhile took care of putting a bandage on Jack's leg to stop the bleeding there.

Two police cars arrived on the scene moments after the ambulance and they began immediately to investigate what happened. First they talked to Ray Murphy and then moved to the other neighbor to get his version about what happened. More Police arrived and they started a neighborhood door by door canvas of all the houses seeking more information.

Jack remained conscious while the ambulance crew worked on him. Once they had taken the necessary steps to stop the bleeding, they loaded him into the ambulance and raced to the nearest hospital.

Since Sarah, Jack's ex sister in law was the only person on his call list, her phone rang an hour later informing her he'd been shot and was at the hospital. She raced there along with her husband Dennis. He was in surgery when they arrived and were unable to get any information on his condition other than it was serious.

Since Jack was known by the San Bruno police to be a member of the San Francisco Police Department, they too were notified. When Chief Polanski was informed, he ordered Lieutenant Stark and Detective Spooner to the hospital to learn what they could. Sergeant Mike and Detective Jones went to the site of the shooting to talk to San Bruno Police and to conduct their own investigation.

About two hours after Sarah's arrival, the doctor came out of the operating room and was directed by a nurse to where Sarah was seated.

"How is he?" she asked anxiously.

"He should be all right. His chest wounds were the most serious. They didn't hit anything critical but he's lost a lot of blood. I expect he'll be in here for a week or more,"

"When can we see him?" she asked anxiously.

"He's sleeping now. When he awakens, the nurse will let you in but it might be a few hours. Is there anyone else that needs to be notified?" The doctor asked.

"He has a sister in Oregon, but I don't know how to reach her," Sarah replied.

"Perhaps his superiors will know," the doctor answered.

The San Bruno and San Francisco police tried to learn who might have shot him. No case he was working on seemed to give a clue. The car in question was only known to be a foreign model of some kind, Ray Murphy, told the investigators.

Saturday evening Jack started to blink his eyes and re-enter the world. Sarah was called from the waiting room where she had waited all day and told he was now awake.

"Who would do this?" she asked when she arrived at his bedside.

"I don't know," he answered. His voice was weak.

"I couldn't call your sister because I don't have her number," Sarah said.

"Call her for me please. The department should but I don't know if they did." Jack replied. Her number is 555-942-4546

The next morning, the San Francisco news papers carried the headlines: *POLICE OFFICER SHOT IN FRONT OF HOME.*

In her home two hundred plus miles east near Reno, Bunny Hoit sat at her kitchen table having morning coffee. Her two boys had already eaten and were in another room.

The headlines of the Reno paper screamed the news. *POLICE OFFICER SHOT*. Bunny looked down to read the article, not realizing the headlines were talking about the City by the Bay and not Reno.

In the first sentence she saw the words that sent a shock through her whole body.

San Francisco Police Officer Jack Dennison was shot in front of his home Saturday morning the article said.

"Oh my God!" she screamed almost dropping the cup she'd just raised to her lips. She read on and learned he was in the hospital in serious condition. The newspaper article gave no information about his condition or how serious it was.

Bunny immediately picked up her phone to call the hospital. Once she was able to reach the hospital and asked his condition, the on duty nurse asked.

"Are you a relative?"

"No, just a close friend," Bunny replied.

"He can see only family and the only information I can tell you is that his situation is serious."

"Is he going to live?" Bunny asked anxiously.

"That's all I can tell you," the nurse answered.

Putting down her phone, she called her friend and trusted helper, Annette to tell her she had to go to San Francisco immediately and asked her to watch the boys. She'd be back as soon as possible, but probably not before tomorrow.

It was the middle of Sunday afternoon when Bunny arrived at the San Bruno hospital. Stopping at the nurse's station, she asked.

"What room is Jack Dennison in?"

"Are you a relative?" the nurse asked.

"No," she replied. "Just a friend."

"He's allowed to see only relatives," the nurse replied.

"But I must see him," Bunny replied.

"I'm sorry," the nurse said. "Only relatives are allowed in."

Bunny hesitated a moment and then responded with.

"But I'm going to have his baby. I need to see him."

The nurse looked down at Bunny's middle where Bunny had placed her hand.

The nurse looked up, hesitated and then replied.

"Just a moment," and she disappeared down the hall. Going into Jack's room, she found Sarah seated next to his bed.

"Lieutenant. There's a lady here who says she needs to see you. She said she is going to have your baby."

Jack looked up at the nurse and then at Sarah, who was looking at him. Then he replied.

"I guess you'd better let her in."

"Jack?" Sarah questioned. "What?"

"I'll explain later," he answered.

A few moments later Bunny walked through the door. She stopped a moment at seeing Sarah and then went right to the bed, bent over and kissed him on his forehead.

"Bunny! This is Sarah, my sister in law," Jack said.

Bunny turned to extend her hand.

"Ex sister in law," Sarah replied. "I was Jacquee's sister."

"Oh," Bunny replied. "I'm sorry."

"You drove all the way here," Jack asked his voice still weak.

"Yes. I read about it in the Reno paper. I had to come and find out how you are and what happened. They wouldn't tell me on the phone when I called."

Jack went on to tell her he was just washing his car. He'd seen the car drive by once and then it came by a second time, and that's when they shot him.

Sarah could see they needed to be alone.

"I'm going to leave Jack," she said. "I'll be back tomorrow."

"Okay," he replied. "Thanks for coming Sarah."

After she was gone Bunny said.

"I have to get back to the motel honey. I can't stay long, but I will stay someplace over night and head back in the morning. Now that I know you're going to be all right, I need to get back."

The next morning after visiting with him for an hour, Bunny announced.

"If you need recovery time, you can come and stay with me."

"Do you really think I'd do much recovering if I were there with you?" he asked.

Bunny laughed.

"Well, Maybe some at first. At least until you got you strength back," she said.

Bunny left just before noon and Sarah returned right after lunch. As soon as she walked into the room, the first words out of her mouth were.

"Okay. Tell me about her. She's going to have you baby?"

"Yes," he replied.

"Are you sure Jack?"

"Yes. I believe her," he answered.

"Oh Jack. Are you really ready? I know you and Jacquee wanted so much to have a child. How well do you really know her and how did you meet?"

"We were in high school together, although I hardly knew her there. When I took my trip recently, I happened to stop at her motel. She recognized my name and we visited. I learned she had a crush on me during our school years. Anyway, I guess both of us had a bit too much to drink while we visited and talked about the past and; well I guess we both just got carried away. I woke up the next morning and she was there. I never intended for this to happen, but it did."

"Are you going to marry her?" Sarah asked.

"I don't know Sarah," he replied. "I suppose that would be the right thing to do, but I don't know."

"Well, you know I want you to be happy Jack. I really do and I know Jacquee does too, but it's really not been very long. Do you think you're ready for another relationship?"

"I know it hasn't been very long. But at this point I just don't know what I'm going to do. Since I believe the baby is mine, I did tell her I'd help financially. I didn't promise her anything except financial help."

"She appears to care a lot about you, driving here from Reno as soon as she heard."

"I guess so," Jack answered.

"Unless, of course, she's just trying to make a case for herself to convince you to marry her."

"I don't think that Sarah."

"We all love you Jack. We're just concerned."

"I know," he replied.

Chief Polansiki arrived in the middle of the afternoon shortly after Sarah left, bringing him some news.

"We believe we got the people who shot you," he said.

"Really? Jack asked. How?"

"We found a foreign sports car riddled with bullets and two bodies inside. We're pretty sure it's the same people who shot you. We don't know who was responsible, but it looks like the same car and there were two dead bodies inside. What do you know about it, anything at all?"

"I don't know anything about it Chief," he replied.

Jack didn't want to tell the Chief about his kidnapping and the rest of the story. He didn't want to tell him about calling a number and asking for someone named Rocky. It was just best if nothing was said.

Jack wondered if Rocky and his people could be responsible. If so, then perhaps he shouldn't say anything if it were some kind of government operation. If it was Mr. whoever on his yacht, then maybe he shouldn't say anything about that either. Jack didn't know if he got his daughter back, but if he did, then maybe this was his way of payment.

Chief Polanski looked down at him without saying a word. He too knew that sometimes it's better not to question his people too closely. It was something he learned in his thirty five years on the department.

Jack got his answer later that evening, when what appeared to be a hospital orderly in a white gown entered his room. Jack didn't recognize him, but then he couldn't know everyone who worked at the hospital. After all, they did have shift changes and new people were coming on duty all the time while others would be going home. The man walked to his bedside, looked down and said.

"My boss wanted to tell you he appreciates your help in getting his daughter back."

"She's back then?" Jack questioned.

"Yes," the man said and went on. "The boss wanted you to know that the people who shot you won't be bothering you again. He says he still owes you and if he can help in anything, he'd be happy to see what he could do."

Jack didn't say anything in reply, thinking that perhaps it would be better never to ask for his help. He just looked back at the man in the white garment for a moment and then without hesitation, the man turned and walked out of the room without saying another word.

Well, I still don't know who is responsible for getting the girl back, but I guess it's all right, Jack thought. I wonder how Viola got free. Was it Rocky's doings or something else? I guess it doesn't matter as long as she's back.

Sarah came again the next day and Bunny called to see how he was. Don Perry called after learning what happened and said he'd come to visit, but Jack told him it wasn't necessary. Julia Davis, who had proposed to him earlier also dropped by to see him. She was there to let him know she thought he needed a woman to care for him and as soon as he was allowed to come home, she would come to see if there was anything she could do.

Jack's sister called to check on him several times and talked to him once he was feeling better. She couldn't come down and Jack told her it wasn't necessary.

By week's end, he was well enough to go home. The doctors told him it was best if he just took it easy for at least another week or better still two weeks. They asked if he had someone to help and he replied yes he did. Julia came by the first day he was home and stayed all day. Sarah also dropped by and knowing that Julia was there, didn't stay long.

Jack looked through the mail that piled up while he was in the hospital. Among the many things was an envelope form the publisher of the stories he'd been giving to Henry Mullins. Jack tore open the envelope and found a statement of earnings along with a check for one hundred twelve thousand dollars. He stared at it for a moment not able to comprehend that it could really be that much money.

"One hundred twelve thousand," he said out loud.

"What?" Julia asked not knowing he wasn't talking to her."

"Oh nothing," he replied.

When Bunny learned he was going home from the hospital, she drove over to see him with plans to stay a few days. When she arrived, she was dismayed to find Julia there.

"Hi," Bunny said when Julia opened the door. "I'm Bunny Hoit, a friend of Jack's. Is he home?"

"Sure," Julia replied wondering who is this person she didn't know?

"Bunny," Jack said upon seeing her. "What are you doing here?"

"I thought I'd come over and see if I could help out."

"You don't have to do that," Jack said. "Don't you need to attend to the motel?"

"I made arrangements to spend a few days here to care for you," she told him.

"You don't have to do that," he repeated. "You've got a business to attend to and two boys who need you."

Julia looked on not quite sure who this person was and why she felt she needed to be here.

Where did she come from and how did Jack know her?

"My friend Julia will look after things for me for a few days. I'm not your responsibility Bunny. You have other important obligations."

Then he turned to Julia and said.

"Julia. This is a friend of mine from high school. I met her while I was gone on my extended trip."

"Yes, we met at the front door," Julia replied and then said. "I guess if you're going to have live in help you won't be needing me."

She turned to get her coat.

Jack followed her toward the front door.

"Julia. I didn't know she was coming. I'm sorry. I really do appreciate your help."

"It's okay Jack." Then after a moment's hesitation she asked. "She looks pregnant, Jack. Is she?"

"Yes," he answered.

"Yours?" Julia asked.

"Yes," Jack answered.

Julia just stared at him a moment, then without saying anything, turned and walked out the door.

Jack watched as she walked to her car and drove away. He knew she wasn't happy. He was sure she still had thoughts of them being a couple. He closed the door and turned back to find Bunny across the room looking at him.

"Did I interrupt anything I shouldn't have?" Bunny asked.

"She's a long time friend," he answered. "She came to help because she cared."

"Do you like her?"

"Yes, I do," Jack said.

"Well, I'm here now and I'll take care of you." Bunny replied.

Sarah wasn't too happy when she learned that Bunny was there and staying a few days. But then he was an adult and he could make his own decisions she thought. Besides, it wasn't any of her business except she'd grown very much attached to him being her brother in law for that short time. She still felt like he was a part of her family and as such she was concerned and interested in his well being.

When Bunny left three days later, Sarah made sure to come over. She needed to talk to him.

Friday morning she was at his front door.

"Sarah," he said at seeing her. I didn't know you were coming. What's up?"

"I need to talk to you Jack."

"Okay. Come in. Can I get you anything?"

"No, I don't think so. Jack I wanted to talk to you about this Bunny person."

He was a bit surprised. He knew that Sarah was not comfortable with Bunny being in what she considered Jacquee's house, and yet it was now his house and he could do what he wished. There was something else and he wasn't sure what it was.

"What about Bunny?" he asked.

"I know you said she's pregnant because of you and I can understand it happening. She was there and you were vulnerable at the time, but you don't have to marry her. I think she came here on the pretext of helping take care of you, but she didn't need to. I know you are able to take care of yourself just fine and I'm here if you need help."

"Yes I can, but I think she just felt a need."

"Yes a need indeed," Sarah answered a bit sarcastically. "She just wants to make sure that you know you can't get along without her. Are you going to marry her Jack?" she asked.

"I don't know Sarah. I believe her when she said I'm the father. It would be the right thing to do, I suppose, but I just don't know. All I told her was that I'd help financially."

"I care about you Jack," Sarah said a bit fearfully.

"I know you do," he answered. He gave her a hug. "I know you do."

Sarah stayed longer anxious about the situation and they talked more. As she finally got ready to leave, Sarah turned to him and said.

"I want you to be happy Jack. If you'd be happy married to her, then I'm happy. It just seems like now that she's pregnant, she wants to make sure you do marry her. She didn't have to come here, but she did and I think it's part of her plan to get you used to having her around."

Jack gave her another hug and said.

"It's going to be all right. Really it is. Sarah you know I loved Jacquee and I love you too. I know you care about my well being. I hate Jacquee being gone, but life moves on and I need to move on to. I don't know what I'm going to do about Bunny. I believe her when she says the baby is mine. It's true that I don't know her very well, but as far as I know she's a very nice person. When she lost her husband she took over running the motel and raising her two boys and she seems responsible. Anyway, perhaps time will help resolve this situation. That's all that is settled for now."

Sarah gave him a big hug and turned toward the front door.

He watched her drive away knowing she was concerned about him. He understood that.

Jack spent the rest of the day and part of the weekend at leisure and alone. None of the neighbors dropped by to see how he was and Julia never called or dropped by. Jack assumed she felt she wasn't needed and knowing Jack was the father of another person's baby, diminished her chances of winning him over. A lot of reading and sleeping took place as he tried to pass the weekend. On Sunday he decided get out of the house and visit his wife's grave. After that he thought it a good idea to go see Madeline to tell her he'd found her a place to live. Still he'd not found her a job but she had a place to live. He'd paid the first month's rent for her and he'd stocked the cupboards with food so she'd have something to eat. It was a beginning.

On Monday morning after Madeline was released, he picked her up and took her to the apartment and then headed off to the Monkey Tree for lunch before going back for his first day on the job.

The doctor's wanted him to take another week off, but it was boring at home, so he thought he'd try at least putting in some time on the job.

Maria was working when he reached the Monkey Tree and she greeted him enthusiastically. She took his arm and escorted him to a nearby booth. After asking him how he was, she took his order and then went to serve the rest of her customers. While he sat eating his late lunch, Gil, the owner of the Monkey Tree spotted him and came over.

"Jack. How are you doing?"

"I'm better Gil. I'm going to start back to work today. Maybe only part time, but I need to do something. How's Maria working out for you?"

"Wonderfully! I really appreciate your bringing her by and I'm really happy I was smart enough to hire her. She really has a way with customers. They all seem to love her."

"Good. I'm glad Gil."

"I just found out this morning," Gil said. "One of my waitresses is leaving. She's moving back east to be closer to her family, so I'm going to have to find someone. You wouldn't have another gem in your basket would you?"

Jack started to say no, but the thought of Madeline crossed his mind. She needed a job, but he didn't know if she knew anything about being a waitress.

"How much experience does someone need Gil?"

"Why? Do you know someone?"

"I do, but I'm not sure if she'd be up to it. I don't know if she's ever done anything like this."

"Bring her by, Jack." Gil said. "Let me talk to her."

Jack arrived at the office while some of the day shift detectives were still there. They looked up at seeing him arrive and one of them said.

"Some people will do anything to keep from coming to work." They all had a good laugh.

Jack noticed a large pile of cases on his desk. They must have been saving them until his return he thought.

Mike, his assistant was back and greeted him when he walked in.

"Welcome back boss," he said.

"Mike. Good to see you." Jack said. "I'm glad you're back."

"I hear someone tried to put you away while I was gone."

"Yes, but I survived."

"That's good. I'd hate to have to break in someone new."

"Thanks a lot," Jack replied and they both laughed.

Then changing the subject Jack asked. "How's your wife?"

"You know, I think she's better. The doctors in Denver thought she made progress and the last tests before we left looked good."

"That's great news Mike. I'm glad to hear it."

The day didn't seem too busy. Jack looked through the pile of cases on his desk and assigned a few to each of his detectives. At dinner time, he drove to see Madeline and tell her he'd come by in the morning to take her for a job interview. She was elated and the next morning when he arrived, she was dressed in some of the new clothes he'd purchased for her."

"I've never done waitress work before," she told him.

"That's okay. Gil is a pretty nice guy and if you show you're interest and have a willingness to work, I think he'll be impressed. If that doesn't work out, I'll try and find something else."

Jack sat and had coffee while Madeline and Gil sat at an empty table in the corner and talked for about fifteen minutes. Finally they both got up and walked back to him.

Madeline looked down smiling and Gill spoke.

"Take her down to get some uniforms Jack. I think she'll work out just fine."

After getting uniforms for her on Wednesday, he drove her back to her apartment. When she got out of the car, she turned and said.

"Why don't you come up? You've done a lot for me and I appreciate it. Perhaps I can find a way to pay you back."

He could see the tiny smile on her face and he knew what she was hinting.

Jack looked up at her standing just outside the passenger side door of the car. Her invitation was not difficult to understand.

"I'd really better be going,"

"Are you sure? I know you're not married Jack and we aren't really strangers. After all you've done for me, - - -Well I need to do something to show some appreciation. Besides, Maybe I'd enjoy it too.

"Good bye Madeline. I've got to go to work."

Wednesday and Thursday were quiet and he was glad. He'd been out of the hospital almost two weeks and still he noticed working a full day was a bit much. He did manage to put in five hours each day, but that did make him more tired than he expected.

CHAPTER SIX

THE COPY CAT

Friday morning saw workmen arrive to start fixing Carl and Trisha's home, and a couple of the crew members started working at replacing the siding of his house. Jack talked to one of them and was told they were sure they could finish in one day. After breakfast, he drove to visit Jacquee's grave. Then he was off to work.

By late afternoon he could tell he was beginning to feel tired once more. He decided that apparently he wasn't at full strength yet even though he'd been here part time all week. About seven P.M. he got up and walked to his now repaired car for the drive home.

As he turned into his driveway he noticed the workmen had finished the repairs to his home. But it was dark and he couldn't be sure. Once inside, he sat down, tired from his day's activities and was starting to doze off when the door bell rang.

When he opened the door, there stood his neighbor Ray Murphy from across the street.

"Hi Jack. I saw you come home and my wife sent me over to see if you've had dinner. We are eating late tonight and she cooked a lovely pot roast and wanted me to invite you over."

"Gee, Ray. That's nice. No I haven't eaten and yes, I'd love to accept your invitation.

It was a very nice meal and Jack finally learned a lot about them. Ray worked for the city of San Bruno and his wife worked part time at a local arts and craft store. They lived here for about ten years. Both were originally from Caldwell, Idaho, he learned, and came here after a short stint across the bay in Redwood City. They had four children. One son was in the military. Two worked for the federal government and one was a teacher in Oregon not far from where his sister lived.

He enjoyed the evening and when it ended Jack decided on his walk home, that when he was better, he'd have to invite them to his place. The only problem he could think of was who would cook the meal? Oh he could manage some things, but it needed to be something better than what he felt he could prepare. That's really the problem with not having someone who was a good cook available, he thought to himself as he crossed the street to his house.

He knew several ladies who might come, but then he was afraid they might think it was a permanent invitation. He wasn't ready for that. At least not yet.

His week end was spent resting. Jack visited Jacquee's grave site on Saturday and went to visit Sarah and Dennis for awhile on Sunday, but spent the rest of the week end just trying to recover. Reading occupied most of his time and except for eating out both days he stayed home.

Jack's phone rang shortly after one P.M. on Monday as he finished shaving.

"Lieutenant?," the voice asked.

"Yes," Jack replied.

"We've just had a lady shot on Montgomery Street across from the Union bank. She's wounded but we think she will be all right."

"Okay. Why are you calling me?"

"Well, it looks just like a repeat of the other ladies who got shot. This shot was also from a building top. At least so it appears at the moment. It looks just like the case you worked on a few weeks ago."

"Yes, I know. That guy's still in jail," Jack replied.

"We think we may have a copycat Lieutenant."

"A copycat?"

"Yes sir. That's what we think. It looks like the same kind of situation."

"Okay," he replied. "I'll be in there soon."

He hung up the phone and then said out loud. "Just what we need. A copycat shooter. Is everyone out there nuts?"

Arriving at work he was greeted by Detective Brennan.

"They gave us the case since we had the other one. I know Ryan worked with you on it, but he's tied up helping the prosecutor so I thought I'd help you with this one."

"Okay. Do we know what building the shooter used?"

"We think it was the Union Bank building from the angle of the shot, but it might be from one nearby. We just aren't sure. One thing we know. It wasn't from as high a trajectory as the others."

"Could the shot have come from someplace inside the building and not from the roof top?"

"Don't know yet," Brennan answered. We think the windows are sealed and cannot be opened. We are having all the building windows checked now."

"Okay. Is there anything else happening?"

'Only the usual overnight stuff."

"Okay," Jack replied. "Let me know any other information you get. He turned to read the report of overnight activities that lay on his desk. It was quiet that afternoon and he was beginning to feel tired even before the evening hours arrived. He was still not up to staying too long, so after giving it some thought, he decided to just call it a day. Before he could leave however, Detective Brennan came in.

"Lieutenant," he said. "We learned that most of the bank building windows are sealed and cannot be opened. We did find a few, six I think, that can be opened however. We have been talking to bank employees and checking into their backgrounds. At the moment that's all we have."

"Okay. I'm going home so if anything happens you can find me there."

"I'm going home Mike," he said to his assistant. "I'm feeling pretty tired."

"Okay," Mike replied. "See you tomorrow."

As Jack started toward the doorway to get his car, the phone rang on his desk.

"I'll get it," Mike called and Jack continued walking. He was almost to his car in the lot when Mike came running after him.

"Lieutenant."

Jack stopped. "What is it?"

"We've just had another lady shot near where the other one was earlier."

"Two in one day? How is she/?" he asked.

"I understand, from what I was told, this one's pretty serious. This time it wasn't just a slight wound."

"Who is on the case?"

"I sent Spencer and Harris. They were the only ones in the office."

"Okay," Jack turned around and headed back to his office. After getting a cup of coffee, he waited at his desk to hear from his two detectives. It took about an hour until his phone rang.

"Dennison," he answered.

"Oh Lieutenant. I didn't know you were still there."

"What have you learned?" Jack asked.

"The lady who was shot is Evelyn Strong. She was just leaving the bank to go home. I learned she's an employee at the bank. She's sixty some years of age and one employee of the bank told me she was getting ready to retire in two weeks."

"Do we know how serious her wound is??" Jack asked.

"Pretty serious I understand. She'd already been taken away before we got here. Harris is on his way to the hospital to find out more. I'll be back after I talk to more of the employees. I've got several patrol car officers helping me here."

"Okay. Isn't the bank closed now?"

"Yes it is. The shooting happened just before closing. The lady who was shot was leaving an hour early for an appointment I was told."

"Are all the employees still there?"

"Yes. We have talked to some and we have the names of everyone. Should I let them leave?"

"Yes. Go ahead. We can talk to them in the morning. Meanwhile you stay and have the custodian show you around. See if you can find any indication where the shot may have come from. Don't forget to check the roof. I'll be gone when you get back here, so just leave me a report."

Jack hung up the phone and turned to Mike and said. "I'm going now. I'll get the details tomorrow."

The blinking light on his phone answering machine told him someone had called. It was Sarah wanting to know how he was. A second call was from Mo Harrison in Kansas City.

"Jack. I just missed you at work. I have bad news, but I knew you would want to know. Jane passed away this evening. She had a heart attack today in the office. We called an ambulance and they took her to the hospital. When I got there I learned they couldn't save her. Call me when you get this."

Jack sat down on a nearby chair. He was shocked at hearing the news. He liked Jane, he really did.

"She couldn't be too old," he said out loud. "Maybe in her late fifties. Maybe. I'd better call Mo in the morning. It's too late back there now."

The next morning after Jack got his coffee he sat down next to the telephone to call Mo.

"Jack Dennison here Mo. I got home too late to call you last night. I'm terribly sorry to hear about Jane."

"Yes. Me too! She complained about not feeling well and I told her to go home, but she said she'd stick it out the rest of the day. When I walked back out from my office awhile later, she was slumped over her desk. I called her name but she didn't answer, so I checked her pulse. I couldn't feel it, so I called an ambulance. I was told she was still alive as they took her away, but when I got to the hospital, the doctors told me they couldn't save her.

She'd apparently had a heart attack in the office and another more severe one at the hospital."

"That's terrible," Jack said. "I really liked her."

"Yes, I did too. I knew you'd want to know Jack."

"Yes. Thanks Mo. Let me know if there are going to be services. I don't know if I can come but perhaps I can. I just don't know."

Mo hadn't heard about his being shot a few weeks before, so Jack spent time telling him all about that.

Later his phone rang as he was getting ready for work.

He answered to learn it was Lieutenant Stark.

"Jack, I knew you'd want to know. The lady who was shot outside the bank last evening died from her wound. If the shooter was the same person who took a shot at someone earlier and only wounded her was trying again, he wasn't so fortunate this time. If he wanted to be a copycat shooter, he failed. We need to catch him before he tries again."

"Do we know anymore about where the shot came from?"

"We are pretty sure it came from inside the Union Bank building on Montgomery."

"Inside?" Jack questioned.

"Yes. At least from the angle of the shot that's how it appears. We're looking into it now."

"Thanks. I'll be in there in a bit."

Bunny called him a few minutes later to see how he was doing and to tell him she'd had a visitor from a large national firm interested in buying her motel.

"They said they are looking at sites in our area for a new store. It would be perfect Jack," she said. "I could sell and move to where you are. Then we could be together."

He could tell she was hinting at their relationship becoming more permanent.

"Well, if you do think about selling be sure you get someone to help you with all the details. Selling a big property can be complicated. You want to get as good a deal as you can."

"I will," she assured him.

After she hung up, Jack stood thinking to himself. *I don't know if I want her moving here. I suppose it would be convenient once the baby is born to be able to see my child, but she'd sure expect our relationship to become permanent.*

"What have we learned that's new on the shooting?" he asked Brennan when he arrived at work.

"It's the same caliber gun that shot both ladies. It's also the same that was used in the last shooting. We are still talking to employees. So far we have nothing."

"Has our forensics team gone over the roof area and the windows that can be opened to see if there is anything?"

"Yes, but I don't know anything yet."

"How do the bank employees get into the building when they come and go?" Jack asked.

"What do you mean Lieutenant?"

"Well, the front doors aren't open before banking hours, yet employees start earlier."

"Oh!" Brennan replied. "They all have keys and they enter though a door in the back of the building. There is a key pad inside the door and they need to enter a code to pass through a second door that will get them into the bank proper."

"Is there someone there who is always the first person to arrive? You know someone who checks them in."

"I don't think so, but I can check."

"Is it possible anyone might get in who doesn't have a key?"

"I wouldn't think so. Why do you ask?"

"If someone forgot their key, how would they get in?" Jack asked.

"I understand there is a button they can push and someone will show up to let them in."

"So the person, who lets them in, would have to know all the employees."

"I suppose so. Why?" Brennan asked.

"How many bank employees are there?"

"About fifty or so I think."

"Do you really think that any one person knows every employee who works there? Sure they will recognize those they see all the time, but I'll bet there are some others they never see."

"Good point," Brennan replied. "I'll find out. You think someone who is not employed at the bank could get in?"

"Yes."

"Find out if anyone has been let go lately and what is the procedure after a person is no longer working there."

Sarah called wanting to see how he was doing. She'd tried his home but Jack had gone to work early and he wasn't there. After Jack finished talking to her, he went across the street to have dinner at the Monkey Tree. Maria was working and as usual she was glad to see him. Madeline wasn't working that day, but Maria told him she thought Madeline was doing okay.

Once he returned to work he managed to stay until early evening before leaving. He knew that perhaps next week he should stick to his own hours and work a full shift. Coming in early was okay and since he wasn't up to working a full day yet, he was leaving the evening hours to his assistant Mike.

Jack was up early Wednesday morning. It was a good thing because after he finished breakfast, the lady he'd hired to do his house cleaning arrived. Jack almost forgot she would be coming every other Wednesday and today was her time to be here.

"Good morning Mrs. Benton. I almost forgot you were coming."

"Good morning Mr. Dennison. How are you doing on your recovery?"

"I'm getting better. I think I'll be back to work fulltime next week."

"That will be nice," she replied and then said. "I won't be able to come in two weeks to do your home. I have to go to Texas to be with my daughter. Her husband is away and she is going to give birth to twins. They are due about that time and she wanted me to come and help her. She has two other children ages five and seven. She and her husband wanted to have one or two more, but they didn't expect to be having them both at the same time."

"Okay," he replied with a chuckle. "What does her husband do that he's not at home?"

"He works for the space administration and is currently in Australia at their facility. It's difficult for him to get away sometimes and since I can help out, he doesn't have to try and make arrangements to come home. It's better this way. I brought my neighbor along today to help me. She is going to be doing all my work while I'm gone."

Just then in through the front door came a lady carrying a bucket and several other cleaning items. Jack looked up to see a lady he guessed to be about thirty, blonde and quite good looking.

"This is Jenna," Mrs. Benton said. "She's my neighbor and she will be doing all my places while I'm gone. She's very good Mr. Dennison. She has helped me before. You don't mind do you?"

"No. If you say she's good, then she's all right with me," Jack replied.

Jenna sat down the bucket and extended her hand.

"Happy to meet you Mr. Dennison," she said. He noticed a twinkle in her eye and a smile on her face as she greeted him.

"Well, go ahead ladies," Jack said. "If I get in your way, just let me know."

He sat in the living room reading and thirty minutes later Jenna entered to announce.

"I'm going to start this room now."

"Would you like me to move?" Jack asked.

"No you don't have to. I'm going to dust and vacuum. If I need you to move, I'll let you know. I may be able to work around you."

"It might be better if I just go into the other room," he said and he stood up.

Jenna hesitated a moment before speaking, but finally said.

"Mary told me you lost your wife tragically some months back."

"Yes," he replied. "It happened quite suddenly. We hadn't been married very long."

"I'm so sorry," she replied. I think I can understand a little bit. My mother passed away much too soon and my dad was just devastated at her passing. For the next four years we always thought, my brother and sister and I, always thought he was just going through the motions of living. He seemed to not have an interest in anything. We tried and tried to keep him involved in our activities as well others things we thought might get him going, but it never worked."

"Where is he now?" Jack asked.

"Well, a few months ago he met this neighbor lady at the grocery store. As it turned out she lived just down the street from where Mom and Dad lived for years, but they never knew each other. She was a widow lady and three years older than dad but she was very active. When we met her she told us that, yes she missed her husband terribly, but they'd always decided that whoever survived should live life to the fullest. And that's what she said she was doing.

She was full of energy and always busy. Her energy seemed to light a spark in dad and since he met her, he's like the same old dad we always knew. We're very happy he met her."

"That's good news," Jack replied. "I'm happy for him."

"I'm sorry," Jenna said. "I didn't mean to rattle on."

"Oh, that's okay," he answered and turned to leave. "It's good that you and your husband along with your brother and sister were there for him."

"Oh, I'm not married," she replied. "I've never found Mr. Right. Maybe someday."

Jack looked back at her wondering why she never married. She certainly was attractive enough. He'd seen many other ladies much less desirable, at least in his eyes, that were married and had families.

"Really?" he questioned. "You surprise me. An attractive lady like you, not married?"

He noticed she turned slightly red in the cheeks.

Jenna smiled, hesitated a moment and then said.

"I'd better get back to work." and with that began dusting the living room. Jack walked into the dining area and took a seat to finish the last couple pages of the paper.

He heard the vacuum running and it stopped just as he finished reading.

"I've got to do the dining room now," she announced. He looked up and noticed her smiling down at him. "I hate to ask you to move again."

"It's okay. I've finished the paper so if Mrs. Benton is done in the bathroom, I'll go shave and get ready for work."

He stood up to discover only a foot separated the two of them. She was looking up into his eyes and as they each hesitated momentarily, she released her hands from the vacuum sitting on the floor, freeing her hands and arms. It was as though she thought she might have other uses for them. He looked down and for a brief instant the urge to pull her to him and kiss her flashed through his mind, but as quickly as it appeared, it was gone. His mind told him she would have responded positively, but minds are strange things and not always accurate.

Jack stepped aside and as he did, the look on her face told him, or at least he thought it told him, that she was disappointed.

"I'd better get out of your way," he said.

She did not reply, but turned back to the vacuum to resume her cleaning duties.

Mrs. Benton was indeed done with the main bathroom and had moved on to another room down the hall. Jack could hear the vacuum running back in the dining room as he picked up his razor to begin shaving. He wondered what would have happened if he had kissed her. Would she have slapped him or would she have kissed him back?

"If you were married old man, perhaps you wouldn't have thoughts of other women," he said softly to the mirror. After shaving, he moved back into the bedroom to change clothes. Selecting a shirt and trousers from the closet, Jack walked back into the bedroom only to find Jenna standing in the bedroom doorway.

"You have a very nice bedroom Mr. Dennison. In fact it's a very nice house," she said looking directly into his eyes. His male ego immediately told him she was hinting; hinting at wanting to share it with him. The first encounter in the dining room and now this moment should have told even the densest of persons what the message was. He wasn't the densest person on earth, but there were times in his past he could have thought he was. However this wasn't one of them.

"Thank you," he replied looking into a face he first saw just a couple hours ago. "I like it. Perhaps one day I'll be able to share it with someone again."

She smiled a bit and he knew he shouldn't have said that. It might give her the wrong idea.

"Yes, I think you should. I'm sure some lady would love living here. Especially with" - - -

She didn't finish the sentence as Mrs. Benton called from the other room. "It's time to go Jenna."

"Good bye Mr. Dennison." Jenna said. "See you in two weeks?"

The sound of her voice made it sound like a question and not a statement. Was his imagination working overtime he wondered?

After they drove away Jack finished dressing. Then walking into the kitchen to check and make sure everything was turned off. He spotted a note near the sink. It simply said: Jenna 555-223-7168.

The morning paper reported the death of the lady who'd been shot and died outside the Union Bank and when Jack arrived at work, Brennan was waiting.

"We learned that all employees have a personnel I.D. cards. If they forget their regular card to gain entrance and have to buzz someone, it will identify them. I learned their I. D.'s are all collected when someone leaves the bank's employment. No final pay check is issued until they are collected. The code of the employee who is gone is deleted from the system, so it cannot be used again."

"Okay. Do we know yet whether or not the shot came from inside the bank or outside?"

"We're pretty sure it came from inside."

"And do we know if any of the employees have criminal records?" Jack asked.

"No one that we know of," Brennan replied. "The bank always checks new employees before they hire them."

"Okay. Let's check to see who among the employees owns a gun. In particular one of that caliber."

"I've already started," Brennan replied.

As Brennan walked away, Jack picked up the envelope on top of the pile of other paper on his desk. Ripping it open he started to read.

"I'll be darned. Captain Beecham is going to retire. Good for him Well, that will be an opening for someone. It can't be me because I haven't even taken the test."

Just then, his phone rang.

"Dennison," he said as he picked it up.
"Hi honey," the voice said.
"Bunny," he replied recognizing her voice.
"I just had to call. I needed to hear your voice."
"Is anything wrong?"
"No. I just wanted to talk. I would have called earlier while you were home, but I had to order supplies and time just got away from me. I miss you so much. Can you come and see me this weekend?"

He didn't know what to say. There wasn't anything going on that would cause him to stay here and yet, in spite of the fact that she was apparently going to have their baby, they didn't have an ongoing relationship. He'd never promised to marry her and even though under the circumstances, he probably should, he still wasn't sure. She seemed like a nice person, but they really didn't have a history. What happened between them was not really planned. Besides if he went to see her she was going to think of it as a first step. He knew, at least he thought he knew, that she'd marry him if he asked. He felt sure since she'd already said she would earlier.

"I don't know Bunny. I don't know if I am up to driving all that way. Then the drive back on Monday, - - - I'm not sure I'd be able to go to work. I'm hoping to start working full time next week."

"You could fly over Saturday morning and fly back Monday morning. I'd pick you up at the Reno airport and drive you back to the airport. I really need to see you. I really need to have you hold me. Besides we can start talking about a name for our baby. Will you come? Please!"

She was prepared. If he didn't want to drive, then he could fly. She had it all figured out. It wouldn't take long to fly there. No more than an hour and he could leave his car at the airport in long term parking.

As he sat on the plane Monday morning flying back to San Francisco, his thought were of the weekend past. It did turn out well. Bunny arranged to have some of her hired help do more of the motel duties she would normally do, so she would be able her to spend more time with him. She fixed a nice dinner on Saturday and Sunday they ate out. Most of the time they were together and he had to admit he did enjoy the time very much.

Bunny also told him, when he asked, there was no definite decision from the big company wanting to buy her motel. She hoped they would decide to buy it because moving to be with him was really what she wanted. In the meantime Bunny wanted him to come every weekend or anytime he could but admitted she knew it wasn't going to happen.

She was lonely when he wasn't there.

"I guess it wouldn't be too bad," he murmured and the person seated next to him looked his way at hearing the soft spoken words.

Jack smiled and said to his seat companion.

"I was just thinking out loud."

The man laughed and replied. "I do that a lot myself."

The Saturday mail was still in his mail box when he arrived home and as he thumbed through it, he noticed another envelope from the magazine publisher. Tearing it open, he found a short letter telling him how pleased they were about the sales of their publication and how well it was doing. Enclosed was a check for a considerable sum of money.

"Wow!" he exclaimed out loud standing on his front porch. "I've gotten much more than a couple of year's salary already from those stories. I can't believe there is that much profit from something like writing stories for a magazine. I guess I'd better start looking for more of them to give to Mullins."

There was a call on his answering machine from Mullins, as well as one from Sarah and a third one from Mo Harrison in Kansas City telling him there wasn't going to be any service for Jane. She indicated she didn't want any.

"Well, I won't have to worry about going. What a lovely lady she was. Too bad she never found anyone."

The first part of his day was dull and after dinner at the Monkey Tree where Madeline waited on him, he returned to his desk to be greeted by a familiar face.

"Hello Jack."

"Alexis. What are you doing here?"

"I have some news and I wanted to tell you in person."

"What news?" he asked.

"Remember how startled you were at seeing me the first time?"

"Yes. Why?"

"When I came to your house and saw the photo of your deceased wife, I was shocked at seeing how much we looked alike."

"Yes, I remember that," he replied.

"Well, as far as I knew at that time I didn't have another sister, but I was curious so I did some checking when I got home. I thought it a bit unusual that your wife and I looked so much alike."

Jack waited for her to continue.

"If my research is correct, and I believe it is, your wife and I were indeed sisters."

"How can you be certain?" he asked.

"It took some digging. I talked to some relatives and checked records from several places and it all fits together. In order to be sure I was not missing something, and that I was accurate in my findings, I hired a research team and without telling them I was looking on my own, I had them try and find out. We both came up with the same results. So I really believe your deceased wife Jacquee and I were sisters."

"How did you arrive at that conclusion?" Jack asked curious to know more about this. Alexis certainly did look a lot like Jacquee, but for her to have been Alexis' sister and a daughter to gangster Enrico Del Carlo, seemed a bit off the wall. Anyway he had to know why Alexis was so convinced of this.

"What I learned was," she continued. "Is that at one point my mother and my father broke up. She was very angry at him. She moved back to New York and her family. Dad didn't know that mom was expecting your wife and after mom gave birth, she decided to give the baby up for adoption. Dad never knew. They eventually got back together for awhile, but mom never told him. Dad never knew about my sister. Anyway, I learned that a family from Nebraska adopted her and raised her as their own child."

"And you're really sure about that?"

"The people I hired and I both came to the same conclusion. I'm satisfied that the information is accurate. So now we both know why Jacquee and I looked so much alike. We were sisters."

"That's amazing," Jack replied. "You know that your father always took a liking to me for some reason, even though we were on different sides of the law."

"Yes, I knew that. He told me you were a special kind of person and that I shouldn't let you get away."

Jack laughed slightly as did Alexis.

"Anyway I had to fly out here to tell you in person. I thought you'd want to know. And besides, it gave me a chance to see you again."

"I thought perhaps you left suddenly because you thought since you looked so much like Jacquee, we couldn't make a relationship work," he said.

"Yes, that's exactly what I thought, but the more I thought about it, the more I convinced myself that maybe it would work to my advantage. Especially after I learned we were blood relatives and Jacque was really my sister."

Alexis hesitated a moment and then asked.

"Do you think there's a chance for us Jack?"

He looked back at her without saying anything, but in his mind he wondered if seeing her would be something he'd like or would he really think about Jacquee each time they were together. Even if they were sisters, they would have different personalities. All sisters do as far as he knew. They'd be alike in some ways, but they could be very different in many others. He didn't really know Alexis very well. She was always very pleasant to be around but they'd been together only briefly.

"When do you have to go back?" he asked without answering her question.

"I can stay as long as I want," she answered with a smile on her face. "Well, sort of."

Jack smiled back at the face that so closely reminded him of his deceased wife and said.

"I was planning on working my full shift today, but how about if I bug out early and take you to dinner?"

"I'd like that," she replied.

"Have you reserved a room someplace?" he asked.

"No," she replied with a tiny hint of a smile on her face.

"Then you'll stay at my house," he answered.

He took her to San Bruno to eat. He didn't know many places there, but he'd heard of one in particular that everyone talked about.

The food was very good and the atmosphere was excellent. Jack asked about her work and how she got started. She in turn asked about how he got started in law enforcement. The evening went by fast. When they finished, he took her to his home and they finished the evening with a night cap and a bit of conversation. Alexis took her small bag into the guest bedroom and prepared to call it a day, tired from the long flight from the east coast.

"Have a good night." Jack said as she closed the door to the room.

"Thank you," she answered. "You too!"

CHAPTER SEVEN
EARLY RETIREMENT?

The next morning Jack called Sarah and told her he had a surprise and wanted her to meet someone. When he and Alexis arrived at her house, Sarah opened the door and as she took her first glimpse at Alexis, there was a gasp in her voice and a look of shock on her face.

"Sarah," Jack said. "I want you to meet Alexis Carlson. We have something to tell you."

Sarah was still a bit stunned as she ushered them into the living room. After they were seated, Jack went on to tell her about his meeting Alexis and everything that led up to the current point. Finally as Sarah tried to digest the information, she said.

"We never knew where Jacquee came from or anything about her background." Then hesitating a moment she went on. "I sure wish my parents could have known."

They didn't stay long as Jack needed to prepare for work. After talking a little longer with Sarah asking many more questions, they left and as they drove away, Jack asked Alexis.

"You said you could stay as long as you wanted, sort of. What did you mean?"

"I should go right away. I've got several cases that need my attention. I'm thinking I'd better catch a flight this evening. I'd like to stay forever but I have a court date Friday and I need to prepare." Then after a moment's hesitation Alexis went on.

"Jack. I need to know something. My feelings for you are very strong. In fact I think I've fallen in love with you. I want to know how you feel about me. If you feel we have a chance, I can close my practice in New York and move here. I could practice law in California as well as anywhere else. I know you've not had a chance to get to know me, but while I can be a tiger in the court room, when I'm away from there, I'm a very different person. Do you think Jacquee's memory would get in the way of - - - of our relationship?"

Jack pulled the car over to the side of the road and stopped. He hesitated a moment looking directly into a face that resembled so much the wife he'd lost after such a short marriage.

"Alexis," he said. She looked up at him hoping to hear something that might give her hope.

"I don't know," he continued. "I don't know if seeing you every day would only remind me of Jacquee or if seeing you every day would make any difference at all. I don't know you very well, and I realize from the information you told me about Jacquee being your sister, well I just don't know. The two of you may have many similar traits. In fact I have noticed a couple. But you no doubt will have differences and whether or not that could be a factor, I just don't know.

Do I like you? Yes I do. From what I know and have seen, I suppose there's a possibility we might have a successful relationship."

"Do I want to have a relationship with you?" he continued. "I don't know that either. It's too soon. She's been gone almost a year now and I'm still not over losing her. And with you being on the east coast and me out here, we wouldn't have much time together to explore the option.

Alexis started to say something when Jack stopped her.

"I need to ask you something Alexis."

"What?" she asked.

"Do you think you could really care for someone who had a hand in putting your father in jail?"

She looked directly into his eyes and without hesitation said.

"I know some of what my dad did and I know how he treated my mother and I didn't like any of it. I only went to see him at the end because I felt I should. I don't know why, but I just did. After you came to my office and told me, it kind of bugged and I finally decided to go see him. We had a very nice talk. In fact the best talk we ever had, and while I can't forgive him entirely for all the things he did, I know in my heart that your involvement in putting him in jail, would not stand in the way of our being together.

I have my life to live and I am definitely not a bit like him. I chose to be an attorney because I wanted to uphold the law and I think I've done pretty well. No, I don't believe for a moment it would be an obstacle to our being happy."

Jack started the car and pulled away heading for his home. Then, a short distance down the road he broke the silence. All the while Alexis was quiet as if expecting him to be the first to say something.

"I have to go to work in a couple of hours. Why don't I get ready and I can take you to the airport on my way to work?"

"Alexis looked at him unsure if he was trying to get rid of her or if he really wanted to avoid talking more about their most recent conversation.

"I guess that might be best," she finally replied. "I'd like to stay longer but you have to go to work and I'd need to leave tonight or early tomorrow anyway."

In her head she was thinking he was trying to have her leave so he wouldn't have to answer the question. The question, if he thought they had a chance together. To her that was the answer. He didn't want to have a relationship and he just couldn't say it. She was sure of it.

He took her to the airport and waited with her until it was time for her to depart. They didn't talk any more about their feeling for each other but simply passed the time discussing other items in each of their lives. Finally they called her flight and she stood up. Jack stood next to her looking down into a face so familiar.

Then she reached up and kissed him passionately. When they separated she said,

"I love you Jack, very much," and she turned and walked toward the entrance taking her to her plane and the flight back to New York. Just before she disappeared from sight, she turned one last time in his direction, smiled and was gone.

When she was out of sight, Jack stood watching the place he'd last seen her, his mind racing with thoughts about her, his deceased wife, a possible relationship and even about the lady who was now carrying his child. Finally he turned, walked back to his parked car and drove on to work.

No sooner than he arrived at his desk, then Brennan walked in.

"I'm glad you're here Lieutenant. I think we have a lead on the person who shot and killed the lady at the bank."

"Okay. Tell me," Jack ordered.

"A man by the name of Jason Hughes quit the bank over the weekend."

"What's so unusual about that?" Jack asked.

"Well, he'd been there about six years I'm told and well liked. Those I talked to this morning were shocked at his abrupt departure. He gave no reason other than to say he had to leave. He left a letter on his boss's desk. They found it this morning and called me."

"Have you checked his home?"

"He lives in an apartment, is unmarried and I talked to the apartment manage and he told me Hughes left Saturday. He forfeited his deposit and the next month's rent he'd already paid. The manager didn't know where he went or why."

"Okay. Keep checking for friends, relatives etc. Try and find out where he might have gone. Check his employment application when he started at the bank. See if that gives you any clues."

"Should we put out a bulletin around the state?"

"Sure. Why not, but he may have left the state for another part of the country. And Brennan,"

"Yes Lieutenant."

"See if he owned a gun of the same caliber."

"Right! By the way Lieutenant." Brennan said. "Christmas is coming up in a week and my wife wanted me to find out if I can get a couple of extra days off. She wants us to spend it with her sister and brother in Merced."

"Sure Brennan. That's okay."

As Brennan walked away, Jack stopped for a moment to think. Christmas! I hadn't even thought about it. I need to get something for Sarah and Dennis and their baby. He looked up across the room to see the small Christmas tree on a stand near the coffee pot. There were a few decorations and he noticed a few small presents under it.

"Good grief Dennison, "he muttered. "Where is your mind? That tree has been there and you didn't even notice it?"

Then all of a sudden another thought popped into his head.

"I wonder if I should be getting something for Bunny and her boys."

His train of thought was broken by detective Spencer from across the room who just hung up his phone.

"Lieutenant. Report of shots fired at a home not far from here. Three men seen running from the scene."

"Okay, take Harris and get over there. Call me when you get there and tell me what you find out."

It was about an hour before Jack's phone rang. It was Spencer.

"We've got two dead bodies Lieutenant. An older couple, probably in their late sixties or early seventies I'd guess. Both shot more than once. I talked to a neighbor and learned they were well liked in the neighborhood. They were a quiet couple. The person I talked to couldn't understand why anyone would do something like this. Another neighbor told me their name and that he was a collector of old and rare coins. He thought that might be a reason for the shooting. I think you should come over."

Jack arrived at the three story house situated up against homes on either side looking over the bay toward the Golden Gate Bridge. Several people lingered outside in the cold as they longed to learn more about why the Police were here. Spencer was taking to a man as Jack approached.

"Lieutenant," he said. "This is Mr. Saum. He lives next door and heard what he thought were shots. He looked out his front window and saw three men running from Mr. and Mrs. Laske's house."

"Yes sir," Saum interrupted. "I went immediately to the Laske home, knocked on the door and called out for Gil and Gertie. Neither of them answered."

"Was the door closed?" Jack asked.

"Yes. Why?" Saum answered.

"It seems strange that if they'd shot someone inside and were fleeing the scene, why would they take the time to close the door as they ran away?"

"I don't know," Saum answered.

"Do you have any idea why someone would target these people? Did you know them very well?"

"I guess as well as anyone in the neighborhood. After I lost my wife last year they invited me over many times. We talked a lot. It was then that I learned that Gil was a collector of rare coins."

"Rare coins?" Jack questioned.

"Yes. He showed me a few, but he told me he kept most of his collection in a safe deposit box."

"Okay," Jack replied. "I'll want to talk more to you later Mr. Saum." Then turning to Spencer, he said.

"Let's look inside."

Once inside, Jack saw the two bodies on the living room floor only a few feet apart. Upon bending down to more closely examine them, he said to Spencer.

"They weren't shot at close range. I don't see any powder marks."

"No sir. I didn't either."

Just then Harris walked in to report.

"I talked to many of the neighbors. None that I spoke to knew them very well. They would speak when they saw each other, but they never visited. That is except to Saum next door and the Olofsky's two doors down. Neither have any idea why someone would want to do them harm."

Just then the Forensics team arrived on the scene, so Jack and his two detectives moved outside to allow them to conduct their work.

"Do they have any relatives?" Jack asked the two detectives.

"There's a nephew Mr. Saum told me. He'd met him once. He's a student at San Francisco State."

"A nephew?" Jack questioned.

"That's what Saum said."

"Ask again about that. Aren't they a little old to have a nephew?"

"I'll ask Saum again." Spencer said.

"Let's get a hold of him. Stay here now and see what Forensics learns if you can and talk to the rest of the neighbors. I'll be back in the office."

The next morning while he was having breakfast, Sarah called.

"I can't believe how much that Alexis lady looked like Jacquee," she said.

"It's pretty remarkable," Jack replied. Sisters can look somewhat alike, but usually you can always tell the difference when you see them."

"I sensed she really likes you Jack. Did you get that impression?"

"Well Sarah, she did tell me she loved me. In fact she flew all the way out here just to see me and see if we had any chance at a relationship. At first she was concerned that because she and Jacquee looked so much alike that it would be a problem."

"What did you say?" Sarah asked.

"I told her I didn't know. Anyway she's gone. She had business in New York and had to get back."

"Did you tell her about Bunny and that she was expecting a child that's yours."

"No."

"Are you going to marry Bunny?" Sarah asked changing the subject.

"I don't know Sarah. I don't know."

"Well, I think you should have someone in your life, Jack. You know we care about you and you really should have someone. I don't know Bunny well, but she seems to really care about you."

"Yes, I guess so, but I'm just not sure I'm ready for that yet?" Jack replied.

"The baby is going to be here before you know it. And anyway! Jacquee would want you to find someone. I know she would," Sarah said.

"Yes. I suppose so," he replied.

Later on his way to work, he took time to drop by the cemetery for awhile to visit his wife's grave and to think. Then it was on to work. Neither Harris nor Spencer were there when he arrived, but his assistant, Mike, was there going over cases on his desk.

"How is your wife doing Mike?" he asked.

"Much better. The new medication seems to be working. We're very pleased."

"Good," Jack replied. "What are you working on?"

"The old Streeter case. Remember years ago, Hiram Streeter was found shot in his back yard. No one ever remembered hearing any shots and we never did find any evidence telling us what happened?"

"Yes. I remember that. What about it? Is there something new on the case?"

"I had a call late yesterday while you were out, from a person who wished to remain anonymous. He said if we were still trying to solve the Streeter case, we should look at someone named Willis Thompson."

"Who is Willis Thompson?" Jack asked.

"Well, he's a prison inmate at the moment. I'm looking at the case to review it before I head to the prison to talk to this Thompson person."

"Okay. Good luck."

Just then his phone rang.

"Dennison," he answered.

"Lieutenant? This is Myron Candoo the attorney."

"Oh yes Mr. Candoo. I remember you. What can I do for you?"

"Remember Molly Herald?"

"Yes, of course. How could I ever forget her?"

"Anyway." Candoo went on. "She's in Germany with the Herald boy and she's being held by the German Police on charges of stealing government secrets. We are working through the American Embassy to get the case solved, but I want the boy brought back here. Right now he is being held by embassy personnel. The German government has agreed to let him return to the U.S., but I need someone to escort him back. The boy knows you and I'm sure he would be comfortable traveling with you. If I talk with the Chief and get permission for you to fly there and back, I'd be most appreciative. Of course we will pay any and all expenses."

"Well, I don't know. I'm still just getting over having been shot. I just started working full time this week."

"Yes, I know about that, but I really need you to do this."

Jack thought for a few moments and finally said. "Okay. If you can get the Chief to let me go, I'll do it."

"Thank you Lieutenant. I'll talk to the Chief and get back to you. Can you leave tonight?"

"Tonight?" Jack asked.

"Yes. Tonight. I need you to go right away."

"I guess so Mr. Candoo."

It was less than an hour later when Jack's phone rang. It was his Chief.

"Jack. Myron Candoo just talked to me about your going to Germany to bring back the Herald boy. I told him you could do it only if you wanted to. Do you want to?"

"I guess I can if he really needs me. He seems to think so. I told him I would if he got your permission."

"Well you'll only be gone a few days," the Chief said. "You'll be back Saturday or Sunday. Candoo will call you in a few minutes with the details."

"Okay Chief," Jack answered and no sooner had hung up the phone, than it rang again. It was Candoo.

"Lieutenant. I just talked to your Chief and he agreed to let you go get the boy. I've booked a flight for you. It leaves in an hour."

"An hour?" Jack exclaimed.

"Yes." Candoo answered. "It will get you into Newark in time to make connections for a six a.m. flight to Berlin. You'll arrive in Berlin at 8 a.m. Thursday morning. I've booked you into a hotel near the airport. Get some rest and then pick up the boy on Friday. You're flight back leaves at 8 A.M. Saturday morning. It changes in Frankfurt and arrives here about noon the same day."

"I need to go home and get some clothes and my passport," Jack replied.

"There's no time for that." Candoo said. "I'm sending a messenger to your office right now with a credit card you can use. He'll have a letter with all instructions for you as well. When you get there, use the card to buy whatever you need. Buy clothes and anything else you might need. I want to get the boy back here as soon as possible. I'll feel more comfortable when he is here. I don't know how long this mess will go on with Molly, but I'll feel better having the boy here."

"What about my passport?" Jack asked.

"I've taken care of that," Candoo said. "Someone will meet you at the airport in Newark with a temporary diplomatic passport. It will get you through."

"Okay," Jack replied.

It was only moments later when the desk clerk downstairs called him to inform him there was a young lady to see him.

"Bring her up." Jack ordered.

A minute later in she came escorted by the desk clerk from the floor below.

"Mr. Dennison?" the young lady asked.

He could see she was very young. Perhaps in her teens and dressed in heavy wool like pants with boots covering to just above her ankles. She was wearing a thick green coat and a wool cap, pulled down over her ears. A small amount of reddish hair peaked out from under the cap. He thought she couldn't be more than about sixteen. But then who knows?

"Yes," he replied.

"This is for you," she said as she handed him an envelope.

"Thank you," he replied.

Then she turned and walked away followed by the Officer from below.

Jack opened the envelope to discover a letter and an International American Express credit card in the name of the Law firm of Candoo, Alott & Moore.

"Looks like I'll be spending Christmas in Berlin," Jack said to the ticket lady at the airline as he was checking in.

"How long are you staying?" she asked.

"Only a day or so. It's business."

"Too bad. It can be beautiful in Berlin at Christmas time," she replied.

"You've been there?" Jack asked.

"Yes. I grew up there. Well, sort of. My father was in the army and he was stationed in Germany when I was young. We were there for almost four years."

"Did you like it" Jack asked.

"I guess so. I was young and I don't think I really thought much about it. I just remember it was lovely in the winter with the snow and all the decorations. Here's your boarding pass," she said as she handed it to him.

"Enjoy what time you have."

"Thanks," Jack replied.

He slept part way to Newark. With the three hour time difference, the plane arrived at the Newark airport at just after five in the morning. His connecting flight to Berlin was scheduled to leave at six. He had to hurry to get to the area for international departures. With no luggage to worry about it was going to be a fairly easy connection. He wanted a cup of coffee but the lines at the coffee bar he passed, were long. Spotting a coffee machine nearby, he slipped a few coins into the slot, pushed the correct buttons and a paper cup appeared. A moment later the machine poured a dark liquid into the cup. Taking a sip of the very hot liquid he muttered.

"Better than nothing I guess."

He walked some distance toward his loading area juggling his hot cup of coffee from one hand to another. Soon his loading gate was within sight. As he walked quickly toward it, he could see passengers already passing down the passageway to board. Then he heard his name announced over the loud speaking system. Jack walked up to the airline attendant's desk, coffee cup still in hand.

"I'm Jack Dennison," he said.

"May I see some identification please?" the lady in the airline uniform asked.

Jack pulled his wallet from his pocket and showed his I.D. which included his Police badge. The lady looked at it and then motioned to a man nearby. The man came forward and also examined it and said.

"I don't know who you are sir, but bringing this to someone here is very unusual."

He handed Jack an envelope, glanced at him one more time and then turned and walked away. Jack opened the envelope, saw the temporary passport, and stuck it into his pocket.

"You may board now Mr. Dennison," the airline attendant said as she handed him a boarding pass to the first class section of the airliner.

He found his seat next to a window and was no more than seated when the airline attendant arrived to see if she could get him anything. Jack had never been in the first class section of an airliner before and had to admit, the larger seats were nice and all the attention passengers here received wouldn't be hard to take.

Once they were airborne, drinks were offered and a meal was served shortly after. When he finished both, Jack leaned back and soon closed his eyes. He slept most of the way and arrived early the next morning Berlin time.

After checking into the hotel, he tried to get some sleep, but he wasn't very successful, so about noon, he looked to see where he might find some additional clothes and toiletries to purchase. Then, once he did it was back to his room to shave, shower and change into the new clothing he'd just purchased.

Jack used the credit card to obtain a minimal amount of cash from the front desk, had lunch and then took a German taxi to the U.S. Embassy.

He walked inside to be greeted by a man seated at a desk just inside the door.

"May I help you?" he asked.

"Yes. I'm Jack Dennison from San Francisco. I'm here to see about the Herald boy."

"Oh yes. Just a moment," he said and picked up the phone, dialed a three digit number and said.

"Mr. Dennison is here." He hung up the phone and said. "Someone will be right here."

"Thank you," Jack replied.

A few moments later a slender, but tall lady, perhaps in her late twenties with dark shoulder length hair came walking down the hall. When she arrived at the desk, she said.

"Mr. Dennison?"

"Yes," he answered.

"May I see some identification?"

"Of course," Jack answered and pulled out his California driver's license, his Police I.D. and his passport. The lady looked at the photo on each and at him, then said to him and the man at the desk.

"It appears to match our copy of his fax picture."

She turned to Jack and said.

"Welcome to Berlin Mr. Dennison. Or should I say Lieutenant?"

"It doesn't matter," he replied.

"I'm Janine O'Hara. I'm an assistant to the Ambassador's secretary. I was given the job of watching after young Mr. Herald.

"Come with me. The boy is down the hall. I understand your flight tomorrow is early."

"Yes it is," he replied.'

"I have arranged for one of our cars to bring the boy and pick you up at your hotel in time to connect with your flight."

"What's the status of Molly Herald?" Jack asked.

"The German authorities have her confined while the investigation goes on. We are doing what we can to help."

"I'd like to see her," Jack said.

"I understand you and she had an affair."

Jack looked a bit surprised and replied.

"Well, not exactly. She wanted one I felt, but I was married, so it never happened."

The boy recognized him when he entered the room and smiled up as Jack bent over to greet him. Janine could see the boy knew who Jack was.

"Hello Bobby," Jack said.

"Hello Mr. Dennison," he replied.

"You can call me Jack, Bobby."

"He seems to know you Mr. Dennison." Janine said. "How come you call him Bobby? His name is Helmet."

"Yes it is," Jack replied. "It's actually Helmet Hans Herald, but he likes to be called Bobby. So that's what I do."

"Oh!" she replied. "I didn't know that."

"I've come to take you home," Jack said talking to the boy.

"Okay. I don't like it here," he replied.

"And why is that Bobby?" Jack asked.

"My birthday was the other day and I didn't even get a birthday cake."

"I didn't know that," Janine said a bit shocked.

"How old were you Bobby?" Jack asked.

"I'm eleven now," he replied.

"Well, when I get you home, I'll get you a real nice big birthday cake," Jack said.

"And I'll get you birthday cake this evening," Janine said trying to make up for the over site.

The visit lasted only a short while and Jack told the boy he'd be back in the morning to take him home to California. After they left the room, Janine turned to Jack and asked.

"Have you ever been to Berlin before?"

"No, I haven't"

"We still have some time this afternoon to look around. I can have a car drive us to a few places and I can give you a short look at the city. That's better than you going back to your hotel with nothing to do the rest of the day."

"I'd like that," he answered. "But first I'd like to see Molly Herald."

She drove him to the location where Berlin authorities were holding her and while Janine waited, Jack was escorted to a room down the hall. A few minutes later Molly entered. At seeing him she ran into his arms.

"Oh Jack. It's all wrong. I didn't take those documents." She gave him a big hug. "I'm so glad to see you. Can you get me out?"

"I don't think so Molly. The Embassy is working on it I understand."

"But I didn't do it. We just checked into the hotel when the Police came. They found these things in my luggage. I don't know how they got there. Really I don't."

"They will work it out Molly. In the meantime I've come to take the boy back. Myron Candoo asked me because the boy would remember me."

"When I get back, can we see each other?" She asked looking at him with expectations.

"I don't know. Let's just wait until you get out of here."

He wasn't sure he really wanted to see her. All he could remember now was the occasions back when he was on the kidnapping case and she was trying her best to snare him, even though he was married.

"You're not married now," she said. "I thought maybe you might be interested in having a relationship with someone. I thought maybe it could be us. I've got money Jack. You could retire early and we could spend all our time vacationing and having fun."

There was a smile on her face as she mentioned '*having fun*'.

"We'll see when you get back Molly."

He didn't want to say no, but still he didn't want to encourage her. He had to consider other things like what was he going to do about Bunny?

Finally he told her he needed to go and when she was released to come and see him. Jack wasn't sure why he said that, because he felt she would and he wasn't sure he wanted to see her.

"I will Jack. I promise."

He bid her farewell, but he didn't get away without a hug and kiss. A good long kiss."

Janine O'Hara was waiting and asked.

"How is she?"

"Oh, she'll be just fine. I told her to come and see me when she got out."

"She will, you know."

"Yes, I'm sure she will," Jack replied.

"By the way, I thought you were going to have someone drive us around?"

"I decided that we might be out late, and I didn't want to tie someone up. They like to go home on time, so I decided to drive."

There were far too many things to see in the short time left. It was dark early in December and while there was only a small amount of snow on the ground, there were many Christmas lights decorating many of the buildings.

Finally when it became too dark to really see anything of importance, Janine said.

"How about some dinner? I'm hungry and I'm sure you must be also."

"Yes, that sounds good. I was going to eat at the hotel, but if you know a better place, I'd like that."

"Yes, I do know a better place. I think you'll like it."

It was on the top floor of another hotel located near the center of Berlin. It looked very formal, but not overly so. When they arrived, Jack saw that the host recognized her immediately. She was apparently well known there.

"Ah! Miss Janine," he said.

"I don't have a reservation Rupert. I didn't know we were coming but I have a special guest who is Berlin only for tonight. I wanted to have him taste some of your exquisite food."

"For you my dear Janine, we always have a place."

She was apparently known here quite well Jack thought. The place seemed too formal and classy to just be able to walk in unannounced and be able to have dinner, but Rupert escorted them to a table in the center of the room. Jack noticed he removed a reserved sign from the middle of the table. Had she reserved this earlier or was she so special in Rupert's eyes, that she had enough power to have someone else's reservation cancelled or moved to another location? Jack thought the whole thing was just a bit strange.

"A bottle of wine perhaps?" Rupert suggested.

"Yes," she replied. "My special," she smiled up at him.

Rupert bowed slightly and said. "Of course." Then he walked away.

"I love eating here," she said.

"It looks like they know you quite well." Jack said.

She didn't respond to his remark, but said.

"So tell me all about yourself Jack. You don't mind me calling you Jack do you?"

"No. Not at all."

"Okay, then tell me. How did you get into your line of work?"

"I was looking for a job and they were advertising, so I decided to apply."

"That simple?"

"Yes. Pretty much. How did you get into your line of work?" he asked.

"My uncle. He was an assistant to the Ambassador in Belgium and France for a number of years. When I was younger, I asked a lot of questions about his job, and I guess he saw my interest. He told me how to apply and what courses in college would help, so I took them, applied and eventually they called me."

"Is this your first assignment?"

"No, after I was trained, I was sent to England. I was there for three years and now I am here."

"Do you like it?"

"Oh, yes. I hope that one day I might be something more than an assistant to an assistant."

She laughed and Jack did as well.

Rupert arrived with the wine, poured a bit for her to taste and when she approved, he filled both their glasses to an appropriate level.

She lifted her glass to her lips, took a sip and announced.

"Umm! Good."

They ordered dinner, ate when it arrived, had an after dinner drink and finally it became time to leave.

"I guess you can take me back to my hotel." Jack said.

They made their way to the car and when they were both inside, she turned to him.

"I was thinking. You're flight leaves early and rather than have the embassy car bring the boy to your hotel to pick you up and then have to come and get me, why don't you just stay at my place. I have plenty of room. Then they can just pick us both up at the same time."

Jack looked at her a moment and said.

"I didn't know you were going to the airport with me."

"Well," she hesitated. "Actually, I'm going all the way to San Francisco with you."

He looked at her, not knowing whether to respond or not.

"The Ambassador thought it best if I went along."

They drove to his hotel, picked up his things and then drove to her place.

"What are you going to do with this car, if they are coming in another vehicle to transport us?"

"Oh, they will pick it up," she replied.

They arrived at her apartment and once inside, she said.

"Here you are Jack. You sleep in my room. I'll take the couch. It makes into a bed."

"I don't want you to have to do that," he replied.

"No! No! It's okay. I don't mind. I'm usually home alone every night and it's nice to have someone here to visit once in awhile. I know you're going to want to retire early since you have to get up early and I'm going to be up for awhile anyway. I'm reading a book and I had to stop last night at a very interesting part. I am anxious to get back to it. So don't worry."

"Okay, if you insist," he replied.

She was sitting on the couch reading when he closed the door and lay down to sleep.

Much later, he wasn't sure when, he felt someone else in the bed.

"It's okay," he heard a voice say. "I couldn't sleep out there. Sorry."

He soon discovered she couldn't sleep in here either. Neither could he; at least until much later.

"Get up Jack," she ordered. "We're going to be late."

She was standing in the bedroom door, already dressed.

"I thought you might need a bit more rest, so I let you sleep longer."

The Embassy car arrived on time with the Herald boy, and the two of them got in and the driver delivered them to the airport on time.

They had three seats in the first class section. Janine sat next to Jack with Bobby Herald across the aisle. All three of them slept for a good portion of the flight. The layover in Newark wasn't long. They had time to walk around and stretch, have some decent food and then it was the six hour flight to San Francisco.

As they walked up the ramp and into the arrival area, Myron Candoo was waiting.

"Jack," he said. "Glad you're here." He then spoke to the young lad, asking him how the flight was and how he was. Myron didn't know who Janine was, so Jack had to introduce her.

"This is Janine O'Hara from the American Embassy in Berlin. They wanted her to come along."

"Oh!" he replied. "Nice to meet you Ms. O'Hara."

Then he turned to Jack and said.

"I really appreciate your doing this."

"It's okay," Jack replied.

"How long are you staying Ms. O'Hara?" Myron Candoo asked.

"Not long. I have to get right back," she replied.

Then Candoo turned to Jack and said. "Why don't you use the credit card and show Ms. O'Hara around our fair city? I'll get it back from you next week."

"Okay," Jack replied.

Myron Candoo took the boy, bid the two of them goodbye and left. Jack and Janine retrieved his car and he drove to his home in San Bruno.

On the way there, she turned to him and said.

"The Ambassador didn't really send me along. It was my idea."

Jack smiled across the seat at her and replied.

"I know."

"You knew?" She asked.

"Sure. It didn't seem necessary to me, so I checked. I was told you asked for time to make the trip and they gave it to you."

Janine started to laugh and then said. "And I thought I'd put one over on you."

"I'm a detective Janine. When things don't look or seem right, I check into them."

Now they were both laughing.

"Are you sorry?" she asked.

"No. Not at all."

"I'll bet you think I'm terrible," she said.

"No! Why would I think that? I had a very enjoyable time uh - - - showing you around and being shown around."

On Monday morning he took her to the airport and after she checked in, he walked her to the departure gate. She was still going to have a couple of hours to wait, but he had to leave and go on to work.

"Have a good flight Janine. Thanks for help with the boy."

She turned to him and said.

"By the way Jack," Janine went on. "I really like your bedroom. Maybe someday I'll have one like it."

She kissed him good bye when it was time for him to get on to work. Jack walked back toward the parking area for his car, but before he was out of sight, he turned one more time to look back. She was standing in the walk way and when he turned to look in her direction; she waved and threw him a kiss. Jack waved back and again turned and walked to his car.

"So what happened while I was gone?" he asked Mike when he arrived at work.

"There is nothing new on the disappearance of the bank employee. We haven't found him yet. On the shooting of the couple in their home, we talked to the nephew and he seemed very distraught about the whole situation. He knew they seldom kept any rare coins at home unless it might be some they just acquired. As quiet and reserved as they were, he didn't understand why they might let strangers in.

"By the way! He's not really a nephew. He's actually a nephew of their daughter's husband. They lost her to cancer last year. She was divorced a few years before but had a close relationship with the young man. He'd been to her parent's home several times and they considered him a nephew."

"Have we checked on the daughters ex?"

"Yes. I spoke to him Friday. He's very upset. I think he liked his ex wife's parents better than he liked his ex wife. At least that's the impression I got."

"No leads on who might have committed the crime?"

"Nothing yet."

Forensics doesn't have anything. No prints, except theirs and the nephew and a couple as yet unidentified. They do have shoe prints that indicate the shoes worn by at least two people had heavy thick soles. The kind that might be worn by construction people or dock workers.

"So perhaps we are looking for someone who does that kind of work?"

"Perhaps, but that's not much to go on," Mike said.

"No it isn't. What's going on with the Streeter case?"

"I talked to Willis Thompson at the prison and he denies knowing anything about the Streeter case. He still claims he's innocent of the robbery charges that sent him to prison. Friday I got another call from the unidentified person wanting to know if we had talked to Thompson. When I said we had and he denies knowing anything, the caller said I should ask him about a lady named Joan Devers."

"When I asked why, the caller told me to just ask him. Then the caller hung up."

"Nothing more?"

"No. Only I should ask him about her? I'm going up there again tomorrow morning."

"Okay. Keep me posted."

A few minutes later Jack's phone rang.

"Dennison," he answered.

"Honey! It's me. Where have you been? I haven't heard from you."

He recognized Bunny's voice and he went on to explain how busy he was and his trip to Germany. Finally she said.

"When am I going to see you again?"

"I'll come over this week end," he answered and she then asked.

"Are we getting married Jack? We are going to have a baby and it should have both a mother and father." Then after a moment's hesitation on both their parts, Bunny went on.

"If you don't love me and want to marry me, just say so Jack. Don't keep me in suspense. Our baby is going to be here before you know it. I need to know."

She sounded anxious for him to give her an answer of some kind.

"I know," he replied. "I'll be over this weekend and we'll talk."

She wasn't exactly happy with his answer. A more positive response would have been more to her liking but it was all he was giving now. Jack asked about the prospect of her selling the motel and how her boys were and then he broke off their conversation, telling her he needed to get back to work.

He knew she wasn't happy at his changing the subject and not giving her an answer, but he wasn't sure what he was going to do. Maybe by this weekend he'd make up his mind.

Detective Brennan came in just after the phone call ended.

"Guess what Lieutenant? We've found Jason Hughes. While you were gone, I sent out an all points to all fifty states, and the Midland Texas Police found him. He's in custody there. They just called me."

"Did they talk to him? Did they get any reason for his shootings?"

"Detective Warder told me they didn't question him, but he volunteered the information that he really didn't mean to shoot anyone. He didn't know why he did it, he just did. He only thought he might wound someone, but his shot didn't go where he wanted it to. Warder said he seemed really remorseful."

"Okay. I guess you had better arrange to bring him back."

"I will. Who should I take with me?"

"Take Harris. He likes to travel."

On Tuesday Mike returned from his visit to the prison and talking to Willis Thompson.

"When I mentioned Joan Devers name," he told Jack, "he became very upset. He wanted to know where I learned about her. When I told him we got a phone call telling us to ask him, he really exploded using some words even I'd never heard before. When he settled down a bit, he said he knew who told us. When I asked who it was, he answered that it was his so called friend Ed Rouch. He told me it was Rouch who killed Streeter years ago. He was just an innocent bystander. Thompson told me they only went there to rob Streeter, not to kill him, but Rouch shot him anyway. Now he figures that Rouch has double crossed him and was living it up along with his girl friend Joan Devers."

"Didn't we always think there was a second person in on that robbery and killing?" Jack asked.

"Yes." Mike answered. "But we never could prove it. Thompson had never been in trouble before and he acted very remorseful at his later trial for robbery of the gas station. Because of that he got a pretty light sentence. He's up for parole in a few months. Anyway Thompson went on to tell me his friend Rouch convinced him to take the blame for the gas station robbery they were caught on later, because Rouch had been convicted twice before and it would go harder on him. Thompson said Rouch told him he'd keep the rest of the money they stole from Streeter safe until he got out and then the two of them could live well."

"And now Thompson believes Rouch has stolen his girl friend and they are living it up on the money from the Streeter killing?" Jack asked.

"That's right." Mike answered.

"So what else did he say?"

"He wasn't happy. When I asked him if he knew where Rouch was, he said we should check the Florida Keys. He told me to check a place called 'Sandy Inlet.' He told me Rouch once mentioned it to him a long time ago and he doesn't think Rouch remembers telling him."

"Did you ask how Joan Devers was involved in the killing?"

"I did and he said she wasn't involved at all. She was away at the time."

"Well, I guess we should check down there and see if we can find 'Sandy Inlet'." Jack said.

"Right! I'm going to call the Florida State Police and see if they know where this is and if they do, maybe they can find Rouch and Joan Devers for us," Mike replied.

As Mike went on to pursue this case, Jack turned to cases on his desk and moments later his old friend Don Perry walked in.

"Don!" Jack exclaimed at seeing him. "It's been a long time. How are you and the wife doing?"

"We are just fine. How about you?"

Jack turned to his friend, hesitated a moment and then said. "Let's go into the office. I need to talk to you."

Once inside, Don looked at his long time friend and waited for Jack to say what was on his mind. Finally after a few moments hesitation, Jack turned to his friend and said.

"I've got a problem."

Jack then went on to explain about his meeting Bunny, a young lady from high school and what happened since, bringing Don up to date on the subject. Don said nothing during the entire time, waiting for Jack to finish. Finally when it appeared Jack was finished talking, he asked.

"Do you love the lady?"

"I don't know," Jack replied. "She's very nice, but I don't have the same feelings with her that I had when I met Jacquee."

"Don't expect that," Don replied. "You were hit hard when you met Jacque and you will probably never meet another lady that impacted you like she did. That doesn't mean you cannot love another and be married to her and be very happy. Remember Jacquee hasn't been gone very long. You still have very strong feelings for her and your memory of her just doesn't want to let go. It's normal and it may be some time before you ever feel the need to look for another lady. Did Bunny say it's okay if you decide not to marry her? Don asked.

"Yes," Jack answered. "She said that she is capable of bringing up our child and that I could come and visit and be a part of its life. I told her I would certainly be there financially. I'm going to see her this weekend. She called and wanted us to talk about our relationship and whether or not we might be getting married."

"Well, what are you going to tell her?" Don asked.

"I don't know. I really don't. I suppose I should marry her. It would be the right thing to do, but I just don't feel I'm ready. I just can't get Jacquee out of my mind."

"Then tell her that." Don said. "Tell her it's too soon. You can't get over losing Jacquee and are not sure you'd be a good husband. Let her know that perhaps in time the two of you might still get together. You said she is a nice person and you like her. Would it really be so bad being married to her?"

"No. I don't think so."

"Besides, I'm sure her two boys could use a father," Don said. "Could you be a father to them?"

"Yes, of course," Jack replied.

"Then tell her your feelings Jack. If she's the person you say she is, she'll understand."

"I really feel she wants us to be married," Jack replied.

"I'm sure she does. Especially since she's carrying your baby."

Neither of them said anything for a moment and then Don asked.

"Is there anyone else in your life Jack? Another lady perhaps?"

"No. Not really. I met a lady in New York who is a dead ringer to Jacquee in appearance and I learned recently that she is Jacquee's sister. When I first met her, I was startled by how much they looked alike. She came here and when she saw that she and Jacquee were almost identical, she thought that it might be a problem in our having a relationship. She did some research and she also hired another firm to do some research. The end result is that she and Jacquee are sisters. Anyway she told me she'd move here if I thought her looking so much alike would not be a problem."

"Would it?" Don asked.

"I don't know. I can't say I really know Alexis. I've already seen some things in her habits that remind me of Jacquee, but I don't know if that would be a problem. I suppose if we had more time together it might work, but right now I have to decide what to do about Bunny and the baby?"

"Well, then talk to Bunny. Be frank with your feelings and if you think you care enough about her, then don't worry about it being such a short time since Jacquee's passing. Get on with your life. Besides if you have a wife and family to keep you occupied when you're not at work, you may find that everything will work out just fine. Jacquee would want you to have someone. I don't believe she'd expect you to live alone all the rest of your life."

"I suppose your right."

Jack looked at his friend a moment without saying anything and then giving Don a hug, he made one final statement.

"I'll talk to her. We'll see what happens. We don't know each other too well, but — well, we'll see."

Wednesday morning Jack went to visit Jacquee's grave and talk to her. When he came away from the cemetery, he felt much better about the situation. It was as though she was able to transport her feelings through to him and tell him it was okay to consider getting married to someone. His spirits seemed raised, and he drove immediately to Sarah's house to talk to her about his feelings and thoughts.

"I think I'm going to marry Bunny, Sarah." He told her after they were seated and she brought him a cup of coffee. "I hope you don't think it's too soon for me to consider doing that. With her being pregnant, I should be a responsible person and do that."

"Do you love her Jack?" Sarah asked.

"I don't know. I'm really confused. I loved Jacquee so much that it's hard to think of loving someone else. I like her a lot and she certainly is nice. I believe we could be happy and I have to consider the baby."

"You don't have to marry her just because of the baby," Sarah replied.

"I know. I told her I would help."

"You could still do that and not marry her. Maybe you should wait awhile."

"I'm going to see her this weekend and tell her my decision."

"And you've decided you are going to marry her?" Sarah asked.

"I think I should."

"Well, if you've made up your mind, then why are you here?"

"I just felt I needed to tell you."

"You were worried about how I would feel weren't you?"

"Yes. I guess so."

Sarah took his hands in hers and said.

"Jack, I know how much you loved my sister and I know what's going on in your mind. But if you want to marry Bunny, then do it. I want you to be happy and I know Jacquee would want that also."

The Florida Police couldn't find any place called 'Sandy Inlet', but said they were going to check with some of the old timers who lived along the string of small islands to see what they might learn.

Detectives Brennan and Harris left Thursday morning for Texas and on Friday the Florida state Police called to say they believe they learned where 'Sandy Inlet' was. An old timer told them he'd heard of a place referred to by that name. It was a small uninhabited island near the wild life refuge. It's almost down to Key West. The Police were going to check it out.

On Saturday morning Jack drove to Bunny's motel just east of Reno. He saw her out front with the cleaning cart used to make up the used rooms from the night before. She saw his car drive into the lot, and she stopped what she was doing and ran to greet him.

"Hi honey!" she exclaimed rushing to throw her arms around him and standing on her tip toes, she reached up to kiss him. Jack lowered his head to meet hers and their lips met.

"I'm so glad you're here," she said when they parted. "Would you like some lunch? I just filled the cart and I was going up to the house to feed the boys anyway before I continue. I suspect you didn't have much breakfast this morning before you left."

"No I didn't. Lunch does sound good," he replied. "What about your work?"

"Oh, I'll get to that. Let's go up to the house."

When they had finished eating and the boys were gone back to do whatever they wanted to do, Jack turned to her and said.

"Bunny."

She didn't say anything, but looked across the table and the dirty dishes they'd just used for their lunch, waiting for what he was about to say.

"I've made a decision. About us," he hesitated for a moment before continuing.

"It's not been very long since I lost Jacquee and I miss her very much. What happened between us should never have happened, but it did. I don't know that I'm ready for marriage again this soon, but given the circumstances, I should probably do the responsible thing. We don't know each other very well, but I do like you allot.

You seem to be a good parent and you're a responsible person. That's evident from the circumstances I see you in since your husband died. I think any man would be lucky to have you as his wife." Jack stopped for a moment before going on as she sat and just looked at him, waiting.

"Bunny, I think we should get married."

She broke into a wide smile. Her eyes were sparkling and she got up and went to him and kissed him.

When they parted she said.

"I think so too. Yes, I will marry you," and she kissed him again.

When they parted again, Jack said.

"I'll do my best to be a good husband and a father to your boys."

"You'll do just fine," Bunny replied.

"I know we don't really know each other very well, and at times I can be difficult but, with the baby coming."

"Don't just marry me because of the baby honey. I want you to marry me because you love me. I know I love you but you shouldn't marry me just because I'm pregnant."

Jack didn't say anything at first and Bunny didn't say anything either for a moment and then he went on.

"I'm not sure I'm over losing Jacquee yet, but I promise I will try to be a good husband to you and a good father to the baby and the boys."

"I know you'll do just fine," she replied. "For me it would be my high school dream coming true."

She never did get back to the cart in front of the motel rooms where she'd left it until much later.

By the time Jack left early Monday morning, they decided the wedding would be a quiet affair to take place in six weeks here at the motel. Bunny would be only a few weeks away from giving birth at that time. Rooms would be provided free of charge for all wedding guests and the restaurant next door was reserved for the wedding dinner.

Bunny also told Jack that the corporate firm interested in buying her motel had once again contacted her through her attorney. They still had an interest and she was now even more interested in selling and moving to be with him.

Jack was almost late in getting to work on Monday. His departure from Bunny's motel was delayed by her reluctance to let him go. He'd not even had time to go home first and change.

Brennan and Harris returned from Texas just an hour earlier than his arrival at work with their prisoner and Mike was there to let him know the Florida State Police called to let them know they'd picked up Ed Rouch and Joan Devers. They were being held pending the San Francisco police's decision on what to do with them.

Jack then told everyone about his decision to get married and of course he was congratulated by all.

Henry Mullans showed up a bit later to announce a movie studio was interested in doing a movie based on some of his and other detective's magazine articles.

"Whatever happens Jack," he said. "If they go ahead with the idea, they will be paying all of us a few bucks for the movie rights."

"Any idea how much?" Jack asked.

"I don't know, but it might be very lucrative. Depends on how much they feel it's worth. I've hired an agent to negotiate with them. I just wanted to let you know. You will get a cut of course on your share as will any of the other detectives I've dealt with."

"I'm surprised by how much those articles have already generated. I'm glad I decided to cooperate with you and provide some background. I may even be able to retire early if this goes through."

They both laughed at the prospect.

"I could use the money." Jack said. "I'm going to get married again and raise a family so I need all I can get."

"Yes you will." Mullins replied. "Congratulations."

The next morning Jack drove first to the cemetery to tell Jacquee of his decision and then he was off to see Sarah.

"Come in Jack," she said when she opened the door.

"I've come to tell you something," he said.

Sarah looked at him and without waiting for him to tell her, she said.

"You're getting married. You decided to marry Bunny."

"How did you know?" he asked surprised by her statement.

"I knew. When you were here before, I just felt that you would go through with the idea and marry her. You are a responsible person Jack. You need to be happy and I know Jacquee would want it that way."

"I hope you don't mind."

"No. Of course not I care about you Jack."

He gave her a big hug and she fixed coffee and served cookies while they talked about when it was going to be and where.

"Where are the two of you going to live?" Sarah asked.

"Well, she still has the motel to run and until she can sell it, she'll be there and I'll be here. I'll drive over on as many weekends as possible and when the motel sells, I guess she and the kids will move here. Beyond that I don't know.

"Will you be selling your house and getting something larger?" Sarah asked.

"I don't know. It's way too early to decide. It's a nice house, but Bunny will probably like to have a place of her own. I don't want to be too far away. I still want to be able to visit Jacquee."

Sarah reached across and took his hand, squeezed it and smiled.

THE END

EPILOGUE

Jack and Bunny were married and six weeks later she gave birth to a little girl they named Emily Ann Dennison.

She continued to run the motel and he traveled back and forth almost every week end.

Jack continued to provide story material for Henry Mullins and the movie company did buy movie rights to several stories the two of them put together. It provided each with a tidy sum of money.

Ten months later, the big nationwide firm bought Bunny's motel and she moved to be with him in San Bruno.

Eighteen months after her arrival, Jack was promoted to Captain in charge of training where he worked for three years and then decided to retire early. Money from the movie rights along with money from magazine stories and his retirement provided him with a very good financial position. Besides Bunny made a nice profit from selling the motel.

They moved into a much larger home down the coast in Monterey.

A few months after their move to Monterey, Bunny gave birth to a baby boy they named Jack Randolph Dennison Jr.

Jack served a few years on the Monterey city council and the two of them continue to spend their time enjoying the fruits of their labor and raising their children.

And the murder of Mr. & Mrs. Leske was solved when detectives learned their nephew casually mentioned to a classmate about their rare coin collection. This led to the three people responsible. They were found and captured.